# RED, WHITE &
# BETRAYAL

# RED, WHITE &
# BETRAYAL

## A.J. WOOD

Red, White & Betrayal

Copyright © 2018 by A.J. Wood

All rights reserved. No part of this book may be reproduced, stored, or transmitted by any means—whether auditory, graphic, mechanical, or electronic—without written permission of the author, except in the case of brief excerpts used in critical articles and reviews. Unauthorized reproduction of any part of this work is illegal and is punishable by law.

Because of the dynamic nature of the Internet, any web addresses or links contained in this book may have changed since publication and may no longer be valid. The views expressed in this work are solely those of the author and do not necessarily reflect the views of the publisher, and the publisher hereby disclaims any responsibility for them.

This is a work of fiction. All of the characters, names, incidents, organizations, and dialogue in this novel are either the products of the author's imagination or are used fictitiously.

ISBN 978-0-9905249-3-9 (paperback)

Published by:
Waterton Publishing Company

# PART 1

# 1

THE MORNING SKY was bursting with clouds, providing a great spattering of shade around the city. Yet, it was eerily hot, and muggy, despite the clouds' best efforts to keep the heat at bay. Two ends of a spectrum, colliding into a confusing outcome. This was to be the scene of his birth; the first words of the first chapter written in his book. His Life Book, which, not unlike the weather when he was born, also became a tale of two conflicting stories he was destined to survive. He came into this world, born Edward Alex Watters (Eddie for short obviously), in the Midwest to your everyday, average family. Just enough money for vacations, food on the table, and a nice little house (even if it was in a crappy part of town). But he always wanted out. First off, he hated the cold. Winters were depressing, and he wanted to live near the ocean, to feel there was a more infinite world out there outside of a few chain restaurants and the same people with the same drama, day in and day out. Some people truly loved the cold, the seasons, and all that. Eddie never understood why. It was always so ugly during the winters; how could one spend half his or her life in the doom and gloom just waiting for that first flower to blossom?

The conflicting nature of his life began to really take hold of Eddie at a young age, beginning with his personality, where he had developed a cool, calm manner, punctuated by a hair-trigger rage. If he was that smart, funny kid to some kids, that was fine. However, it only took a few nudges here and there... maybe a little push of the right buttons, to send him off the deep end. But who could blame him? We all have our demons to fight—Eddie just tended to fight those demons with no regard or with no thought of the consequences.

This personality trait became apparent early on his life, in his elementary school years. A small kid with a talk-back, punk-ass way about him invited all kinds of trouble. Early one fall, at the beginning of fourth grade, he discovered how his "lose your mind in rage" would both hurt and help him all at once.

"This kid keeps staring at me all day. Do I have boogers on my face or what?" he asked his best friend, Tommy.

"I don't see anything there, Eddie. What did you say to him this time? You always are talking smack!"

"I didn't say anything! Especially to Hulk Johnson! He's the toughest bully in school!" Eddie was right; nobody back-talked Hulk Johnson. The kid was rumored to carry a knife and that he even killed his own brother (as elementary-aged rumors would go, of course). He was originally from Brazil and believed the best way to integrate himself in the American way was to use his size to scare people into liking him.

"You'd better stay clear of that guy. Seriously, dude," warned Tommy, which was the best advice Tommy could give.

"Hey, Eddie! Why you keep looking at me?" Here came the Hulk, deciding he would target Eddie for that week.

"I wouldn't look at you, Hulk. You're too ugly to look at. It hurts my eyes!" Eddie responded in his wittiest fourth-grade-level response.

"Oooh, you're dead!" yelled some bystander kid as more and more children started to approach the developing scene.

"Oh, you little shit!" responded the Hulk, which of course created a giant buzz around the library the kids were in. Not only did the Hulk kill his own brother, but he cursed like an adult too! What a true bully! And the Hulk continued, "I choose you, Eddie. Right now!"

Now Eddie had heard of this term *choose you* before. It meant he wanted to fight, right there and then. But Eddie would smart-ass his way out of it if he could, especially in front of the other kids who were witnessing the ordeal.

"Choose me? Do you mean choose me to be your date or something? Choose me to be friends, so I can protect you from the mean kids? Ha-ha!"

And right there, *bam!* The Hulk threw a punch straight into Eddie's tiny fourth-grade face.

"I choose to knock out all your baby teeth!" yelled the Hulk, laughing himself silly at his own joke while Eddie was bent over bleeding from the mouth.

But the Hulk underestimated Eddie that day. The kid had heart and, of course, the little rage monster that lived inside him. And with that, Eddie stood up and swung back. A full-fledged fight erupted, and it was classic. One who witnessed it would not say Eddie won the fight that day, but one would not say he lost either. It was determined to be a tie, little Eddie versus the Hulk, and when the teachers ran in to break it up, Eddie had earned the respect of the biggest bully in school.

The rest of the school year, something amazing happened. As it is with all bullies, once someone stands up to them, the bullying stops. The Hulk even wanted to be friends with Eddie, always saying things like, "Eddie, let's sit together at the lunch table," or "Eddie, is anybody picking on you? I'll take care of them for you." The two became fast friends, Eddie teaching the Hulk how to assimilate better, while the Hulk, in return, taught Eddie all about Brazil. Eddie really *dug* hearing about such a remarkable foreign country. He thought how cool it would be to visit one day, as the stories the Hulk gave him planted a seed about visiting and understanding other countries, especially Brazil.

As the years passed, as young friendships go, the two drifted apart, but Eddie never drifted from that little travel bug the Hulk had planted in him, especially about Brazil.

# 2

Eddie's next Life Book chapter eventually progressed through high school and even the state college just over an hour from where he grew up. Upon graduation, he moved to Southern California. It was great being a twenty-something living in California with the beach on the weekends, drinking all week, and working just as hard. Life was good, but one needed money to sustain the lifestyle. Women of Southern California tended to like guys who could afford *things*. Probably obvious, but what about just loving a guy for his traits, personality, or heart?

Being a hopeless romantic, Eddie also discovered that his hair-trigger personality pushed him right into relationships. Although on occasion the romantic approach was a benefit, it became a liability throughout life. Eddie started to find himself distraught, continuously searching for the right *one*. At that point in life, he was ready to escape the bar scene, wanting to settle down and push strollers, change diapers, and celebrate anniversaries in nice restaurants (or whatever else family men did).

To continue his despair, life at work just plain sucked. If one has ever worked for a large corporation, in a low- to mid-level position, as another cog in the big wheel of corporate profits and shitty bonuses, well, then, he or she knows the feeling. The typical workday was the same as the previous and the next: wake up at 5:00 a.m., go to the gym, home by 6:30 a.m., get ready and shower. Dress in business casual (which is about fifty dollars a week for dry cleaning), and off to sit in a road-rage-filled, 1.5-hour commute to the office. Now this was where it really sucked: arriving at the office, it was off to the diminutive cubicle, which was basically a five-foot-by-five-foot jail cell.

Eddie always shared his frustrations with coworkers, which didn't help with his office reputation.

"What the hell is wrong with people here?" he asked his peers. "I finish all my assignments for the day by lunchtime—that is, if I'm not in pointless meeting after meeting, listening to some knucklehead try to sound smart about something that really does not matter in the grand scheme of things in the world."

"Dude, be careful what you say around here. You're starting to piss people off, making them look bad," they warned him.

"But it's shocking how passionate people like us work in the corporate world. I mean, who cares if you modernize some system to increase capacity and the company sells an extra shipment of semiconductors or whatever the hell it is they sell? It's not like these monstrous corporations are curing cancer or anything. They definitely don't pass the increased profits to the worker bees, so why take it so seriously?"

"We get paid, don't we, Eddie? Chill out, man!"

"No way! Look at this place—it's a damn prison!"

Eddie was right. The office was nothing but off-white plastered walls, with the occasional crappy painting and corporate logo spread out sporadically, slightly brightened by the dimly lit energy-saving bulb, enough to cause a migraine by morning coffee. Eddie often wondered if they tried to make it depressing on purpose, maybe just to show the workers that the power rested out of their grasp.

"I can be accomplishing so much more in life right now," Eddie complained. "I pass the time just exhibiting the appearance of actually doing work. There's only so much time you can spend on ESPN.com, or CNN, or even Facebook. I'm frickin' bored silly here!"

Eddie spent his spare time just standing up about thirty times a day… seriously, thirty times. Not just to stretch the legs or anything but to descend the elevator and literally just walk around the building… multiple laps. "What the hell am I doing here?" he would scream out in the parking garage. He *really* felt like it was a prison, and he couldn't bear the thought of living like this the next forty years. Every day by 6:00 p.m., he'd be ready to bolt out the door and sit in another 1.5-hour commute back home, only to eat dinner and get in bed, prepared to wake up at 5:00 a.m. the next day. "Holy shit. Shoot me now!" he lamented every single night.

But weekends were his great escape. Friday night, the drinking would start the minute he got home. Life was bleak at best. Passing time on the beach, wandering around aimlessly, and so on and so forth. But the beach helped cure his depression. The smell of the ocean lifted his spirits. The saltiness of it all gave him freedom. The stickiness and humidity of the air was fantastic.

Every Friday was like a weekend reprieve, conjugal visit, and visitor pass all rolled into one. And then there was Saturday. Cruising up and down the beach, seeing all the delighted people, moving around and around with no worry in the world. That was probably because, where he lived, there was no concern for money; everybody had it. Everybody but Eddie, that is. But still the weekend was great. Pickup basketball games, surfing, chasing girls, and drowning out his sadness. But Sunday would always arrive like a slap across the face.

One Sunday night, Eddie's start-of-the-week depression began to hit. He settled down to decompress with a movie. Wouldn't you believe it, but the damn universe was speaking to him! *Office Space*, the anticorporation, antiestablishment, "free us all" flick was speaking directly to Eddie.

"I am this guy!" Eddie screamed out loud. "They wrote this for me!" One could imagine many young corporate hacks had also screamed this while watching the movie. "I can't do this anymore." He really couldn't.

"I'd almost rather mow lawns and rake leaves for the rich and be totally done with it. I'm twenty-three years old, single, and there is an entire world outside of my cubicle!" Eddie pondered, *Why don't I quit, buy a backpack, and hit Europe? I mean, people still do that, right?*

Every day the entire next week, instead of studying his Fantasy Football lineup, he researched Europe and what it would take to just bail. But then, he realized, with the limited funds in his bank account, he'd make it about a month over there till he'd be sleeping in Hyde Park or some hostel in Nice. And everyone hates hostels. Young Americans from California at least needed a hotel room with its own bathroom.

*Wait a minute,* Eddie thought as he looked over the nice little globe he'd bought from some store that shouldn't be selling globes. "Why not South America? What did my buddy Hulk say? Rad beaches and great weather? Bet they have hot chicks there too! I could learn another language, be free from all this corporate bullshit!" This life-altering idea hit him as hard as that punch to mouth the Hulk gave him. Brazil! The exchange rate was like four to one!

Being that he was still young, stupid, and had nothing to lose, he immediately went about selling his truck for about $10,000, which, when calculated, could last him about eight months in Rio de Janeiro. Only problem left was confronting his boss with a resignation letter and a crazy-ass idea like giving up a good job with a nice career path to move to some third-world country. Eddie's Life Book was getting quite interesting indeed.

"Mr. Crowder?"

"Hey, Eddie. How's the project going? You here to give me a status report?"

"Shit, here's a status report. Your leadership: *red*. Your shit bonus: *red*. Me resigning: *green*!" Of course, that's what Eddie wanted to say, but he knew not to burn any bridges, so he went with the more thought-out version.

"Oh, well, that is going fine. In fact, we're about three weeks out to completion."

"Great! Let me know when you have that status report for me," Mr. Crowder responded, his head down, focusing on other work.

"Actually, I wanted to discuss another matter," said Eddie quite sheepishly.

Mr. Crowder peered up over the thin glasses resting on the front of his nose. "Okay, shoot."

"I have been thinking a lot about my career. I really want to get into international business, but I have no experience. After a lot of thought, I'm thinking of taking some time off, go learn another language and culture, and really use those skills when I return."

This was a load of shit, of course; he really wanted to go fuck off the next few months, but the line about the language was true.

"Eddie, have you really thought this through? What this really means?"

"Absolutely. I know you are a tough negotiator, but on this one, I've really made up my mind." Eddie was ready for the onslaught of advice he wasn't going to take.

"You know what?" asked Mr. Crowder, a big smile across his face. "I actually agree with you. When I was your age, I lived in Australia for a year. Best time of my life. It never hurt my career, and I look back on that time and smile a lot. You doing the same, plus adding a language, before you are married with kids... hell, I would do it again if I could!"

And, well, that was it. Done. Bingo. He was moving to Rio de Janeiro, with $10,000 US cash, not a lick of Portuguese skill, and no friends in the country. A lot of people called him crazy, but in the end, when Eddie would lay his head down, looking forward to his move, it was quite simple. The answer to every question was always the same: "Fuck it. I am out."

# 3

Natalia da Silva Pacheco was at a crossroads in her life. Being upper-middle class and living in a decent house outside of the central neighborhoods of Brasília, Brazil, she was not unlike many her age. Being an extremely successful high school student with a ton of family connections, she had the whole world in front of her. But no matter how hard she tried, she just couldn't escape her past.

*Pacheco* was a pretty common family name in Brazil, but this was no common family. These particular Pachecos were the most famous of that name. Generation to generation of famous artists, they were very well respected and could basically do whatever they wanted. Even so, it was hard to be both an artist and a businessperson, as her grandfather before her father and even her father himself found out. This family could have owned not only Brasília but the entire country, but they were extremely wasteful and made investment mistake after investment mistake until they could just scrape by while maintaining the image of the famous, successful artist family.

When Natalia was just sixteen years old, her dad sat her down and said, "Natalia, girls in Brazil have it very hard, but you can make it easy on yourself. You will have the power over men that most girls have—but to really understand how to use it, now that is the trick. I want you to wield that power and be in control of everything."

"But, Dad, I'm sixteen years old. Why are you telling me this now?"

"I see you, Natalia. Every one of your boyfriends is older, some in their twenties. You think I like seeing my sixteen-year-old daughter out with a twenty-year-old man? They are using you and taking from you what you should take from *them*!"

"So, act like a boy, you are saying? Use men like they use women? Is that your point?"

"Exactly!" Natalia's father beamed with pride. His daughter wouldn't be a typical girl, gushing over boys but thrown aside at will. His daughter would play the game her way.

But even if Natalia could hold up that charade for a while, that just wasn't who she was. Sure, she went out and hooked and up, then dumped boys as her father had instructed, but she also felt empty about the whole trick. She felt remorse, or as much remorse as a teenager can feel about love. But she stayed strong, and for the next three years, she bounced around from relationship to relationship, never truly subjecting herself to an honest connection. To say she built a wall that day her father sat her down would be to say the ocean is a puddle of rain. She didn't just build a wall; she built an entire fortress around her, where nobody could penetrate through to her heart.

At eighteen, Natalia stared at herself in the mirror. *What am I doing with my life? I'm so worried about meaningless crap. There has to be something more out there, something deeper. Fuck, I can't live off my parents forever; I need to get into college and find my true destiny, my true self!*

And that destiny was the Catholic Church. At least for the time being.

Like most Latin American countries, Catholicism is *the* religion. Sure, there are some branches of Mormonism, the Lutherans, and the remote native religions where you sacrifice sheep and all that, but Catholicism was really *the one*.

Natalia knew all about the importance of the church in Brazil, but she wasn't really into it until she made her way to college and started to acquaint herself with certain students.

"Girls! This is my new friend Natalia," pronounced one young woman at Natalia's arrival at a local house party. And the rounds of "Hi, nice to meet you" flowed in as Natalia made her way around the room. She ended up in the corner by herself after some time, not being extremely excited about such social situations.

"Aren't you in my physics class on Tuesdays?"

Natalia turned, searching her memory for both voice recognition and possible names.

"Umm, I think so. Yes, that's right," Natalia responded a bit quietly.

"Don't worry, this isn't my *scene* either! Hi, I am Susanna. Nice to meet you."

"Hi, Susanna. Sorry, I usually don't go to many parties."

"But I always see you after class with a bunch of boys. I thought this would be your thing!"

"No, not at all! Those boys are crazy! They like me because I treat them how they treat all the girls. I think they see me as a challenge, but to be honest, I am completely over all that... all that bullshit! I am just so tired. I'm tired of boys, tired of acting like I want to be at these parties—" Natalia caught herself venting to this new stranger. "I'm sorry, Susanna. I don't mean to complain; I just really don't want to be here. I'll talk to you later. See you in class!"

"Wait! Natalia!" Susanna didn't want to let her go quite yet. "Listen, I've been there, believe me! Actually, I'm still there. I only came here tonight because... well, actually, I don't know why I come to parties like these either. But let me tell you, I don't know if you go to church or not, but I met someone who completely changed my life around. He gave me the gift of opportunity, of a future, and I want to share that gift with you. Are you free tomorrow night?"

Susanna was right; she did know a very, shall we say, *influential* man. He was a priest at one of the churches in town, or at least he said he was a priest. Indeed, nobody really knew if he was actually a priest, which might sound strange, but well, this guy was a trickster. They called him *Padrinho*, which was Portuguese slang on the word *Padre*, or *Father*, but in a caring type of way (add the *-inho* to the end of the word and it's endearing). It also had a double meaning of the term *Godfather*, which fit him nicely.

Susanna walked Natalia into a room in the basement of the church in the Asa Sul neighborhood of Brasília. The city of Brasília is a planned city, the newly shrined capital of Brazil built in the 1950s, and the architect who drew it up designed the city as a giant airplane. The body of the plane is somewhat like the Mall in Washington, DC—a large grassy area specifically planned to be a gigantic open space so if there were any government protests, no matter how many of them showed up, it would seem like a small gathering within that space. One end housed all the federal government department buildings, everything from the State Department to the Brazilian IRS. The other end had towers, the soccer stadium, a gigantic communications tower, and other symbolic structures. The "wings," or *asa* in Portuguese, sit in the north and south sides of the city and are the planned apartment communities for the citizens to live—hence, Asa Sul, or South Wing, where this particular room in this particular church was located.

The room was dark, lit only by a series of candles about a foot apart along each wall, with a stage up front for the Sunday school teacher or, in this case, where Padrinho preached. Padrinho was in his sixties, very personable and dynamic, and Natalia was immediately drawn to his comforting disposition.

"Welcome to the beginning of your new life, my girl," he proclaimed as he looked down at her and the rest of the class, kneeling for opening prayer in their respective pews. "Students, I hope your hearts are open for the truth."

Padrinho initiated his sermon, a powerful and somewhat different type of preaching from what Natalia had heard in church before. "Children of God," he began, "tonight I want to talk to you about the greatest evil that threatens the world—the *elite* sinners, who own and control our bodies and minds. Do you know that government, militaries—essentially everything that represents power in this world—are all puppets of a small, select group of leaders, used as powerful weapons to control the world civilizations?" Padrinho raised his voice. "Who controls the puppeteers? Who is the master of the planet? Five to ten elites in the United States of America! The rich! Do they care about us? Do they care about the planet? No! An example: here in Brazil, the great Amazon forest lives. The Amazon is *Brazilian*! Why are the Americans involved if we want to cut down trees, build factories? It's *our* Amazon! They control our government. They control every government. And they control you!"

Natalia became quite curious at this point. Everyone knew the Americans had great influence over the Brazilian government, along with most others—that was not too controversial—but who was this small, elite group of people at the top? So many questions.

Padrinho went on like this for an hour. The evils of the world, conspiracies all over the place. Of course, the impressionable young students ate it up, but the end was where he hooked them.

"There is only one event in store for us. The rich and powerful leaders, they are the devil! They are driving us toward Armageddon! The Bible tells us it's going to occur, and it is in fact happening, under the covers. Nobody wants to admit it. But there is one thing you can do. Take God into your heart, and pray every day for your soul. Pray for the deaths of the elite and for the deaths of the wars they wage. When the *end of days* rolls upon us, we who have our eyes open and live only for God will survive in eternity."

With that, the students gathered around, held hands, and repeated over and over to believe in God, believe in Christ, and believe in the Catholic Church.

Over the next few months, this was a usual Friday night for Natalia. These classes took a subject, like how diseases were all curable by the body and that the rich knew how to make it work but withheld this information for complacency and power. Or how wars were held for the perception of conflict but were really there to subjugate the population to borders and poverty. Padrinho provided Natalia a new reason for living, a new way of being, and it engulfed her like a tsunami. The man became a powerful human-God to her, Susanna, and the others.

Likewise, Padrinho took a liking to Natalia as she became fully committed to him and his beliefs. Natalia's Life Book showed she was easily influenced with out-of-the-norm ideas, and this was just another example.

One late Saturday afternoon, after a day spent with family and friends, Natalia couldn't push her excitement for that night out of her mind. She and Susanna were invited to a private sermon upon completion of Natalia's first semester of school. It was as a celebration of achievement, also billed as a way to use her university-gained knowledge to fight back against the rich. The primary lessons of late were Padrinho's continued hatred of the United States. For him, the United States really was the "Great Satan," as the radical Muslims called it. The United States was responsible for pretty much everything wrong in the world, and Padrinho wanted to talk to the girls about this and how they could fight back.

But first, before the sermon began, he wanted to set the environment right. "The Amazonian Indians live free, without guilt or worry, and the United States of America is trying to take that from them. Put yourselves in their consciousness. Why does the rest of the world wear clothes, and not the freest of the free on earth? They don't need the control to hide themselves from the world. Their bodies are their temples, and they know no disease because the body is free."

Natalia heard this, but she wasn't sure where he was going with it.

"Girls, release yourself from the *burden* of the norms of the world. The primitive people knew how to live, and only a few know today." With that, Padrinho removed his clothes and sat there stark-naked. He grabbed Natalia's right hand with his left and vice-versa with Susanna. "There is no shame in being free and exposing yourself to God."

Natalia began to shudder. She didn't know if it was nervous energy and whether she should get up and run or if God was speaking to her through Padrinho.

"I see you shaking." Padrinho glanced over. "That is your guilt and anxiety trying to escape your body. Be like me, and be free."

Susanna immediately removed all her clothes, and Natalia felt obliged to do the same. There they sat, three bodies, Padrinho and the girls, completely naked. Padrinho commenced with some humming trancelike prayer.

"Language is control too, girls. Follow my lead." Closing their eyes, the three hummed and released gibberish-type sounds as Padrinho explained, "God knows no language. He can understand our hearts."

Natalia and Susanna glanced at each other, and they must have known what was about to happen. As Padrinho forced himself on the two girls, one at a time, there was nothing they could do to stop it, nor did they believe they *should* stop it. Not only was Padrinho physically abusing two younger girls, he was abusing them in another profound way—mentally. Added together, it was the worst kind of act a man could impose on another, especially on two younger victims full of trust and respect for him.

The end of the night arrived with the sun slowly making its way above the horizon. Natalia and Susanna made their way back to Susanna's house to sleep off the rest of what was left of that morning. Upon awakening later that Sunday, Natalia was quite sure it was all a dream, or a nightmare, or was it in fact reality? Her confusion was massive, and she didn't know where to go from there. Susanna didn't want to talk about it, and Natalia was fine with that. She decided she would skip church that day and go try to sort out what just occurred.

In fact, Natalia didn't make it to church again for a full month, and she couldn't get ahold of Susanna, who dropped off the face of the earth. But she knew she had to confront Padrinho and at the very least to try to understand why he'd done what he did. This was a priest when all was said and done, and she thought, *Maybe he is right and God wanted him to be with me?*

Arriving early at one of the Friday-night sermons, there was a commotion in front of the church. Natalia finally found Susanna, crying hysterically by the front gate.

"What's happening, Susanna?"

"I don't know! When I pulled in, I saw some girl running out the front door screaming! I could only assume what happened to her, right? I waited about thirty minutes, and all these police cars showed up! Natalia, I'm so sorry I've been avoiding you. I've felt so ashamed I brought you into this." Susanna began to weep as Natalia put her arms around her.

"It's not your fault, Susanna. I've been so confused too. I know what he did was wrong… at least I think I know."

"It was wrong, Natalia! He was absolutely wrong! He's a predator! And look, he has another victim. How many of *us* can there be?"

And with that, Padrinho appeared from the door, but not so fatherly this time. At least not the same father he was. This time, he looked like a plain, dirty old man, handcuffed and surrounded by police. His hair was scuffled, he had tears coming down his eyes, and he was headed for a miserable rest of his life, just as he deserved.

Natalia truly believed she had found what she needed, what she was really looking for in Padrinho. She had grown skeptical about the rich, and about America. But with this experience, she didn't know what to believe anymore. She would have to continue her search. How would she now fill the void in her heart? How would she quiet the grumbling desire inside her to lead a fulfilling life? One thing she knew for sure: this story in her Life Book would be locked and sealed forever, and she would never trust another man again.

# 4

THE SWARMING HEAT, humidity, and overwhelming number of people speaking a difficult foreign language hit Eddie like a ton of bricks. As he departed customs into Galeão International Airport in Rio, he kept thinking, *What the hell am I doing here?* It was a total onslaught of culture shock. Having traveled internationally—Mexico, Canada, Europe—before had given him some experience in the matter, but nothing loses you, confuses you, and excites you into utter disbelief more than the first time you walk into a third-world country. Without knowing the language or culture and without any friends, Eddie's life began to move in slow motion.

Finding his luggage and out to the curb, he hopped into a taxi, attempting to orient himself to his new reality. *"Zona Sul, por favor."* Eddie did pick up a couple of helpful phrases before he made out for this new venture. His research also told him where to stay away from and, conversely, the best place to situate himself.

Zona Sul is the tourist area of Rio, where the beaches of Ipanema and Copacabana form a perfect South American paradise. His plan was simple, underwhelming, and especially unprepared and unorganized—to identify some cheap hotel to set up shop and go from there. At the ripe age of twenty-three, knowing everything and nothing all at once, that was all Eddie could organize.

Now, there is a difference in Brazil between a motel and a hotel, as anyone who's been there might know. A hotel is what it is, and that's where you go to stay on vacation. A motel, on the other hand, is where young Brazilians take their significant others for a little alone time. In Brazil, most young people cannot afford to just go rent an apartment and start their lives like back in the United States. They usually live with their parents and families until they get married, so if you want to try to get a little action from your girlfriend, it's kind of hard with the parents, kids, nannies, and maids running around the house. Solution: you take her to what is essentially a sex motel.

Eddie showed up at Motel Amor, alone, with suitcases and no accompanying girl. "Wow, this is like being in a red-light district!" he exclaimed out loud as he walked into his room, which was furnished with a hot tub, some weird sex chair in the shape of a heart, and an ice bucket full of condoms. "Disgusting. Bedbugs would be an upgrade for this shithole!" Eddie was used to the first-world cleanliness of even the worst places. So with that, he grabbed all his belongings and exhausted the extra spending money for the week on the Sheraton. So much for saving every nickel.

The first night in Rio was extremely lonely for him, lying in bed, staring at the ceiling, scared, jet-lagged, and starting to really question his decision. However, the next day, after about three hours of sleep, Eddie went full assault on the town. He was up out of bed and dressed, and he immediately bought an English-Portuguese dictionary, along with a notebook and pen. The idea was simple. As he started to learn the language, if there was a word out there that escaped his knowledge, he would write it down in the notebook and look it up later. He transformed himself into a studious beach bum.

Ipanema, the locals' beach, was often a site of visitation, as opposed to Copacabana, which was a bit more famous and popular with the tourists. Copacabana was expensive and seedy, with prostitutes everywhere all aimed at making money off the European tourists who walked the streets in their black socks and Teva sandals (better known as "mandals," or as the creative teasers call them, the "Air Jesus"). Always the talkative hosts, the Brazilians took pride in Eddie's interest in the place.

As he strolled into the local bakery for his morning coffee and sandwich, he struck up a nice friendship with the proprietor of the place.

"So, Mr. Gringo, you are liking my city, yes?" the man asked every day.

"Ipanema is frickin' awesome! Ya know, this is like South Beach in Miami. And holy crap, there are some beautiful people, all in their little Brazilian bikinis! Both the women and the men!" Eddie immediately noticed the famous bikinis—something between the American-style bikini and the thong. He also perceived how the men essentially wore the male version themselves, something requiring acclimatization.

"Mr. Gringo, but you need to watch out for the sun down here, amigo!"

"I know, I know. I'm so white I light up the beach. Blah, blah. I hear it from all you Brazilians!"

But Eddie wasn't alone. It was around Christmastime, which is the summer in Brazil; the beaches and surrounding city were full of tourists, even the local spots. As he mingled and worked his way through the beach, he realized the decision to relocate to Rio was spot-on.

Looking down in his trusty notebook, the notes and words started to saturate the pages:

1. Organization of the Ipanema lifeguard towers (Portuguese: *Postos*):
   - Posto 8: Arpoador, the gay section.
   - Posto 9 through Posto 11: The cool surfer crowd and beautiful people.
   - Posto 12: Do not go. The lagoon behind the beaches drain the polluted waters there, and it's nasty.

*Okay, now I know where the cool kids and hot chicks hang out*, he thought. *First box checked! Now what? Oh yes, that pesky language barrier.* Eddie realized the easiest way to learn the language was to force himself to speak it, but this was easier said than done. So many young Brazilians wanted to learn English from a native speaker that everywhere a gringo visited, English was the preferred communication, not Portuguese.

However, that did provide Eddie some relief for a trickier situation: finding a place to live. After five days at the Sheraton, cash-flow could be an issue, unless he found an apartment. Eddie figured he'd try his luck with the concierge at the hotel.

"Excuse me. Can I bother you for some help?" Eddie began.

"Yes, sir. How may I help you?"

"Listen, I am checking out tomorrow, but I need your help finding a place to live. I have no other friends, nobody else to help. Can you give me anything? A name? An apartment agency? Anything?"

"Sure thing, sir. Most gringos love living in Copacabana, right near a beautiful nightclub that's very popular. It's a great spot—it's called Hello Nightclub. In fact, here, take this card to the club tonight and tell them I sent you.

"Wow, that's very nice of you! Thank you, man!"

Eddie headed up to his room to clear up and start to organize his life. As the hours passed, he decided it was time to have a couple of drinks and try out this club.

Dressed in his swankiest outfit, Eddie popped in a taxi and instructed, "Hello Nightclub, *por favor*!"

The cab driver gave him a look, rolled his eyes, then sped off down the road.

*That was frickin' weird*, Eddie thought.

The front entrance of the place was lit up, both from signage and the bounty of women outside smoking cigarettes. Eddie exited the cab and looked around in disbelief. So many women. As he meandered up to the front door, they all stopped to peek over at him.

*What the hell is going on? Every single one of these girls is checking me out. They must love the gringos here!*

As Eddie made his way into the club, he headed straight to the bar. One after another, girls approached him to strike up some conversation. Not one of them was especially great looking, but he was receiving so much attention he didn't bother worrying about that.

"Hey, mate. You're loving this place, eh?" Some Australian man patted Eddie on the back, wearing a huge smile as he continued, "The girls love us foreigners here, eh?"

"I know. I can't believe it! Maybe the Brazilian men are all dicks! This place is full of girls lined up for us!" replied Eddie, still in awe.

"Live it up, mate! It ain't like this back home!"

And as the Australian stumbled away to hit on his next target, an especially nice-looking young lady made her way next to Eddie.

"Hello. What is your name?"

"I'm Eddie. What's yours?"

"Marianna. Are you American?"

"Yes! Nice to meet you. I love being here! Tell me about yourself, Marianna."

"Oh, sorry. I don't understand. My English is very bad."

"Oh, no problem. My Portuguese is bad too!" Eddie shot her an awkward smile, and Marianna half smiled back. But Eddie continued, "So, maybe we can practice our language with each other?"

"Sorry, I don't understand!" Marianna was very bashful. "I cost $500 for entire night. Or just buy one hour."

"Excuse me?" Eddie asked, not quite understanding her, thinking maybe she was asking for him to buy her a drink.

"I cost $500 for entire night."

Now the entire scene became crystal clear. No wonder these girls loved the foreigners—they were all prostitutes looking for companionship, but the foreigners were confused enough to think these girls were actually hitting on them. Not true; they were only after the wallet.

"I think it's funny you are fluent enough to say that! What, did you take English for Prostitutes?"

"Sorry, I don't understand."

"Yeah, yeah, whatever," Eddie responded, and he headed straight for the door.

Steaming from being duped by the concierge, Eddie decided to do it on his own, with no help from anyone, because really, who could he trust?

Although it took him a few more nights at a hotel, Eddie eventually met a nice couple one day who did indeed offer to help him out with his little housing problem. Other than a few outliers like the hotel concierge, Brazilians usually were known for being warm and welcoming, even more so with expats. Most people in the world were trying to move from third-world countries to the United States or Europe, not the other way around, and the fact that Eddie was reversing the trend really intrigued a lot of Brazilians. The couple he'd met connected him with a legit apartment rental agency, and he somehow negotiated a furnished—albeit tiny—spot in between Ipanema and Copacabana. It was about three blocks from Posto 8, but even better, a few steps away from Posto 9, where the beautiful people all congregated. With Eddie handing over enough American cash in exchange for six months of rent, the landlord was quite ecstatic.

Now, for Eddie's American standard of living, the apartment wasn't much. There was no air-conditioning and only a refrigerator and stove in the tiny living room. Plus, the bed reminded him of camping on the hard, midwestern ground. Nevertheless, he *was* three blocks away from the beach.

Next on his list of acclimatizing: finding a school that would teach Portuguese for Foreigners to help solve his little language issue. This turned out to be an easier task than he'd anticipated, as there couldn't be any prostitutes learning Portuguese for him to fend off. Finding one particular little place, he decided to head over and check it out.

"Hello, my name is Eddie. I'm living here but need to learn Portuguese. Can you help?"

"*Oi*, Eddie. *Sim*, we can help. How much do you know?"

"Nothing, but I took three years of Spanish in high school."

"You really don't know anything, do you?"

Eddie eventually filled another page in his notebook with the subject line: *Never confuse Spanish with Portuguese. This is a* big *no-no*.

Brazilians are extremely proud of their Portuguese descent and make it clear that it is *not* Spanish. Yes, both are Romance languages, so if one understands verb conjugation and such, then one would have a bit of a head start. Other than that, confusing the two in Brazil is practically cause for deportation.

"Please take this grammar test in the room back there, and we will place you in the right class," instructed the extremely nice language school girl, even after he offended her and the whole history of Brazil.

"I don't know a damn answer on this test. Three years of high school Spanish, all for naught. Watching *La Bamba* and learning how to curse in Spanish aren't much of a help. Shit!" Eddie muttered to himself as he looked over the entrance exam.

- Question 1 – Circle the adverb in the following sentence:
  - Kindly remove the luggage from the car.
- Question 2 – Circle the sentence clauses:
  - We parked the car, then entered the store.

And so on. For him, it felt like being back in school, but he was there to learn, not shoot for an A in Portuguese.

# 5

WHILE EDDIE WAS doing his best trying to understand the difference between future subjunctive and slang speak, activities affecting this gringo forever began to take place just a few kilometers down from Copacabana, just past Ipanema, and a straight shot from the Sheraton, where he'd previously holed up. You see, this is where the biggest favela in South America is located. A *favela* is the Portuguese word for *slum* or something to that effect. These favelas are little shanty structures or brick huts built by homeless and impoverished people, who then tap into the city's electricity and water grids. The growth of the favela then becomes a neighborhood, followed by a few blocks and so on and so forth until it gives birth to its own functioning suburb—much like this particular favela, named Rocinha. Calling Rocinha a suburb is like calling an aircraft carrier a boat. Rocinha is actually its own city, and in terms of population of the favela alone, it was in the top ten in South America.

A favela like Rocinha has its own laws and regulations too, but it's not the state of Rio's legislature who passes these laws, just like it's not the Rio police who enforce these laws. The entire population of the favelas are governed by the drug traffickers within the favelas, who are armed to the teeth and have more money than a lot of the wealthy Brazilians. In fact, they are so well-organized, -funded, and -stocked with the latest and greatest weaponry that for the most part, the police, or even the Brazilian Armed Forces, wouldn't be much of an opposition to the traffickers. The Brazilian government has tried many times, unsuccessfully, to pacify the favelas.

In a country like Brazil, the biggest motivational drive for breaking the law is hunger. People are dirt poor and starving; there is absolutely no way out if you're born into it. You can't just go get a job as a waiter or something similar and have enough to pay rent at an apartment. So, really, if you want to make it in that country, being born poor, you turn to crime. In the favelas, dealing drugs is the crime of choice. You start at the bottom of the organization and move your way up, much like at IBM or AT&T or any other disciplined corporation.

That's where Luis "Ze" Sampaio was when he turned eighteen, at the bottom. But he wanted to move up, and he wasn't the patient sort to wait for the top traffickers in charge to either die or gift him more responsibility. Ze knew that life didn't have a grand plan for him. He knew the best he could do with a sixth-grade education and literally not a pot to piss in (plumbing was quite the luxury)... was drugs. Ze came from a family of seven, with his older brother in jail and his three younger sisters destined for lives as maids for the upper-class white folks, so he had to do the drug traffic thing. Plus, he really didn't value many of the same necessities in life that a lot of boys from the favela did. In the beginning, Ze was kindhearted, but poverty changed him. It's weird what starvation can do to a person. If he had to kill or rob or whatever, he would. It wasn't like he was some born psycho killer like you saw in America or some kid who was bullied into shooting up a mall; Ze was just starving, along with his family; if it meant killing people or poisoning them with drugs for money, so be it.

One day, Ze's sixteen-year-old sister, Roberta, came home with a story that ignited the engine of Ze's brain.

"Hey, big brother! Have I got a story for you!"

"What is it this time, Roberta? I'm busy. I don't want to hear your stupid *kid* stories."

"I think you'll like this one!" Roberta was pushing a bit more than usual, forcing Ze to turn around and actually have a face-to-face conversation with his little sister.

"Don't waste my time, please. Make it fast!"

"So... I might have lied on a job application, and I might now be working for the richest company of them all!"

Apparently, Roberta was hired by a vendor company that supplied embassies, consulates, and their staffs' living areas with maid services. In Brazil, it's not that hard to stretch the truth a little on applications, even with the complex, bureaucratic notary system they have going on there. The official driver's license or ID card is basically your picture laminated, not a multitude of high-tech anti–ID theft going on.

"What are you talking about? Get to the point already!" Ze was growing impatient.

"Well, I've been assigned as a maid to the US Marines' living house in downtown Rio. I'm going to be cleaning the house of the American government! I'll never be fired from that job, ever! They must have loads of cash lying around there, right?" For those not familiar with it, part of the US Marines' remit is to protect embassies and consulates around the world. It can be dangerous and exciting. But let's be honest the job to guard the US consulate in Rio is downright cushy!

Roberta knew that cleaning the house of the marines gave her an opportunity a lot of others in her position didn't have—a steady job for as long as she wanted as long as she excelled. For the most part, the marines treated their local contractors exceptionally well. Most marines weren't used to having maids, so having that gifted benefit pushed them to treat the help nicely.

But as Roberta described her day and her job to Ze, he wasn't thinking long-term job stability for his sister and family; he was thinking about making money. Ze was smart enough to know the marines didn't just leave money lying around, and he was also smart enough to know that even if they did have a stash of money there, it would be tightly locked up. Although Ze was a smart kid, he was also fearless, which made him completely stupid at times. And what Roberta told him next turned him into the densest dude in Rio.

"Eddie Watters here?"

In Brazil, they pronounce his name *Eg-ie*.

"Here," he replied to his new Portuguese professor.

"*Em Português, por favor*," she said.

"Oh, sorry. *Eu estou aqui*."

Eddie looked around the Portuguese 2 classroom. To his right, he heard the stories of two older Norwegian women who had husbands in the cargo-shipping business and who had lived in Brazil for ten years each. They spoke almost perfect Portuguese.

To his far left was a gorgeous girl, Anna, a typical German—very tall with striking features. She was a photographer who had lived in Rio for quite some time and had great language skills. Luckily for Eddie, sitting in the immediate seat next to him was Dan, a twenty-year-old kid whose parents lived in Brazil as missionaries, and he was there to do one thing—surf. And just like Eddie, he couldn't speak a lick of the language. How did these two find their way in with this bunch? Portuguese 2? Really?

"Hey, Dan. I'm Eddie. I noticed your Portuguese is as shit as mine. No offense."

"Dude, none taken! I haven't even heard a word that professor is saying, let alone understand it!"

"I'm starting to think this whole testing process was crap and they just stick everyone in Portuguese 2!" Eddie joked with a hint of truth.

Dan and Eddie quickly became the class knuckleheads. However, Eddie turned his attention to a more dubious plan: receive outside *tutoring* from Anna. She was receptive to the idea, just not how Eddie had wanted. Being only five foot nine delivered a great disadvantage with German women, as Anna was at least six feet tall; and that difference prevented Anna from pulling the trigger. But Eddie was happy to be at least hanging out with some friends. He started to wonder if he had made a mistake moving to a different country, knowing nobody, let alone the language. Homesickness and loneliness was creeping in heavily.

"Hey, guys," Eddie said to his new crew one day. "We should check out that hippie fair in Ipanema this afternoon. I heard they have some crazy shit there and some weird food from up north. I'm ready for my first bout of Brazilian food poisoning if you guys are too!"

"Ha-ha! Yeah, whatever, dude," replied Dan in his usual, straight-to-the-point surfer style.

"Only if we can counter the bacteria with alcohol!" said Anna, laughing out loud.

"That's the German spirit I know!" Eddie applauded.

Shopping at the hippie fair lasted about twenty minutes until the boredom of arts and crafts set in, so the three foreigners decided to go have a drink at an Irish pub that had just opened nearby. The locals own most bars in Rio, and they were great, but sometimes people just wanted to get back to what was familiar, and for Eddie, a bunch of European tourists at an Irish bar was close enough to California for him.

Up the stairs they went at O'Brien's Pub and into a big dusty-looking room that was unusually loud. Handed their beer-tallying sheet (every bar provides a sheet where the bartender marks off how many beers were bought, which are then paid for at the end), the three continued through the front room.

"See that hot little waitress over there?" Eddie nudged Dan. "She can help me forget about leaving all my friends back home!"

"Eddie, it's not smart to hit on waitresses at bars aimed at foreigners. These girls just want to hook up with the tourists or that kind of clientele. Is that what you're after, some girl who wants a green card?"

"If I'm going to find someone, it's gonna be some girl who's not that! More importantly, someone with a little family money! But what's the harm in practicing my Portuguese with some smoking-hot waitress?"

"Whatever, dude. I'm gonna go play pool with Anna." Dan snickered as he grabbed Anna's hand and led her to the game room.

Eddie, however, was feeling lonely, even with the company of his two friends. But he knew he arrived here partly to learn another language, and hanging out with two English-speaking people all the time wasn't helping. At this point in his adventure, he'd give a conversation with the local waitress a shot.

"*Oi, tudo bom?*"

"*Óla!*"

That's all he got. He had to show off more. The waitresses at those establishments were used to the Europeans who knew a few words, but what was irresistible to most Brazilian girls, whether a waitress or high-class girl, was an expat who was fluent in Portuguese.

Eddie mumbled his way through some ridiculous question about Carnival. To both parties, it was a stupid inquisition; however, she bit and played along.

"Wow, you speak Portuguese?" she asked in broken English, wondering what was going on with this guy.

So, on and on it went, but Eddie couldn't wait to escape what seemed like an eternity, as he only understood half of the conversation, and his embarrassment could not be obscured. In the end, she was busy working, forcing Eddie to give up and walk away, eventually reaching the rest of the crowd, who were playing pool with a couple of Americans. Eddie was terrible at pool, and he knew it, so to hide a second shameful moment in one night, he struck up a conversation with some onlookers.

"Where you from?" asked one of the guys.

"California, but I live here now," Eddie stated with pride.

"Shit, dude, that's cool. Is it for work or something? We haven't seen you at the consulate."

"Umm, not really. I might teach a little English, give private lessons to cute girls, you know. But really just on a leave of absence."

They liked that. But the consulate question was confusing for Eddie.

*Was I supposed to check in or something?* he deliberated quietly in his own mind.

"Ah, gotcha. No, dude, we live here too. We work at the consulate. Usually most Americans are part of the staff," said Guy Number Two. (Eddie learned later his name was Mike.)

"Oh, cool. What do you do there?"

"We're marines."

# 6

Ze Sampaio gathered up his closest amigos. There was Andre, a typical thug who would rob anyone or shoot anything at the first sign of trouble. Pedro, who was a young kid and carried out any order asked of him to show his allegiance and his will to move up the food chain. And finally, Twiggy. It wasn't the first name you'd think of when you saw him. He was a gigantic muscle-head who acted as the enforcer of the group, and he was also quite smart.

The planning happened in a back area of a little bar where they cut the cocaine and packaged it for the rich Cariocas, or native Rio residents. Ze laid out the idea in a way that made sense.

1. Question: Outside of the rich Brazilians, who lived in gated communities and had a false sense of security?

   Answer: Foreigners

2. Question: Who was sick and tired of jacking cars and robbing Brazilians and tourists for chump change?

    Answer: All of us

3. Question: Drugs make us a lot of money, but it's a process. Who wants to make a lot of quick cash?

Answer: All of us

4. Question: What's just as valuable as money and can be used or sold for even more money?

    Answer: Weapons

5. Question: Finally, who has a stash of high-tech, expensive weapons, who would never suspect anyone would be crazy enough or brave enough to steal those weapons, to then sell them for a ton of cash?

Now that was a harder question to answer, but Ze and his little sister Roberta knew where; plus, they had the muscle and brainpower to rob the United States Marines of their weapons.

Unfolding to a genius plot, the climax to Ze's tale became quite interesting: the Rocinha gang of four in the room would dress up as Rio police, purchasing uniforms from the local corruptible street cops. Roberta knew the marines were having a house party, inviting the local in-crowd to share in their stories from whatever the latest happenings were. Before the party started, the marines would be getting ready, and Roberta would need to prepare the house for the night. The marines trusted her and wouldn't watch her too closely.

"Roberta, we are going there for one thing and one thing only: the weapons. As you float from room to room, you need to swipe the weapons-stash room key, unlock it, and put it back before anyone suspects it," Ze directed, setting up the focus. "The rest of us will get to the house before the party, dressed as police, and declare a search warrant to enter the house for possible drugs. Then it's a matter of 'controlling the crowd,' snatching the weapons, and off we will go."

Roberta wasn't so convinced of this plan—they were talking about the United States Marines, after all—but she did trust her older brother completely and would follow him to the ends of the earth, even if she knew deep down that the plan was definitely easier said than done.

NATALIA AND SUSANNA were on vacation in Rio the same time that Ze was planning his heist. The two of them, along with cousins and friends, were a hot group of girls prancing around town, not to be unnoticed by the opposite sex. The marines' grasp was not beyond reach in getting the word out to a troop like this for the big party that Saturday night.

Arriving fashionably late to dinner and parties is a rite of passage for most Brazilians, but not Natalia. She fancied herself different from most and made it a point to be early. Little did she know that her resistance to culture would be her downfall.

Then there was Dan and Eddie, still struggling their way through Portuguese class, workouts, hitting the beaches by morning, class in the afternoon, and bars at night. Dan started to grow a little crazy. He had pierced his nipples, among other places, and would hit on anything that moved, for the most part quite unsuccessfully. Eddie decided he wanted to distance himself a bit from Dan and Anna and maybe try even harder to meet some locals. Still stuck with a minor bout of homesickness, he knew if he didn't immerse himself in the full experience of Brazil, he would end up on a plane back to California much sooner than later.

Making money was another attempt to diversify his circle of friends, knowing the demand for native English speakers worked in his favor. But he needed a way to be a qualified instructor, so off he went, applying to all the various English schools around Zona Sul. The most prestigious was in the Barra da Tijuca suburb, which was a newer, wealthier spot.

Figuring that the application process to work at the English school was going to be a piece of cake, Eddie was full of confidence. *Who wouldn't want a college-educated American and native English speaker to teach English?* But, boy, was he mistaken.

"Óla. *Tudo bem?* I'd like to apply for a job as an English teacher. I'm from the United States. I can start today!" Eddie announced as he walked into one of the more popular schools in Barra.

"Wow, that would be great! Do you have an English degree?" responded the receptionist, completely throwing Eddie off guard.

"Umm ... sorry. I don't think you heard me. I am from the United States. I speak English, fluently ... you know, being from the *United States* and all!"

"Oh yes. I heard you. But as you know, we are teaching students English grammar, not just how to say, 'What's up, dude?'"

"Well, I do have a college degree, and I'm sure my grammar I learned back in the sixth grade—you know, being from the

*United States* and all—should be enough, correct?" Eddie was starting to think he'd royally underestimated this whole process.

"Oh yes, I'm sure." The receptionist was playing with him now. "So, for you to teach here, you need to pass an entrance exam. It's just basic grammar. Should be pretty easy for someone with a sixth-grade knowledge of English, and being from the *United States* and all!"

Eddie took the exam papers into the testing room, sharpened his pencil, and sat down to go to work. Glancing over the first question, then the next, and finally through the whole exam, the only thing he could mutter out was, "Holy shit! This is going to be a bitch! I don't remember being taught any of this shit!" But he plowed his way through it, not knowing any of the grammar intricacies that he really should have known. He was sure the test got the better of him that day.

"So...how'd I do?" he asked the lead professor after what seemed like hours of grading and a magnitude of red ink spilled all over his test like it was a bloody murder scene.

"Well, not so great, to be honest. But, as luck would have it, we do have an opening that might suit you well. There is a class we provide called Conversational English. Any interest?"

Eddie's only real duty was to talk about Carnival, or California, or whatever the hell the group wanted to discuss, just to get them talking. But all in all, he was meeting new people. There was actually a nice young girl in the class who offered to pay him separately to come to her house and do the same thing, one on one. He didn't realize at the time that it was just a ploy to get him over to her house, meet her family, and maybe go from there; he genuinely thought she just wanted to improve her English.

Late in the afternoon hours, he found himself at her apartment chatting away, making *conversation* and convincing her of his interest, when she asked, "Why do you always just want to talk about Carnival? Isn't there anything else you want to talk about?"

"Sure," he replied. "But... what do you have in mind?" He started to figure out where this might be going. He wasn't quite attracted to her, but figuring it had been a while, he just thought, *What the hell. Better than hanging out with Dan all day.*

"My parents are out shopping. They'll be gone for at least another hour. I can also teach you a few words in Portuguese. How much slang do you know?"

"That's exactly what I need to learn!" he said, starting to get a bit excited because although he was learning formal Portuguese in class, that's wasn't really how people spoke. Nobody says, "Hello, how are you doing? I am fine, thank you." It's more like, "What up, man?"

"Hello? Are you coming?" the girl interrupted his rambling thoughts as she grabbed his hand and led him to her room.

"How do you say it? I'm *hot*, don't you think?" she inquired. She must have been watching some American movies.

"Well, in English, I would say you're *smoking*!" he kinda lied, but whatever.

And as she took Eddie into her room, they immediately started to kiss. In Brazil, waiting to make the move was quite disrespectful. The cultural norm goes like this: when you meet someone in a bar or at the beach or whatever, you make out right away. There's no first-kiss drama or anything like that. It makes foreigners imagine that the girls are really into them. Probably not, however; they just like to kiss down there. Even kissing strangers on the cheek as a hello is quite proper, indicating the kiss is a bit more informal than in most countries.

The room was like a kid's room, filled with dolls, a flowery bed, and what looked to be school books. A disturbing sense hit Eddie right off. This girl was about twenty-one years old, but she really needed to upgrade past the schoolgirl look—especially for Eddie, who tended toward maturer, older women—so he was going against his natural desires. But although his interest in this girl was soft, when she began to take her clothes off... well, the cliché speaks for itself. Getting past the undesirable proved easy for him. The initial passion phase moved to hot and heavy, and ten minutes into it came a loud *thud*! Her bedroom door swung open. Her father stood there, situated in the doorframe, wearing a look of hate and bewilderment.

"Shit!" Eddie yelled, jumping off the bed far enough as to almost knock every doll to the floor. Grabbing some hard-headed, battery-operated little figurine in his hand, he was ready to chuck it at the girl's father if he inched any closer.

Some fathers would strangle a guy getting it on with his daughter in his house, even if she were twenty-one and an adult. At least, most American fathers. But that didn't happen. He closed the door, bid the two a good afternoon, and went about his business. Eddie followed him into the kitchen to explain himself, but all the dad did was hand him a Diet Coke and grill him on American politics.

*I'll take that over an ass-whoopin' any day!* Eddie thought.

Apparently, the dad's excitement to have an American with his daughter, tied to his curiosity he had for the United States, led to quite an interesting tête-à-tête. The girl then appeared, not embarrassed at all, mentioning an idea that would lead Eddie down a path that would forever change his life.

"My girlfriends and me are going to party at US Marines' house today at night," she whispered in her terrible, broken English. "Do you want meet us there?"

Eddie agreed to it, mostly remembering Mike, the marine from the Irish pub who he'd thought was pretty cool.

*Why not? What else is going on in my life that I can't hang with some other expats who would surely invite hundreds of locals I can meet?* So there it was, decision made. He was going to his first real party in Rio, even if it was being thrown by the US government.

The party was supposed to kick off at 7:00 p.m., which meant most Brazilians would get there at 9:00 p.m., but Eddie, being a lightweight, knew his drinking capabilities prevented him from lasting all night. Figuring that he'd get there a little early, drinks could then flow, giving him an opportunity to hang with the Americans, feeling nice and buzzed. The Brazilians would show up later, when he could make some moves and be asleep by midnight. Avoiding the girl from earlier in the day would not present such a challenge if he had enough early drinks, another plus for the pre-party arrival.

Natalia and Susanna had similar thoughts. Even being Brazilian, they were planning a parallel routine of arriving on time, downing a couple of drinks, and off to dreamland early (as they wanted to be on the beach at first light the following day). So, right about the time the girls started prepping for the night, Eddie made it back home to his apartment, cracked a beer, and called Dan to come over, figuring he was in need of a wingman, even if he did have metal shit pierced all over his body (which was probably not the coolest accessary to be sporting at a function with some tough marines).

Dan and Eddie partook in some libations and walked to a little bar by Posto 9 to hang out a bit prior to the party. The beach was amazing this time of day. The clock showed 5:00 p.m. on Saturday, and the locals were just wrapping up their beach day. People were still playing volleyball—the local version of kicking it and not allowing their hands to touch the ball. This was very common, being a soccer-crazy country and all. It was a spectacle to watch, because the guys were badass. The beach bar scene carried over from the sun-filled afternoon to help support you through the night. The Brazilian national drink, a caipirinha, was always flowing, and for two gringos, an affordable two US dollars per drink meant there would be many. The drink is pure alcohol, some lime, and a ton of sugar. One could inhale about three of them, letting the sweetness fool you into thinking it was a drink for lightweights. But about a half an hour after the first drink hits the lips, the creeper drink takes its full effect. Perfect start to a nice little fun night.

The two partygoers grabbed a taxi at about 6:00 p.m. and headed downtown to the marines' house. Normally, they took buses everywhere, but these bus drivers were nuts, the ride being almost like a roller coaster at Magic Mountain, twisting and turning the big, metal machine through the curves of Rio's unorganized roads. Not wanting to deal with that madness, the two figured a taxi would have to suffice, praying the guy would understand their Portuguese. About 6:30 p.m., they arrived at the bottom of a long pathway to the front door.

Natalia and Susanna showed up at the exact same time, coincidentally. Eddie immediately thought Natalia was pretty, and she must have reciprocated, as she kept shooting him looks while walking up the pathway to the front door.

Susanna blurted out, "Óla. Quantos anos você tem?" asking Eddie how old he was.

*That's a weird first question*, Eddie thought, deciding to not try to answer her in his still struggling Portuguese. "Sorry, but do either of you speak English?"

"I speak English," said Natalia shyly. "I am Natalia. This is my friend Susanna."

"I am Eddie. This is my buddy Dan."

"What's up?" Typical Dan.

"Sorry. Dan doesn't speak Portuguese or English very well. Ha-ha!"

"Whatever, bro."

"Anyway, let's continue this inside, yes?" Eddie asked.

The group of four reached the front door and gave it a loud knock, and Mike appeared quickly.

"Mike! What's up, dude? Remember we met at O'Brien's the other night? I hope you don't think we are inviting ourselves, but I heard about your party, and I thought you wouldn't mind us showing up if we brought these two hot chicks with us!"

The girls got a kick out of that and laughed.

"No way, dude. Come on in. You're Americans. It's all cool. Some of the guys are chilling inside. We're not quite ready. The maid is just finishing up. There are beers over in the kitchen."

"Awesome. Here, we brought a bottle of Jack too."

"Cool, man. Go have a blast."

It was a bigger house for downtown, and it was nice. There was a large kitchen that had a maid's living quarters extended to the back. Most Brazilian houses and apartments were built with that addition. To the right, there was an open living room, which then led out to a backyard, housing weights, a bench press, and just a lot of random crap. A marine lay napping on the couch—he must have started early. To the left of the living room was a closed door that led to what looked like another smaller space, bolted shut by an array of locks.

"Must be some important shit in there," Eddie said to Dan, not knowing that was the room with the weapons and ammunition.

The world turned slowly for Eddie at that moment. He had been speaking with Natalia for what seemed like hours, though the clock only showed 7:00 p.m. But the realm of time decided to halt to a complete stop when Eddie noticed the maid rushing by them, through the living room, and right out the door. Loud pounding knocks at the front door sounded out as Mike walked over, leaving his place in the kitchen, where he was busy making drinks for Susanna and Dan.

Mike unlocked the door and swung it open, displaying a scene in front of him that was almost unexplainable: a group of police with pistols drawn and scowls on their faces.

Eddie felt an odd sense creeping but calmed down after Natalia leaned over and said, "This is Brazil. Everything that happens here is strange."

"Sir, do you speak Portuguese?" Ze asked in terrible English, being the captain of this particular police assembly.

"No, I don't," Mike responded, looking around for help.

Natalia saw this starting to crumble, so she volunteered. "I can help."

The police began to speak to Natalia, and she in turn translated to Mike.

"They are saying that someone has called to make a complaint about drug use in this house. They are saying you have illegal contraband here," Natalia explained to Mike.

"That's absolutely untrue! We just have alcohol."

More Portuguese speaking between Natalia and Ze led to: "They are saying they have a search warrant to come in and look around the house."

"No, they cannot!" responded Mike. "We are US Marines! They are not allowed in!"

"They are saying it does not matter and that if you just let them in, they can confirm and be on their way."

"Fuck this! It's money they want, isn't it?" Mike shouted.

"Dude, just let them in! We don't have anything here!" yelled another marine in the background.

Mike looked over at Eddie, stared at him, and said, "You didn't bring any shit to this house, did you?"

"Fuck no, man!" Eddie answered.

"Fine." Mike looked at Natalia and continued, "Let them know they can come in."

Ze led his gang through the front door and pointed around, shouting some instructions. Twiggy had the weapons-room key, provided by Roberta, and headed straight for that particular door.

"Wait a minute!" Mike yelled, rushing over to place himself between the weapons room door and Twiggy. "This is off limits. US property!" he looked over and prompted Natalia for a translation.

But before she could get the words out, Twiggy decided he had enough. He took his gun out of its holster, raised it above his head, and pistol-whipped the shit out of Mike. Because Twiggy had the strength to match his enormous physique,

Mike immediately fell to the ground with blood all over his face. Watching all this take place, Eddie immediately had one thought pop into his head, courtesy of Eazy-E: "Homeboy, you'd better think fast."

# 7

"P*OLÍCIA! POLÍCIA!" THE gang yelled as more marines rushed to the scene.* Some memories in life are a total blur, but some are remembered clear as day. That night was definitely an example of the latter for Eddie and Natalia. It's not often one meets his future wife, the future mother of his child, and the person who would cause him the most fucked-up pain imaginable, wrapped in a crazy-ass robbery of a US Armed Forces branch in a third-world country.

Twiggy had knocked Mike so hard that most weren't sure if he was dead on the spot. As more marines filled the room, Pedro came running in with his pistol waving, followed by Andre, and lastly, still by the front entrance, the leader of the gang, Ze.

The robbery was playing out nicely; the next step was to get the inhabitants on the ground, open the weapons room, gather the loot, and escape into the night. However, it seemed Pedro became a bit anxious, knowing his job was to eliminate any threat in front of him. He didn't wait for the entire plan to unfold; he was out for blood, and Dan happened to be next. Pedro pointed his pistol at Dan and took a shot. Luckily for Dan, Pedro was a terrible shot and only got Dan in the arm—enough to knock him to the floor in excruciating pain. They were using smaller, .25-caliber guns, but a gun is still a gun.

The marines were in total confusion at this point. Why were police in the house in the first place? And why were they shooting? As trained soldiers, their first instinct, regardless of what authority figure was on them, was to return fire.

"You idiot, Pedro! There's no need for that yet!" yelled Ze, knowing now that the whole scene had just shifted. The nice little web of fake police and a robbery were untangling into complete chaos.

As the confusing initial first burst by the police moved into a heightened state of disorder, Andre went flying through the living room, jumping on top of the marine who was sleeping on the couch. What a coward. He started whaling on him with all his might, and if the marine wasn't sleeping, he was knocked out cold now. Two marines down and a bum surfer neutralized in thirty seconds. Eddie had a choice to make: go down as a complete pussy and grab Natalia and run or try to go out like a hero. It was a fairly easy choice. Who doesn't want to go out the star? The whole scene felt like a movie or some stage production. How the hell could the Rio police want to come in and fuck up a bunch of marines? But once again, it was Rio; anything and everything happened there.

Eddie flung himself at Andre while he was still on top of the guy on the couch. He wrapped his arm around Andre's neck and pulled him back with all his strength. They rolled off the couch onto the floor as Eddie held on as tightly as possible, back on the ground, and Andre's body on top, both staring at the ceiling. Eddie wasn't letting go, that was for sure. Andre's neck was pulsating, rippling through Eddie's forearm and biceps. Eddie had obviously never killed anyone before, but this guy was attacking the US Marines, which meant he was attacking the United States itself, and he was pretty sure he wouldn't be punished if he happened to subdue one of the aggressors.

While this was happening, the marines were rushing in, shooting at the offenders, taking up strategic positions behind whatever cover they could, with Ze's gang mimicking the same movements. There was so much yelling and screaming. Eddie had a hard enough time understanding Portuguese when spoken slowly, but listening to a bunch of slang-wielding crazy motherfuckers firing off a bunch of words he could never make out, mixed with screaming English and a few gunshots slipped in, proved overwhelming.

Pedro went down in a storm of bullets from the bedrooms. This must have been the scariest moment, yet the biggest thrill in some of these young marines' lives. They trained for this type of excitement, and some of these guys had itchy trigger fingers as it was. Killing someone in self-defense was high on the bucket list for most of those marines. But as Pedro's body exploded across the hallway and into the kitchen, Eddie had bigger problems. Eddie had let go of Andre just slightly, as he couldn't hold his grip much longer. He also noticed that Susanna had made her way over to Natalia, and both had started to crawl toward the backyard.

"Natalia! Stay where you are! Get under the table over there!" Eddie shouted as he continued to fight with the Brazilian.

The girls were trembling with fear, and Susanna was crying hysterically.

"I don't want to die!" Susanna kept repeating over and over.

Big Twiggy saw Eddie struggling to hold on to Andre, and with guns blazing, he fired shots back down the hall as he sprinted toward the two. More marines shot back, with a bullet going right through Twiggy's forearm.

"*Filho da puta!*" Twiggy cursed as he stumbled forward to the ground. But falling to his knee, under a storm of bullets, he caught the girls out of the corner of his eye. Twiggy bear-crawled toward them, grabbed Natalia with his good arm, and put a gun to her head. He started to scream at Eddie, motioning for him to let Andre go.

Eddie was more scared of not knowing what the hell he was yelling than as to what he was actually doing. But Eddie knew if he let go of Andre, Twiggy might just kill the girls and then him. If he held on to Andre, Twiggy most certainly was going to kill Natalia. Decisions, decisions.

Luckily for Eddie, Twiggy had not accounted for the guys in the backyard, and even luckier for Eddie, one of them had a knife. Behind Twiggy came a six-inch blade that penetrated right through his lower back into what must have been his right kidney. He yelped a harsh, high-pitched gurgling scream like a dying animal. Although it didn't kill him, he was rendered ineffective for the rest of the robbery.

So that left Ze and Andre, who was still backward on top of Eddie, but squirming his way loose. During this entire time, Ze had been on his knees, returning fire while fiddling with the door to the weapons room. He was absolutely determined to get into that room, knowing there was enough in there to possibly shoot his way out. Ze finally pulled the lock and swung open the door, right about the time the rest of the marines made it through the hallway to the living room.

They were going in stages, from one cover position to the next, but with only two assailants left, the tables had turned significantly. One of the marines had a baseball bat, which was strange, since they don't play baseball in Brazil. But a lot of these guys brought personal recreational possessions with them in country to try to stay as close to the US culture as possible. He saw Eddie during his struggle and shouted at him to let go of the intruder and get the hell out of the way. Eddie released Andre's neck, and Andre jumped up like a rocket. In parallel, the marine cocked and took a swing across Andre's head, shattering his eye socket and blasting three-quarters of his nose across his face.

"Natalia! Get to the backyard now!" shouted Eddie to the girls, and they bolted out the back door. The three of them were free but definitely not out of danger. Ze was still holed up in the weapons room, and he outgunned the rest of the house by a massive amount.

A couple of the marines had made their way to Dan and Mike, who was regaining consciousness. They pulled them out the front door, where the gang had penetrated just moments earlier. Eddie decided to take cover with the girls in the far corner of the backyard, thinking it might be a good idea to try to scale the ten-foot wall, but deciding the better course was to wait this thing out and hope it ended in the house.

"You girls okay?" Eddie whispered, trying to calm them down.

"I... I don't know," responded Susanna, still shaking.

"What about you, Natalia?"

"I hate this place! I need to get out of here!" she screamed in response.

"Shh! Keep it down! As long as we're out here, we should be okay," Eddie instructed.

"Keep it down? People are getting murdered in there! We could have died!" Susanna insisted, scowling down at Eddie.

"But we didn't, Susanna!" Natalia snapped back.

"Yes, we made it! But we have to be careful. It's not over yet!" Eddie reminded the girls.

Although he was right, the freedom of being outside of that house smelled and felt as good as anything Eddie had ever experienced up to that point in his life. He had so much adrenaline pumping through him from the struggle with Andre that as it started to leave his system, the realization started to set in. One more insane, yet strangely exciting, chapter in his Life Book, dedicated to the craziness of Brazil.

Back inside the house, madness ensued. Ze definitely was off base when he decided to fuck with US Marines. He was holed up in the weapons room, which ordinarily might be a good place to be when you're the only one standing, facing down armed and trained warriors. The problem was, he underestimated the courage and fearlessness of some of these young Americans who were after him. In their minds, the assailants had messed with their friends, the US Marine Corps, and the United States itself. Throwing that out the window, they also ruined a nice little party.

The marines wanted to barrel through the door before Ze could pick out any weapon and load it with the separate ammunition in the drawers, but Ze was one step ahead and had armed himself to the teeth.

"Get the fuck out of there! There's no way out for you!" shouted one of the marines, but Ze couldn't understand his English. Though Ze's original intent was robbery, now he just wanted to stay alive.

"We're going to kill this dude," remarked one soldier to another. "Who here can tell him that in Portuguese?"

"Hey, amigo! English!" one shouted to the Ze inside the room.

"No English! You gringo die!" Ze yelled back, still too timid to start shooting rounds. He knew once he did that, there would be a storm of bullets on him.

"Why don't we just rush this dude?"

"Throw a fucking grenade in there!"

But the marines also understood that if they could end this without destroying their weapons room, they would be much better off. Ze was also in agreement, in his own mind wondering how he could communicate a treaty.

And the marines pulled out a surprise that would satisfy his desire.

Out in front of the house, quite a crowd had formed. One of those gathered was Ze's sister Roberta, who had only left the house before the party was supposed to begin. As she witnessed bloody Americans out on the front lawn, she understood the plan had gone out the window. Out of the front door ran a marine, frantically searching around, yelling, "Does anybody speak English?"

"I do." Roberta immediately raised her hand.

"You." The Marine pointed at her. "Come with me."

Roberta reentered the house to see the bloody scene in front of her. Looking around at her brother's friends, dead or close to it, she immediately began to scream.

"Dude, that's our housekeeper!" shouted one of the guys as they tried to calm her down.

"Where's my brother?" Roberta asked, searching around frantically.

"Your brother? What are you talking about?"

"The policeman is *my* brother!"

Ze heard Roberta's voice, and he poked his head up immediately from his defensive potions within the weapons room.

"Roberta! *Estou aqui!*" yelled Ze, telling her that he was there and alive.

The marines all were completely baffled at this point, but they were just given even more leverage.

"Roberta—that is your name, right?"

She nodded.

"Tell your brother to drop all his weapons, move slowly toward the door, then put his hands outside. If he doesn't, we are going to give him thirty seconds and then blow him to pieces."

Roberta looked up, crying, and translated the words. Ze yelled something back, and Roberta said, "He doesn't believe you. He thinks you will kill him anyway."

"Roberta, aren't we always nice to you in the house? Don't we treat you well? We are honest people. Tell him he can trust it. Also, it's his only choice. The clock starts *now!*"

Roberta quickly translated, stressing the part about trusting them not to shoot.

Twenty-four, twenty-three...

The time was counting down.

Twelve, eleven...

"Marines! Get ready to blast this guy to pieces!"

"Ze! *Por favor!*" Roberta yelled.

Five, four, three... and two trembling hands appeared in the doorway. Two marines grabbed each hand, pulled Ze from the door, and immediately jumped on top of him. With a knee into the neck and with others holding him down and searching his body for weapons, the ordeal came to an end.

In the backyard, the three heard the commotion turn into congratulatory excitement. Natalia turned to Eddie and stared at him, wide-eyed, and he had no idea what she was thinking. But in her mind, she just saw this American, from the worst country on earth, along with soldiers from that country, save her and her friend's life from an attack from her fellow countrymen. She was thoroughly confused, but that was the moment in her life where she started to fall in love with him—or so she later claimed—and the destiny of their lives intertwined and moved together from that day on.

# 8

THE ROBBERY WAS all over the local and national news in Brazil, although for some reason it never made it back home to the States. One would think the whole situation—the characters involved, the craziness of it all—would be made into a blockbuster movie, maybe with some famous actor winning an Oscar for it. But no, just the Brazilian news, and there was a lot of sympathy for Ze and his gang. In the United States, there's so much money, where much of crime is based on boredom or perpetrated by weirdos and nutjobs. Only in the United States are adults kidnapping children and kids shooting up other kids at schools or malls; in third-world countries like Brazil, there's an actual necessity for crime. People are starving. They kidnap to hold people for ransom, to get money for food. And many Brazilians saw this favela gang take on the US Marines, and they liked it. Never mind the fact that Ze's gang already had money from the drug trade, which involved killings and torturing, sometimes involving kids... but it came out as a David-versus-Goliath story.

Natalia, on the other hand, knew that was all complete bullshit. She was there and saw it firsthand. She thought her life was over, taken at the hands of these psychotic thugs, and for the first time, she began to question what she was taught by the likes of adults, including Padrinho. When boiled down, a crime is a crime, regardless of race, color, creed, nationality, or anything else. When you're scared for your life or well-being and you see pain and suffering unfolding before your very eyes, it affects you in a mind-changing, life-altering way.

Natalia and Eddie spent the night of the robbery together but not quite in the romantic setting they had hoped for. Holed up with the *real* Rio police, the players from the various branches of government appeared one by one. The Brazilian military, government officials, and members of the US diplomatic team from the consulate in Rio joined in for the briefing, including a team from the US embassy in Brasília. There they learned that the gunmen were not true police officers but rather drug traffickers from the Rocinha favela. And throughout the night, after they answered more questions than they could possibly bear, Natalia and Eddie had a little bit of time to get to know each other. Through it all, Natalia started to grow fond of the United States of America.

"So, now you know I am good husband material—I will protect you and our future kids!" Eddie leaned over to Natalia, joking, while waiting out the rest of the night. "All that's left is for us to go on our first date."

"Thank you for trying to make me smile. I am so sick of this shit happening in my country. This doesn't happen in America, does it?"

"Well, it depends on what city you are in, to be honest. But no, it's generally just straight-up bank robberies, liquor stores... not many people have the balls to rob the government."

"My friend lived a semester in New York. But some small place, not New York City. She hated it! I think it was... Buffalo?" Natalia guessed correctly.

"Buffalo? Why would you go to America and live in Buffalo? Didn't she ever hear of, like, Miami? Or San Diego?"

"It's where she had an aunt living. She said she would never move back to America."

"Yes, but Buffalo? No offense to them or your friend, but that's like judging the meat loaf by just eating the loaf!"

"What are you talking about? What's meat loaf?"

"I don't even know. I just mean she's judging the whole country on a bland, boring city. The meat is elsewhere! Sorry, it's been a long night!"

Natalia looked at Eddie and wondered who he was. He definitely was brave, but he seemed a little off to her. Plus, he was American, and she had been programmed to distrust anyone with an allegiance to Uncle Sam. Furthermore, in front of her stood a man, and what about her general feelings towards the male species? Was she strong enough to break down the walls of her suspicion towards the opposite sex? At least with this particular man?

But as the night continued toward its conclusion, the two got to know each other just enough to ignite a little spark to keep each other's interest. Natalia described her family of artists, her divorced mother who was dating a pretty affluent man now living in Rio, and her plans for becoming a teacher once she graduated from college. In turn, Eddie gave her his story populated with all its characters and tales—family, past, and so on. They promised to not let the robbery scare away her vacation, even if Susanna eventually vowed to take the next flight home to Brasília.

For Eddie, his time in Brazil was starting to pay dividends. Being a reckless firebrand this time made an impression on a girl, which provided a distraction for him to focus on outside of his homesickness. They would have the next week to really spend some time together, wondering if this might be a nice little summer romance or maybe turn into something bigger. They both quickly started to realize that this was the case of the latter, even with the chasm between them being full language fluency, culture, and the miles apart from their home bases. Natalia was starting to learn who a real American was, which was a complete reverse from what Padrinho had preached, and she kind of liked it.

"Isn't it beautiful here—the beach, the weather, away from the worries of the world?" Eddie mentioned one day to Natalia as they sat alone on Ipanema. "I don't know why people waste away their lives in office buildings. Look at this beach. It's full of people, and it's only Tuesday!"

"That's because there are no jobs in Rio, Eddie. It might be different where you are from, but most of the people at this beach are going to go beg for money tonight, and the others have rich families they can go home to. The real people are working; they are just the minority in Rio."

"Shit, I want to be the minority! Well, I guess technically I am. I mean, I'm sitting here with you, right?"

"So, you want to be unemployed and no job?" Natalia was starting to become annoyed.

"No, absolutely not! I just want to have a work-life balance. I don't want to slave away at a job. How can I do that? Maybe I can, like, import something here that Brazilians don't have. Do you guys like peanut butter? I haven't seen any around."

"What's that?"

"Or what about burritos? Any of that around here?" Eddie's mind started racing.

"Eddie, honestly, it sounds like you are getting bored. Why don't you look for a job down here?"

"Nah, I didn't come here to get a job. I came here to think outside the box, ya know?"

"Well, I'm leaving after Carnival in a few days. If you want, in between importing... what was it? Peanut butter? If you want, you can come to Brasília with me and at least see more of Brazil than just Rio."

This excited Eddie tremendously. He did want to travel but was always a bit nervous about figuring out yet another city on his own.

"Absolutely! Where is Brasília, like way up north?"

"My God! You foreigners have no clue! Let's go find a map, and you can learn about something other than soccer and monkeys!"

"Deal!"

As NATALIA AND Eddie planned the next phase of their romance, Dan was improving quite a bit himself, and before long, he was released from the hospital, armed with a great story to tell and an accompanying battle wound, although his days in Brazil were numbered. That whole ordeal scared the shit out of his parents, and before long, they packed up and moved themselves to a nice quiet town in Kansas. So much for the missionary life.

But the newly growing international couple was just beginning its adventure together. Eddie continued his Portuguese for Foreigners class, and they passed most days at the beach, drinking beer and just hanging out. The great Brazilian celebration of Carnival was coming up, and Rio was alive and vibrant. The scene was a summertime paradise. Vendors walked the beach, offering everything from suntan lotion to food to one-dollar beers. No need to lift a finger; just sit back and enjoy.

One particular day, the skies were crystal blue, the sand was especially soft, and for some reason, the pollution in the ocean seemed to be low. Someone broke out an American football, and a game unfolded on the beach, where the Brazilians were taught the ins and outs of the sport. While drinking beers after every touchdown was not particularly accepted in the NFL, it was perfectly tolerated at the beach in Rio. All the while, the climax of Carnival loomed on the horizon.

Carnival isn't a one-day holiday; it's a weeklong party, and when it hits, it hits hard. The couple stayed up all week long, maybe sleeping two or three hours a day, fueled by alcohol and Diet Cokes, salt water and fun. The celebration is unexplainable, almost weird, including dancing lunatics marching in the streets behind giant trucks inching along while blaring songs from large speakers. The only problem with Carnival in Rio is that it's a complete tourist spectacle. In fact, all the locals from Rio, the Cariocas, leave the city and travel up to the north of the country, creating a void filled with Euro trash from all over and, of course, the drunken Americans. But it is still a great time for all.

The last night of Carnival, Natalia and Eddie decided to visit to the samba competition: a stadium, filled to capacity, cheering for those clubs who would be crowned King of Carnival. The place was a madhouse, with the festivities kicking off late in the dark night, around 1:00 a.m. The environment was not unlike the Super Bowl, with thousands of fans tailgating outside the stadium, beer flowing and barbecuing local flavors on the grills. Working their way inside, they caught the sight of it all like a roller coaster for the senses. People were dressed up in their different VIP T-shirts, sitting wherever they wanted to or where their VIP status told them to. Natalia and Eddie made their way to an upper section.

"This is the best seat in the house if you're not a VIP," explained Natalia, insinuating that Eddie should have doled out a little more cash for a better view.

"I actually like it. You can see *everything* from here, which makes it better," he responded, thinking the only downside was not being close enough to the hotter, scantily clad VIP girls.

Taking their seats next to a group of older Brazilians, Eddie immediately felt their awkward stares. Not knowing if it was because they were being loud and obnoxious, showing too much PDA, or if they recognized Eddie as the gringo involved in the marine robbery, anxiousness crept in. To their left sat a scary older woman, who became more annoyed by the minute till she finally blurted out in Portuguese slang, "Can you please shut the fuck up and stop bumping into me?"

Natalia responded, "I'm so sorry. There's just not a lot of space here."

However, the lady wasn't giving in. "Stay out of my way. Maybe you should move down a row!"

Eddie's Portuguese was just good enough to understand this, and he was in somewhat of a predicament. He always stood up for any of his girlfriends, as his previous experience with Ze's gang had proved, but a bit of a challenge was presented to confront an old woman, even if she was continuously pissing and moaning.

Deciding the best course of action was to go after her husband, in the worst drunken Portuguese, he yelled, "Tell your wife to keep quiet, or I'm going to beat your ass!"

One of the several security guards immediately pulled Natalia aside and began negotiating a peace. It seemed the representative did recognize Eddie from the robbery—and, of course Natalia, being a good-looking girl—they immediately offered a seat down in the first-level VIP box. Away they went to finish out Carnival, savoring the VIP treatment. Eddie started to get used to the good life in Rio.

THE DAY AFTER Carnival ended, Natalia was set to return home to Brasília, and Eddie was set to follow. The thought started to cross his mind of what a future could be like with this girl. They didn't seem to have a whole lot in common other than the circumstance in which they met.

*Am I trying too hard to get a girlfriend? Is she really going to be worth the troubles that go into dating someone from another country?* But in the end, he decided to push on and see what the future had in store.

The morning of her flight home, the two had breakfast together, and from that meal, Eddie could sense that maybe there was something a bit unbalanced going on. She mentioned things and asked questions about the States that could have been attributed to being naive or uninformed, but in reality, she still carried the ideas implanted by Padrinho.

"Eddie, the world is run by the Americans to keep the poor hungry and uninformed so they can divide us and hold us powerless," and "How are you taught to see Brazilians, that we are stupid and you should be able to take what you want from us?" and "Why is it that we all speak English down here, and only a few foreigners like you even try to learn Portuguese?"

Some of it even made a little sense to Eddie. *What the hell. I really don't care, because what do I know about dating a girl from the third world? Maybe they are all a little crazy!*

As the two hugged and gave their goodbyes, at least until Eddie visited her in Brasília, Natalia gave him one last nugget to ponder.

"Take this oil and rub it on your forehead; that will help align the negative thoughts from the robbery experience we shared into a part of your brain where you can overcome its power. Also, if you ever find yourself hungover without me, drink this tea, then put the herbs from it under your nose for two minutes, and your body will heal." These were obvious warning signs of what was to come, but he decided to bypass his logic and go with the flow.

Upon Natalia's return to Brasília, Eddie was back on his own. The day-to-day routine he had previously enjoyed resumed, with only a handful of friends in the city. Becoming a known quantity in the town was a real thing—from the robbery fame and also because his Portuguese was improving, the appearances at several parties, and meeting a lot of upper-tier people. However, he was still itching to explore the Natalia idea. Was there more to her than just the short time they spent together?

Part of being an expat is devouring all the new country has to offer, and that means not just getting into a mundane routine.

Travel is the cure to all that ails an expat, and in a country as big as Brazil, sampling the varying people, places, and cultures while never leaving the border is a goal for many. The north of Brazil is extremely third-world, populated by mostly darker-skinned people (as most of the slave trade took hold in that region). The food, the songs, everything is uniquely different up north from anywhere else in the country. Also, the north encompassed the Amazon, which one could imagine is the furthest place from a first-world reality that can be imagined. Contrast that with the south of Brazil; mainly light-skinned, blond-haired, and blue-eyed Brazilians (stemming from German and Italian immigrants who settled there after the world wars and who brought with them the food and culture of the Old World).

Somewhere in between lies the gigantic hustle and bustle of São Paulo and Rio de Janeiro: two huge cities with cultures of their own, the people a mix of the north and south—a melting pot of the whole country. Finally, inland from the cities, sits the countryside with legit cowboys, open land, and a whole country, Garth Brooks–type of feeling. That is where the capital of Brazil, distinctively named Brasília, rests—where Natalia resided and where Eddie would soon be headed.

Getting off the plane in Brasília, it didn't smell like Washington, DC, nor did it look or feel like it. Eddie had been expecting some extremely clean, brand-new, metropolitan city, only to be given something that resembled Mars or some other alien planet. As it was a planned city, the architect, Oscar Niemeyer, must have been on some space-idea-fueled LSD trip putting that place together. The airplane layout, the futuristic-looking buildings, all provided uniqueness. And as he rode through the various sections, seeing postmodern buildings with government officials and businessmen running around, there were also still sightings of donkeys pulling carts full of trash or scraps or whatever else running through the streets alongside the cars. Yep, still in Brazil.

Arriving at Natalia's apartment in Asa Sul, the South Wing, the first two people he met were her brother and her maid. Her brother was very suspicious of Eddie. "Where are you from? Why are you here? Where are you going? Why are you here again?" he asked over and over. The maid just smiled and went about her business. Natalia's mother spent most of her time in Rio, so the brother was the real hurdle. As the night came among them and the sun began to set, Eddie could tell he had already been through about ten beers and maybe a few joints. During the interrogation, Eddie tried to be as cool as possible, but the more drink the brother consumed, the stranger the conversation. Natalia was translating as much as possible when understanding his broken English seemed insurmountable, but Eddie couldn't help but feel like she was purposely leaving some important points out.

At 8:00 p.m., her brother, João (the Portuguese name for *John*), finally departed, headed for a triumph in some no-name bar. He was almost two years younger than Natalia but very protective and quite aggressive. Natalia and Eddie settled in as the maid gathered the luggage and situated the two of them, amazingly enough, in Natalia's room, where Eddie would be sleeping on a lower bed next to her. João returned that night around 11:00 p.m., hammered and pissed off.

"Eddie, you need come with me down the stairs now," João insisted.

"Umm, okay. What's up, dude?" he replied.

"Some motherfucker stare me down when I came back from bar, and they have carful of punks down there waiting!"

All Eddie could do was sit in amazement, thinking, *Is this a joke? First night in Brasília? A fucking fight? Dude, he's testing you.*

Natalia stepped in and tried to brush it off, as João was beyond reason from the alcohol, but Eddie felt like he had to prove himself to her brother.

"Fuck it, I'm in!" he proclaimed, standing up, ready to go. And for all he knew, it could have been João's friends down there, or they could have been walking into an ass-beating, or the carful of punks might all be gone. Whatever the case, Eddie had to fight. To be quite honest, he might even enjoy it a little.

They headed down the stairway and went outside to the dry Brasília air. As they exited the door, Eddie mused, *Brasília is not much different from, say, Colorado. It has some altitude to it; it's extremely dry. What a nice little place...*

"Eddie! Let's go!" João interrupted Eddie from his happy place.

As Eddie stood there, pondering the environmental qualities of Brazil and Colorado, João immediately took off running toward the punks. Eddie took off after him. João was like a wild man. He was flailing his arms and screaming and cursing. *What the hell?* Eddie thought as he pushed to keep up. João picked up a rock and chucked it at their car, cracking the front windshield. The driver hit the gas, and the tires screeched as the car took off speeding out of the parking lot and down the road.

"Motherfuckers!" they yelled in Portuguese slang, as they flew into the open road.

"Fuck you! Don't come back!" Eddie hollered just to show João his bravery and excitement to be involved in having his back after meeting him only hours before. Eddie stumbled through a translation project to try and say the right words, not being too confident he expressed himself correctly about having each other's back. Whatever—João now knew Eddie was a *man*. And just like that, he was accepted into the family, at least by the overbearing brother.

# 9

As the sun melted away in the distance of the enormous lake, perched between the hustle and bustle of Brasília, so too was the homesickness and loneliness in Eddie's life. His Life Book was starting to reach the point of an official, sincere relationship, even if he still detected something not right in Natalia. But this didn't dissuade his pursuit as he agreed to spend a few extra days in Brasília. After all, even after passing the last few nights sleeping inches away from her, he hadn't made his way past her Catholic beliefs in the intimacy department. Determined as he was, he couldn't leave Brasília without trying to advance the relationship somewhat.

The last night of Eddie's Brasília visit, the two made their way to a local bar and settled on a few beers, then out with friends for the night, but Eddie had a different plan in mind, and he was ready to put the ball in motion.

"What's wrong, Eddie? You seem a little quiet tonight," said Natalia.

"I don't know. Guess I'm just tired. We just keep doing the same thing over and over. Walks at the park during the day, drinks with friends at night. I mean, don't get me wrong, parks and friends are nice and all, but I'm bored with everything. I'm thinking of either taking a trip to the Amazon, or the south... or maybe just head back home to the States." Eddie knew the game. Play a little distant to bring her a little closer.

"Back to the States? Seriously?"

"Yes, seriously. I need to move forward with my life."

Natalia looked off toward the other direction, then back at Eddie and said, "Actually... you are probably right. You are wasting your time here in Brazil. You are young and need to do something with yourself. Probably a good idea."

That wasn't supposed to be the response. She was supposed to beg him to stay. His plan unwound quickly from there. "Oh, really? You want me to move back, then?"

"Well, yes, if that's what you want."

"No! I want to take walks in the park and drinks with your friends!"

"But you just said—"

"I know what I said! I wasn't really expecting you to agree with me! Shit! I suck at this! Honestly, Natalia, what I really want is to take *us* to the next level, you know?"

"Eddie, I can't take *us* to the next level knowing you want to move back to the States."

"No... I don't want to move back! That was my way of telling you I want to stay!"

"Telling me you want to stay by telling me you want to move back?"

"Yes, exactly! Damn, in America, it's the girl who plays this crazy game shit. I know how to respond to it. I don't know how to actually play it."

This was going nowhere real fast. But the message was sent, although not entirely received. The two agreed to call it a night and head back home to just watch a movie, no longer in the mood to go clubbing. But there was still an unfinished conversation to be had, as neither were too clear on the future of the relationship.

"Natalia, this is my last night here. I really do like you a lot. I want to continue this, if you'll forget about all that crap I said earlier. I just don't know how to tell you how badly I want to be with you and really move forward with our relationship."

Natalia looked deep into Eddie's eyes, and being a woman who had been through a lot with this man, she could really now believe in deciphering his true intentions. Concluding that Eddie was being honest, she decided to give in a little. "You know my beliefs, Eddie, but if you can make me a promise... if you can tell me that we are really going to try to make something with each other... that you aren't going to just have me and I'll never hear from you again... then I *could* be open to the idea of—"

"Absolutely!" Eddie eagerly interrupted. "I'm not that guy!" *Wait, am I that guy? No, I do really like her. Can I commit now? Sure. She's great.* And as Eddie continued his internal argument, Natalia just watched and wondered if he was going to make the move after she'd given him the green light.

"Eddie, are you here with me?"

"Huh? Oh, sorry. I was just thinking... actually, I wasn't thinking. Actually, I was thinking too much. Oh, never mind!"

"Let's go to my room, Eddie, and I can help you clear your thoughts."

THREE MONTHS LATER, as Eddie continued his progression in Portuguese school and was trying to make a little money on the side, his life in Rio was a bit dull without Natalia there with him. She had visited him once, and he had also gone back to Brasília, but now that she was officially his girlfriend, his nights in Rio were spent home alone watching movies rather than out and about on the town. He wasn't 100 percent sure how he felt about this, as he was involved with a long-distance relationship all while also being long distance from his homeland, but then the call came that completely changed the script in his Life Book, forever and for the rest of his future.

"Eddie..." Natalia was trembling so badly that Eddie could detect it over the phone. "Eddie, I need to speak with you about something."

"Is everything okay? What's the matter?"

"I'm... I don't know how to say this other than to just say it."

"Don't be afraid, Natalia. You can tell me anything."

"I'm pregnant."

Hours spent on the phone, reassuring each other that everything was going to be all right, but not entirely sure if those words were true, Eddie was now sitting in a very different set of circumstances than just the day before. No more teaching English. No more days at the beach. The time had come to be serious in life... to be *responsible*. And he knew exactly what he had to do.

Making his way to the best jewelry store in Rio, debt-free at the time but looking to reverse that trend, he had his credit card in hand and ready to go. The bonus of saving potentially hundreds on sales tax (buying jewelry in Brazil as a tourist) sealed the deal. "Can you show me the best diamond engagement rings you have?" he muttered to the saleslady, being a bit shy.

"Umm, I'm sorry, but here in Brazil, we don't really give diamonds as engagement rings," she responded.

Now this was both good and bad news. The diamond ring selection wasn't too extensive, which obviously limited him to a reduced choice. The flip side to that, though, was that Natalia wouldn't be like the typical American girl, expecting some XX–plus carat ring surrounded by even more diamonds and whatnot. But Eddie wanted to stick to the American custom, and so he would have to figure out how to get the best of what they had.

"What've you got, then? Just anything. Let me take a look."

The woman brought out three diamond rings, very simple—the last rings in stock. One of them looked perfect enough for him, with such a limited selection and his limited knowledge in asking a girl's hand in marriage. Immediately choosing this extremely simple, circular diamond upon nothing more than a plain band, the purchase was finalized. For a girl being in her early twenties now, not even expecting a diamond, he assumed this would blow her mind, even if it was less than one carat.

As Eddie hopped on the Rio bus to head back to his apartment, his eyes darted around. He had never been so scared for his life, traveling across all of Rio de Janeiro, on a public bus, with some very poor, very scary-looking guys, staring him down like they wanted to steal his shoes—and he was on that bus with a $5,000 diamond ring in his pocket! *If these guys knew what I was carrying, holy shit, they would rip this bus apart for a piece of me!* But even though he had sweat trickling down his face and looked extremely nervous and suspicious, the other guys didn't say a word or make a move. Alive and well arriving home, he felt as if his apartment had never looked so safe.

The proposal was planned in about five minutes, with Eddie not giving it a lot of thought but knowing it would be fine. He flew Natalia out to Rio for another long weekend, as she was getting used to not working and having that kind of spare time. Picking her up from the airport, Eddie went total first class on her—well, a taxi pickup at that time was first class enough!

"We can take the bus back to your apartment," she proclaimed.

"No, I have a special day planned today. I still haven't been to the Christ the Redeemer statue. Are you in?"

"Oh my God! That would be so much fun! Yes!" she yelled happily. She was in a good mood that day, and he could only hope she would repeat that *yes* just as excitedly in a few hours.

Driving up to the famous Cristo statue in Rio is a contradiction in the country itself. Most think Rio is like the Amazon, with animals running around everywhere, native inhabitants, and so on, but it's not. Rio is quite cosmopolitan and becoming more international every day. The bottom of the mountain that holds the statue turns from a nice suburb to a bit poorer yet safe tourist attraction. However, ascending the mountain, the Amazonian vibe comes into play. Wild monkeys hopping around in the trees become visible, and is a sight to see for those who are used to just cats and dogs. As the summit of the mountain approaches and the statue comes into full view, the breathtaking scenery engulfs one's eyes. A 360-degree view of Rio can be found at the base of the statue: to the south, the rich area and beaches of Zona Sul, with tall building, hotels, and the beaches themselves. To the north, nothing but favelas and poverty, with the famous *Maracanã* soccer stadium thrown into the middle. The line between rich and poor in this world can't be any clearer.

Standing at the foot of Cristo, it was the perfect setting for a proposal, with barely a cloud in the sky and just enough altitude on the mountain to suppress the wild summer heat felt within the city. A slight breeze swished by as the different tourists snapped pictures of the scenery. Almost every language in the world can be heard up there— from the Spanish from the visiting Argentinians to the different tongues of Western Europe. Natalia being so religious, Eddie knew being at the feet of Cristo would put her in the right frame of mind.

"Natalia, I want you to know that even though we have only known each other for a short time, I love your laid-back, cool way. You're just so... cool. Really cool. But at the same time, you are beautiful, and there is no one else I would want to say this to." As he got down on his knee, he kept thinking, *Wow, I really fucked that one up. Cool? Laid-back? That's not what she wants to hear! But what else can I say? I haven't known her long enough to have sufficient adjectives!*

"Eddie! Hello!" Natalia caught Eddie off in never-never land again.

"Oh, yeah, sorry! What I want to know is... will you... will you please marry me?"

Natalia had watched enough American TV shows and movies to know how it worked, as the bend-the-knee thing is really for certain cultures. Yet she began to cry, which Eddie took to be a good sign. After what seemed to me a full minute, she screamed, "Yes!" in Portuguese and English.

"There you have it. We're engaged!" was all Eddie could muster. The engagement wasn't even as spectacular as the scenery around them, but in Eddie's mind, it would have to do. Natalia didn't know the ins-and-outs of American proposals to the extent that she would realize what a crap job he had done, so she was content too.

And as Natalia and Eddie embraced, with tourists around clapping and whistling to the delight they had just witnessed, Natalia thought, *I can't believe I am marrying an American and having an American baby. I am going to hell.* And on the other end of the hug, all Eddie could do was wonder, *Shit, what have I done?*

BYPASSING ANY MAJOR wedding event, the couple decided on an extremely intimate celebration. No reception, no dancing, no drinking and carrying about. Natalia was pregnant, after all. The two wanted to tie the knot with just the local Brazilian family and maybe do the same in the States at some point. Natalia's family was exceptionally supportive of the pairing, although many of her cousins, aunts, and uncles had questions about Eddie seeing how he was American. Her father was the tougher sell, but in the end, he respected the fact that Eddie had learned Portuguese and seemed to come from a good family.

After the wedding, and as the days turned into weeks, the daily grind of family life was starting to encroach on their lives. From his free-spirited days in Rio de Janeiro, a life full of current and future responsibility was pulling Eddie down like a brick tied to a butterfly. The tide was also starting to turn on the relationship itself, as maybe Eddie wasn't so attractive to Natalia anymore without a job or any prospects. Being on vacation for a few months when they met was all fun and games, but now it was starting to annoy her.

"My family is really wondering how you are going to take care of me. You don't even have a job. What are we doing here?" she often asked, and he consistently replied, "I'm still on vacation, learning a language, and having fun. There are plenty of years left to slave away at a job." He knew that wasn't the right answer, but he wanted to pull a reaction. "If your family has a problem with that, you should have married some rich Brazilian!"

"We're just wasting our lives here," she pressed. "I too want to work and start a life. Why can't you just get a job here so we can buy a house or an apartment?"

"I'm not working in some corporate job in Brazil just to make one-eighth the amount of money of the same job as in the States when that's the whole reason I left in the first place!" he argued, frustrated that nobody could understand that.

"Well, you'd better figure it out fast, because in a couple of months, you will not only have yourself to look after but two other people!"

"Wait, you just said you wanted a job... but now I am taking care of both of you? Why don't you work and I'll stay home with the baby?"

"Are you kidding me?" This was definitely not the way in South American cultures.

"Well, just saying... but anyway, I have a plan that I've been working on."

"Better not be to win the lottery. I've heard you say that about ten times, and that's not a plan."

"Ha-ha. No, seriously, Natalia. I love being an expat, traveling the world, and learning new cultures. So why not get paid to do that? And at that, why not let my employer pay for housing and lifestyle and allow us to experience the world? What employer would do that?"

"Well, how about the airline companies?"

"Shit, I didn't think of that. No, anyway, think of another, even richer company."

"Shipping companies? Cruise ships? The list goes on and on, Eddie."

"Damn it! Okay, so there are a lot. But hear me out. What I was going to say was... Uncle Sam, that's who. The US State Department is always searching for foreign service diplomats to work overseas in their embassies and consulates. I've researched it, and it's a tough job to land. If a potential resource does not have a specialized skill, like information technology, I can apply as a general applicant."

"So, yes, that would be really cool!" Natalia was proud of him. This was a life she could love.

"It's a two-step process, and the first step means I have to study and pass a written exam, consisting of multiple-choice questions and essays. It's going to be in a couple of weeks at the US embassy here in Brasília. I looked it up, and stats show something like only 5 percent of all applicants pass the written test. Screw it. Why not me?"

EDDIE WAS BACK at it, studying hard for a test. Natalia's family were on board for it too, so it was a nice boost for the couple. As the day of the written test came and went, the couple waited nervously for the result. Lo and behold, luckily for Eddie, his result was included in the 5 percent. It was not an easy accomplishment, but it was a big "screw you" to all of Natalia's family who were starting to think of him as a bum. But if the written test was no joke, passing the in-person interview was almost impossible.

Eddie was greeted back at the embassy with the other applicants, all top 5 percenters. The proctors required the hopefuls to produce more essays, then analyze the group as they argued over issues and aimed to resolve the problems of the world. Next, one-on-one interviews were conducted, all over an eight-hour period.

Eddie failed miserably. He was still a twentysomething-year-old beach bum, going up against army captains with war experience or older, high-ranking corporate execs who were looking for a challenge. He had no shot.

Failing the foreign service interview further established him as a complete loser to Natalia's family, and it even got her thinking about why she'd agreed to the marriage. Even with her initial hesitations, maybe the idea of marrying an American was better than the reality of it all. Natalia began to feel the pressure, and it was soon too much for her to bear.

Pregnant and feeling a lack of hope, she spent less time with Eddie and more with her family, which was further building the strife between them. Her family continued to harp on the couple, constantly pressuring Eddie to find work in Brazil. But he hunkered down, dug in, and wasn't going to do what anyone else told him to do. Until finally, the weight of it all collapsed on top of them.

"Natalia, you knew who I was when we met, when we married, and even now. I will never change, but I am sick of your family dictating our lives! They keep telling you to tell me to stop being a lazy ass. You know I'm not lazy. I just don't like to work!"

"That's the definition of *lazy*, Eddie."

"You know what I mean!"

"They are right, Eddie. You need to support your family, and you don't do shit all day, and plus, on top of that, you drink all night with João. You're becoming him, and I didn't marry my brother!"

"You know what? I'm over it. I'm over your family, I'm over this town, and I'm over Brazil. Pack your shit. We're moving to America!"

"Why America? Calm down, Eddie. We just need to find you work."

"I can find work in one minute. Just not here. If you want me to work, I'll work. I'm going to be the hardest damn worker you've ever seen! But I'm not doing it here. There's a reason people go to the States, and that's for more money than they can make here."

"You know what? I am willing to go to America if that's what it would take."

This really took Eddie by surprise. Again, he'd tried the reverse-psychology move, and just like before, Natalia had called him out on it. It wasn't supposed to work that way.

"Well, fine. Let's do it, then! But don't come complaining to me every day about living in another country. If we do this, we really do this."

"Then let's do this." Her response was all it took. Those words concluded another chapter in Eddie's Life Book, one as a free-wheeling, all-night-partying, beach-bumming, expat American living in the third world.

# 10

A MARRIAGE CAN BE like a kiss. In the beginning, the first kisses are all passion and desire, but then kissing might become just a day-to-day part of life, almost like brushing one's teeth or putting on deodorant. And many times, just like a marriage can taste bad as it nears its end, so too can the kiss. It becomes all cheek kisses and no tongue, until finally the kisses fade away into hugs.

Natalia and Eddie were nearing the end of the passionate phase very quickly. Deciding to move to Southern California, as she was averse to cold weather, was an effort to maybe stir up the relationship. The plan was to relocate somewhere between Los Angeles and San Diego, someplace with good schools, close to the beach, and as cheap as possible. In California, *cheap as possible* is over $3,000 a month for rent, a stove, and a few rooms. Therefore, a good job for Eddie became even more important, growing his responsibility from just taking care of his family to keeping up with the Joneses.

Deciding to move on from his previous employer and look for work where he wouldn't be traveling much while staying home with his soon-to-be-born daughter was top priority. And he was really lucky. On the flight home from Brazil, the couple happened to sit next to a young American man who had struck up a conversation about work and careers. He had recently started a company that did a lot of technology work in South America, and he asked Eddie to keep in touch. Deciding this could be fate, Eddie kept the man's business card, knowing at some point in the future it might be an ace up his sleeve.

Finding work for a kid who had spent the last months running around Rio de Janeiro proved tougher than first believed. Eddie had spent days searching for work and applying online, receiving no response or maybe the occasional hit, yet the pay was too low, and so on it went. Frustration crept in, cutting deeper into the relationship as the stress piled on to an already tense situation.

Desperation hadn't quite knocked him down, but it was landing enough punches for Eddie to have to reach down and attempt to throw a haymaker of his own. He dug into his junk drawer and found the business card that the seatmate on the flight home from Brazil had given him, and he dialed the number. The very next day, he was in the stranger's office building, looking to get back into the corporate world that he had previously tried so hard to abandon.

"Hello. This is Eddie Watters, here to meet Mr. David Carlton," he said nicely to the receptionist.

"Right this way. He's expecting you," she responded, smiling.

*Not a bad-looking receptionist*, he thought. It was the first time he'd started to really think about girls other than Natalia.

But never mind that; he had a job interview to crush.

"Eddie, what's up, my friend? Glad you reached out to me. Let's sit down and chat," opened David excitedly.

Actually, he was more excited than Eddie thought he would be. But Eddie also had more than just a light résumé; he had the bilingual thing, providing a bit more arrogance and optimism in his chances of landing a position.

"Thanks for meeting me. I have really been looking into what you guys are doing here—seems super interesting. I'm definitely looking forward to learning more," he countered.

And on and on it went. It seemed David's company was young but growing. They couldn't hire enough to keep up, and now David had grand plans to really grow in Brazil, and he loved Eddie's background, especially the fact that 1) he spoke Portuguese, 2) he had a permanent visa for Brazil, 3) he had many Brazilian connections through Natalia, and 4) he knew the country pretty well.

"Eddie, I want you to know that there are sacrifices to be made here; we don't pay high salaries, but I will grant you a healthy amount of company stock." He followed with a doozy: "Let me introduce you to our vice president of human resources, Lisa Manning."

The stock thing was great, of course, but it posed a major challenge. How was Eddie going to afford rent on a crap salary? As he thought things through, out of nowhere, she walked into the room. The VP of HR, Lisa. Eddie shook her hand, and stood in complete awe.

Lisa was stunning upon first impression; she was one of those who dressed amazingly, with fashionable clothes that accentuated her gorgeous body, and eyes that matched beautiful color with an intellectual presentation that one could somehow decipher by peering straight through them. She was a perfect blend of beauty and brains.

But contrary to the nerves that generally accompany meeting the VP of HR, Eddie felt oddly at ease in her presence. She carried both respect as a businesswoman, and an easy feel about her where Eddie felt comfortable enough to discuss anything. As they began to speak, he could only muster one thought. *Oh, shit. Wait, I'm married.*

LISA ANN MANNING was living the life, or at least the best she could make it after a tough divorce a few years back, and raising two boys as a single mother. However, she had worked her way up from no college degree or work experience, first taking a job as a receptionist in a small, whatever-the-hell company to eventually landing a position in human resources. Showing off her hard work and toughness, she parlayed those traits with her outgoing personality, climbing her way up the chain. Being in the male-dominated corporate world, the executives still ensured she was a part of their inner team, till one day she was hired as the vice president of HR into David's small but thriving company. All this in the span of three years, very impressive for a twenty-seven-year-old woman who had children at home.

But it wasn't always that easy for her. As she spent her days with David, trying to recruit and grow a start-up, she couldn't escape her past. Her ex-husband, Tom, was always on her case for one thing or another. First, it was to not pay her any child support or alimony, which was fine with her, to now being a total asshole. She was armed with grit, however, and the time came in her life where she had to fight back.

"Tom, I'm sick of you taking advantage of me at every moment! You don't see your kids, and I paid for you to go through the police academy. I need more from you now, or I want full-custody of the kids!" It was not an unreasonable request seeing how she was the one who paid for the two boys' sports, schooling, clothes, and everything else. Tom had been a good dad, but since he'd dreamed up some harebrained idea to become a police officer, he was starting to become jaded with society and really just becoming a dick. To be fair, Tom had spent the last several years in the Los Angeles County jail system. There he dealt with the worst of the worst, accustoming him to the power trip and speaking to people a certain way, which was starting to percolate into his personal relationships.

"Lisa, you have no idea what you're dealing with. I know every judge, every bailiff... you don't want to take me to court—I'll own you there, and you'll lose everything that you have with the kids," Tom threatened constantly. And so it went, on and on like this until Lisa couldn't take any more of his bullshit.

"You know what, Tom? Don't talk to me like I'm one of those criminals in the Castle." The *Castle* was what they called the jail Tom worked in. "You want to fight over a few hundred dollars? I just want you to do your part! I can't be a full-time mom, paying for everything, driving the kids everywhere, while you don't do shit!" It wasn't an unreasonable request. Any single mother knows how hard it is to balance school, homework, dinners, extracurriculars, shopping, and everything else, all while trying to climb the corporate ladder as a woman. And Tom was living the good life. He had the kids on the weekends, even though it was technically fifty-fifty custody, and he didn't have to lift a finger and could be a Disneyland dad. The problem was, since he had that custody, he was supposed to be splitting the bill for everything, which he was not, so the reason for taking him to court was to motivate him to help.

But Lisa made a huge error. She'd underestimated the friends Tom had in the court system. The day came for their court hearing, and shit went down, just not in the favor of Lisa.

The judge asked Lisa to present her case, which she laid out beautifully. She opened with, "If I can show you receipts of everything from soccer teams to clothes to haircuts, I'm sure you will see that I am doing 100 percent of the raising of the kids and paying 100 percent of the bills."

Tom rebutted, "Your Honor, nice to see you again. Hope your family is fine. I look forward to seeing them next week at the BBQ. Anyway, here are receipts of all the clothes I've bought in the last two weeks alone. You can see I've bought over ten articles of clothing in one shopping trip, which I do once a month."

"But your ten articles are from Old Navy, and you spent $50 for cheap clothes, while I spend $500 on nice clothes that last the whole year!" Lisa countered. "Furthermore, the kids live with me Monday through Friday, and I pay for the weekly expenses."

"Well, Your Honor, I have been generous in not trying to disrupt the kids' weekly schedule, but, if I may, I feel the kids' grades have been slipping since I graciously let Lisa have the kids longer during the week, so I'd like to request that they switch schools and live with me."

"Are you kidding me?" Lisa was shocked. She'd expected an argument but not a full 180-degree flip-flop.

"Ms. Manning, can you explain the drop in grades?' asked the judge.

"Well, the kids are working hard, and I'm trying to help with homework, but I work late hours trying to keep everything afloat."

The judge countered, "Well, maybe if they lived with their dad, as he is requesting, their grades would improve and you could focus on work."

"I can't believe this. I came for help with the bills. He won't be there for them; he won't take them to sports or any of that. He just doesn't want to pay his share!" she argued.

But this is how the world works, unfortunately. When you have friends in all the right places, you stand to win the battles, and it was an impossible fight in which Lisa was engaging. In the end, the judge agreed to let Tom off the hook with no support for any bills. In fact, he told Lisa that she was irresponsible, only working so hard to buy nicer things for the kids, and he gave her six months for the kids to get their grades up or she would lose custody. Talk about reversal of fortunes. Had she never taken Tom to court, this wouldn't have been an issue. Now, not only did she have no help, she was in danger of losing custody.

Lisa came out of court and headed straight to work. David met her as she walked in and immediately had something for her.

"Lisa, we're interviewing a great candidate to run business development growing the team in Brazil. He's American and will be based here, but he has experience, has country knowledge, and is a great guy. I'd like you to meet him today."

About an hour later, David came to get Lisa out of her office, and she was visibly flustered. She had been crying, completely stressed out, and ready to just head home for the day to curl up with a bottle of wine. But she wiped off her tears, threw a coat of makeup on, and rallied. And as David brought her into the next-door office, she looked at the interviewee and thought, *Wow. Cute guy. Hope he doesn't see the kind of day I'm having.* But, of course, as David spoke the magical words—"Let me to introduce you to our vice president of human resources, Lisa Manning"—the two shook hands, and the spark was immediate.

"First, let me apologize for my appearance; I had a bit of a rough start this morning," opened Lisa.

"Not at all, you look great," he said. *Oh, shit. You can't say that in an interview to the VP of HR! Crap!* he immediately yelled within himself, hoping Lisa wouldn't walk out on the spot.

"Why don't we get started?" she responded. Quickly through the questioning, Lisa felt like Eddie was an interesting candidate. After some time on the job details itself, the subject of family came up, and although not entirely appropriate, the two got to chatting about their lives a bit.

"I'm actually expecting my first child, a daughter," Eddie told her. "I'm so excited, but it's really stressing out my wife and me. Hopefully when she's born, that all goes by the wayside."

"Well, I'm pulling for you, because you seem like a good guy—but it's hard having a kid, keeping a marriage together, work, and all that. I don't want to scare you, but it is what it is!" Lisa was obviously a little pissed. "But anyway, I guess we are supposed to be discussing more about the position and the company." She looked at her watch and noticed the thirty minutes were already up.

"I'll tell you what," she explained, "let me give you my card, and if you have any further questions, we can always discuss more anytime you'd like. I think you'd be great here, just based on your personality and fit for the company. I'll let David sort out the technical stuff. Great speaking with you, and I hope you make the right decision!"

To Eddie, the company was fantastic, but he wondered, *Is it really the right place for me? Is this Lisa woman making the job seem that much better?* Deciding it was a question he couldn't quite answer, he opted to move forward if offered the position, even if he would have to wrestle with his well-being of returning to the corporate world. For now, he could provide for Natalia and his daughter, which might smooth over some of the edges that had formed in their continuously declining relationship.

# 11

THE APARTMENT THAT night was eerily quiet. No TV, no music playing, even though Natalia had invited her old friend Susanna to town to keep her company till the baby was born. Eddie had been working up a storm, and Natalia herself was growing homesick. Life in the United States was good to her in many ways, but in the same breath, she'd lost her friends, her family, and support back home. In fact, in her mind, she was losing her Brazilian identity.

So with Susanna in town, most nights meant samba music playing loudly, both of them singing Brazilian songs and acting like it was still Carnival. But there was none of that going on this night.

*What the hell is going on?* Eddie wondered. As he took in the sight of the apartment, only to see clothes everywhere, the recently built crib, with its diapers placed neatly on the side, he grew worried over the possibilities. Running through different scenarios in his head, he figured maybe they'd just gone to grab some dinner.

Driving down Pacific Coast Highway, searching about in all the various spots they normally frequented, he noticed Natalia's car parked where the happy hour was legendary. Not even getting an invite, he thought to surprise them just to see what the response might be. As he walked through the front door, out toward the balcony where there was a separate bar, he saw the two of them talking up a storm with two guys in their midthirties.

Watching them for a while, he saw Susanna throw back a few martinis like they were Perrier, laughing and flirting with one of the guys. The other guy was in a separate conversation with Natalia. Since Eddie had been around the culture for some time, he knew right away that the one hanging out with Susanna was Brazilian (she didn't speak English well, so it didn't really take a detective on that one). Natalia's suitor was definitely American. Both men were adorned with rather nice work clothes, this being their place to go hunting for willing women—or even pregnant, girls for that matter.

"Hi, girls," Eddie said in Portuguese. "Didn't see you at home, so I thought—"

He was interrupted by the guy talking to Natalia.

"Excuse me, dude. Can't you see we're in a conversation?" said the American. He obviously didn't understand Portuguese, so Eddie thought he'd cut him a little slack.

"Oh, I'm sorry. You must be this young girl's doctor. I mean, she's very pregnant and in a bar, so I figured you're here to make sure that if she pops, you could deliver. Either that or you're a total slimeball hitting on a pregnant girl at a bar." Eddie's lifelong trait of bursting in every situation was starting to creep up. Since his first fight in elementary school, this attribute had hung around, sticking by his side like a stalker. While it did help him out of some sticky situations, when was he going to learn to let things go?

"Who the fuck are you?" The guy started to get in Eddie's face.

"Eddie, this is Don. His friend Marcel is talking to Susanna, so he is keeping me company," explained Natalia as she cut in.

"Do you know this asshole?" Don asked Natalia.

"I'm the asshole who's the father of the her soon-to-be-born kid and who is about to beat the living shit out of you if you don't get out of my face and leave this bar!"

Susanna jumped in with her man. "Calm down, calm down!"

Eddie pulled Natalia aside. "What the hell, Natalia? I'm out hunting for money all day, and you're at happy hour, ready to burst at any minute, fucking talking to these idiots?"

"He's harmless. I would have told you, but Susanna dragged me down here, and she's hammered."

Right on cue, Susanna ran to the balcony and threw up over the ledge, while Natalia looked at Eddie and grabbed her abdomen in pain.

"Eddie, I think it's happening!"

Quickly grabbing a hot mess in Susanna, Eddie took Natalia by the arm and led her outside while flipping off her friend Don simultaneously. Hurrying down the stairs and out into his car, they drove to the apartment, gathered the suitcases, and threw a pot of coffee on so Susanna could sober up.

"Susanna, we need you here!" Eddie yelled, trying to get all men on deck. In his mind, the more help he could get, the better, because deep down inside, he knew the two of them alone had no idea about babies. At least an extra pair of diaper-changing hands could be a benefit at some point.

Rushing to the hospital, the three were greeted with a mix of encouraging smiles and confused faces. "Are you really having a child?" asked the nurse, trying to be humorous as they checked in. "You look like children yourselves!"

"I promise you, I am a child!" Eddie proclaimed excitedly. "But yes, this is real, and you know... us being children still and all... we have no clue of what's about to happen, so maybe your best room and about ten nurses and three doctors would be great, thanks!"

"Well, I can promise you, every room here is great," replied the nurse.

"Eddie, can you stop joking for just one minute!" The pain was obviously putting Natalia in a more serious mood. Then she turned to the nurse and said, "Please... it hurts. Can you get us to our room?"

As the doctor entered the room where the three had now been situated for some time, Natalia's contractions were starting to become more and more frequent, and Eddie witnessed the severe stubbornness of her beliefs. He knew that she had always been a more holistic-leaning woman, but it never bothered him much. If she didn't want to take antibiotics and instead rub lotions and drink potions, well, so be it. But here, he could tell the pain was intense beyond description, but she refused to accept anything to kill the agony.

"Natalia, please let them give you something!" he yelled, watching her sweating profusely, all while breathing in quick, shallow breaths.

Natalia's face was scrunched up in agony, red as a tomato, as she screamed between bursts, "Nooo! Ahhh! No drugs! Please, God, help me!"

"Please, Natalia..."

"I said *nooo!*"

Even Susanna tried to reason with her. "Natalia, they are safe, I promise you."

"I said *nooo!*" She turned her head to shoot Susanna a nasty glare.

Soon afterward, Natalia committed to the task, and the baby was delivered, screaming her head off as the doctor pulled her out and immediately placed into Natalia's arms.

Eddie fell in love with his daughter right upon looking at her. "Oh my God, little girl... you are a treasure!" he said to her, simultaneously counting her fingers and toes just to make sure everything was okay. He turned to Natalia and said, "We did it! You did it! Can you believe this?" He knew deep down that nothing could ever come close to this feeling again. He couldn't give two shits about any guy hitting on his wife or Natalia's family not liking him or how he was going to afford college. Nothing.

As Natalia slept off the emotional and physical drain of the day and Susanna went out for some food, Eddie looked now to his daughter and was hit with massive ambition. "I am now on a mission, little girl; I am going to give you the best life possible, to have you grow up without worry, without drama. You are going to have the most devoted, caring, and loving dad. I will never abandon you or let anyone harm you. I promise you that."

THE PAIR WERE all alone after Susanna returned home with the exception of Isabella. They settled on calling her Izzy, knowing that it was easy to pronounce in each of their native tongues. The realization hit hard and fast that the name was the only easy thing about the baby. Days and nights were spent feeding, sleeping, crying (sometimes all three), and generally not knowing even the hour. But they eventually locked themselves into a groove. Eddie returned to work, but really all he wanted to do was finish his days and get back to his family.

Natalia, on the other hand, didn't enjoy being a mother as much as most would expect. Sure, she loved the baby immensely, but changing diapers and cleaning a house wasn't exactly what she thought of for her future. It wasn't long before the stress of the relationship reappeared, and they were back to arguing more days than not.

"You brought me here for a better life! You know, in Brazil, we have nannies and maids who take care of the babies and the house! I am not a nanny or a maid!" Natalia constantly harped.

"I don't understand, Natalia. You are a *mom*. You get to stay home all day with Izzy while I have to go off to work. What's so bad about that?"

"I wasn't put on this planet to just be a mom. I need *more* in my life than baby food and *Barney*!"

Eddie was in complete shock. He thought maybe she had a bout of postpartum depression, but as the days turned and the months rolled, Natalia never let up. He could see the agony in her eyes; she loved her daughter on one hand, but on the other, she wanted to live her own life without the overbearing responsibility of being a mother. It was clear the parents were polar opposites. One liked the working world, one didn't. One liked to be at home with the kid, and the other, well the point has been made.

"Natalia, I can't give you what you want. I am not a rich man who can afford a nanny and all of that. It's different here. In Brazil, nannies are dirt cheap for what they do. Here, they're expensive."

"Well, maybe we should return to Brazil?"

"Hell, no!"

"Why not?"

"We have a nice life here. I have a decent job, with stock that will eventually vest. Other than the help, you have everything you need here. Plus, Izzy is safe. Brazil is dangerous, and you know that!"

"I don't have a nice life here. You do! I am stuck with a baby all day!"

"Oh, I'm sorry you get to stay home and have no stress other than when does the baby take a nap! My bad!"

"You have no idea. Working is so much easier than raising a kid!"

"Well, I do both, so..." Eddie was right. The minute he entered the door from work, Natalia would hand Izzy over, and it was up to him. But honestly, he didn't mind. "Anyway, I'll make a deal with you, Natalia. How about you find a job, and I stay at home? Or better yet, you find a job that pays enough money to hire a nanny here, and we can do that!" Eddie threw a dagger right through her. Yes, she wanted to have a life, a job, a career... but only on her terms.

"You know I can't find a job that pays that much!"

"Oh yes you can. You just don't want it. Somehow in your head, you want a job that pays you what you want, lets you make your own hours, where you don't have to go sit in some office building all day. That job doesn't exist! Don't you think I want that job too? Don't you think *everyone* wants that job?"

"Eddie, I could have a nice life in Brazil, but you took us here, so now you need to find a way to make it happen. Period." And that was that. Eddie was in a no-win situation. All he could do was keep working hard and hope that as Izzy grew a bit and became less dependent on her mother feeding her every few hours and whatnot that maybe Natalia would calm down and they would figure it out.

Not being an extremely lucky man, Eddie quickly had to deal with the next little nugget of strain offered up to him. Time did pass as it always does, and Izzy did grow from a squirming little bundle of organs and muscles to a moving and crawling little one-year-old. But even as Natalia had to spend less time on baby duty, her free time was still spent on searching for a future that fit the ideals she so stubbornly desired.

So, as she worked her way through the daily internet searches and "research" for the day, she came across a site that asked the question, "Do you feel that your body is imbalanced and that through a natural healing process, you can change your consciousness to perfect your natural state?" Now that kind of statement garners the "What the fuck?" reaction in most people, but to Natalia, it was like someone hit her with a homeopathic slap. She bit hard, reading deeper into the article: "Consciousness Healing is a homeopathic tool used for chi development and balance. What if you could heal your own body through touching and tapping of sensory areas on the body, creating energy sources for natural betterment?" Natalia was off and running.

"Eddie, I found my calling today!" she screamed excitedly when he returned home.

"Oh yeah? What is it? Nurse? MRI tech? What?" he asked, excited that she might have found a job.

"It's called Consciousness Healing, and that's what I'm going to do with my life! I'm going to heal people!"

"Oh... great," he mumbled, trying to sound excited but also trying to hide his disappointment.

"I've already signed up for my first training course for next week. It only costs $5,000, and I am sure to make it up as soon as I start building clients."

As Eddie ran through the math with her, he discovered that there were probably four or five required training sessions to become certified, all in all costing about $25,000. "How many damn clients would you need to pay that shit back?" he wanted to ask her. "Natalia, we can't afford that! And really? Are you really going to have a career in this? What about something more traditional with a 401(k) and health insurance?"

Natalia gave her standard response: "You always stifle me! You don't believe in me at all! You don't see who I really am! I am a natural healer, and this modality will certify me and give me the tools to do that!"

"Modality? Natalia, this is some whack-job who is preying on people like you to make money! If this 'healing' actually worked, why do we have antibiotics and medicine?"

And on and on it went...

"You're a fucking asshole, Eddie! Why can't you just believe in me? All you care about is Isabella. You don't care about me at all! Lately, I'm just a warm body for you to have sex with, and then you move about your day. I can tell you would rather be away from me than to have to hear about my wishes. I want to heal people. You need to deal with that!"

"Well, Natalia, I want to play for the LA Clippers, but unfortunately, one of us needs to be responsible and actually make money. What if I decided not to have a *real* job? We'd be living in a car! I don't *see* you? Fuck that. I work all day, come home, and take care of Izzy while you go up to the room searching for bullshit ways to spend money on some cult hippie group? Fuck this. If I left tonight, you'd have to get a real job. Good luck with that!" As he started to leave with Izzy, Natalia followed him out of the apartment, screaming like a wild woman.

"Get back here now, Eddie!"

"You know what, Natalia? I'm fucking out of here. You want to spend $25,000 of my hard-earned money when that should go to Izzy? You're a selfish person! Act like a mom and think of your daughter!" That hurt her, he knew it did, but not the kind of hurt that came next. She threw a right cross to the left side of his jaw, through his lower face, and around the other side.

"What the fuck, you crazy-ass Brazilian! You just fucking punched me while I'm holding your daughter?"

"That's right. You're an asshole! You don't think I care for my daughter? Well, I do! Just because I don't want to spend every second of every day with her doesn't mean I don't love her!"

"You suck at being a mother! Most moms would love to stay at home ... to not ever have to work. You're some crazy woman who would rather leave your daughter with a stranger so you can go to a job. You're crazy!"

"I'm crazy? I'll show you crazy!" Natalia picked up a glass bottle and smashed it on the floor. She then took the jagged edge of the bottle and cut herself down her arm.

"Are you fucking nuts?"

"Give me Izzy or I'll tell the police you hit me and cut me, *now*!"

Eddie had to make a choice. He didn't want to go to jail over this craziness, and deep down, he knew she'd return anyway.

So, he reluctantly handed Izzy over, and she jetted out the door and to her car.

"Well, Natalia, I hope Consciousness Healing can cure crazy, because then I'm *definitely* paying!"

# 12

Lisa Manning was still battling her way through the days, trying to balance the single-mom thing while maintaining her thriving career. Eddie was right there next to her in the company, having quickly built the work relationship into a friend-and-confidant pairing. Lisa had learned all about Natalia's slow decline into homesickness and holistic searching, while Eddie was quite aware of Lisa's dickhead husband. It was immensely inappropriate to have shared all of this with each other; however, having insane significant others in common gave them the reason to be able to share things with each other that quite honestly should have been prohibited.

That said, nothing ever happened between them up to that point. Eddie was married, and regardless of Lisa's hotness and coolness, even attempting to cheat on Natalia felt too forbidden for his taste. But now that Natalia had verbally abused him, coupled with the emotional assault she had been inflicting, Eddie relied on his confidante now more than ever.

Natalia had disconnected from Eddie for close to three weeks, with no communication whatsoever. All he could do was sit in the apartment and stew. Quite frankly, he'd had enough of the constant bickering and carrying-on himself, and for that reason, he started planning his escape. He knew that as a next step, he would reach out to Lisa Manning as a possible landing spot, who spent more time in his mind now than did his estranged wife. But planning and execution never seemed to go hand in hand for Eddie, and as Natalia strolled back into the apartment, three weeks after taking Izzy and after not contacting him that whole time, he couldn't muster the courage quite yet. He immediately leaped over to check on his daughter, asleep in her stroller, before starting in.

"Just looking at you walk in here infuriates me, Natalia. Where the hell have you been? Three weeks of being worried sick about my daughter! Three weeks worrying about you too, unbelievable! Three weeks wondering why I ever married you!"

"Eddie, we obviously have serious problems now. I needed to get away and search my true feelings about everything."

"You couldn't have searched your feeling here? Or alone? You needed to take Izzy too? Why? You don't even *like* being around Izzy!"

"That's so unfair! I love my daughter! See? This is why we fight! Just because I don't want to stay at home all day with my daughter doesn't mean I don't love her! You Americans, you think the whole world revolves around your children! Let me tell you, it doesn't! It revolves around the marriage, around the adults! The children come second. It doesn't mean we don't love them; it means we have lives!"

"I just can't believe what you are saying. I guess it's the cultural differences—if that's what they really are—because I know Brazilian women who would love to be stay-at-home moms. But anyway, maybe the differences are just too much, Natalia."

Eddie was searching for an opening. Maybe Natalia would walk out the door and they would separate; or maybe she would fight for the marriage. He was fine either way.

"I don't want to fight with you right now, Eddie. I'm exhausted, Izzy is out... let's just get some sleep."

Eddie knew the fights were actually his fault. She was right; if she wanted to be in a cult and pursue her dream of healing people, who was he to stop it? She should do what she wanted, and it wasn't his job to dissuade her. His initial reaction, once Natalia exited to the bedroom, was to call Lisa with the latest information.

"Hey, it's me. She's back!"

"Oh, wow! How's Izzy?"

That was the major difference between the two women in Eddie's life. Lisa's concern was immediately for Izzy, while Natalia's was for herself.

"She seems okay. She's asleep right now," Eddie replied, knowing physically she was okay but not as confident in the poor girl's mental state after all of this.

"Well, good, Eddie. You have your family back, so now you can go to work on repairing your relationship." Deep down, Lisa also was growing quite close and quite fond of her new pal.

"Yeah, but I don't know how much I want to, ya know? I don't want to be a divorced dad, but honestly, I'm not that into her anymore. Every conversation we have—when we're not fighting, that is—every conversation is about something *deep*... healing, energies, the universe. I just want to take care of my daughter and maybe watch a little football!"

As the conversation continued, Eddie couldn't help but detect some whimpering coming from the bedroom. He knew it wasn't Izzy, because she was in her own bed, napping.

"Lisa, I have to run. Something is going on here. Call you later."

"Okay, Eddie. Let me know if you need anything." Lisa hung up the phone and wondered if she was smart to get so close to a married man, but then again, she knew the poor guy was drowning. She wrestled with the idea of cutting off the friendship but then confirmed to herself that he really needed support, and if her conscience disagreed, so be it.

ENTERING THE MASTER bedroom, Eddie witnessed the depressing scene in front of him. Lying in an almost fetal position, with a pillow over her head to suppress the noise, was Natalia, crying her eyes out.

"What's the matter, Natalia? What happened?" asked Eddie, wondering what he was now going to have to deal with.

Natalia rolled over and looked at him in the eyes. "I don't know. I just don't feel right. I don't feel right with you. I don't feel right being with you. I just feel totally depressed."

Eddie sat on the edge of the bed and decided to only slightly feel the temperature of the pool rather than jump right in. "I thought you wanted to rest. Don't you want to talk tomorrow?"

Natalia now wanted to jump in feetfirst, right there and right now. "Eddie, I have a lot going on inside me right now. I am struggling here in the United States. I hate it here, and I feel like I am really resenting you for bringing me here."

"But we agreed together." Eddie immediately grew irritated for the blame being placed squarely on his shoulders.

"No, you agreed to, and I followed. Now I am stuck at home, every day, cleaning, cooking—"

"Yeah, I've heard it before, Natalia," Eddie interrupted.

"I know, but what you don't know is that I can't do this anymore. I don't want to be here anymore. I want to go home."

"We can't go home, Natalia. I have a job here."

"I don't want you to come with me either." Natalia's words cut deeply.

"Natalia, you know I would fight for this marriage. Plus, what about Izzy? She is *not* going to Brazil!"

"I know. I realize you will never let us leave. I'm trying hard to find my way here, but I have a lot of negative energy inside of me. I told you once about Padrinho and what he did to me. That is still killing me inside. Also, I almost died in that robbery down there, and now my marriage is falling apart because my husband wants me to be some nanny and maid and not have a career! To top it all off, I don't get any support from you. All I receive to help with my depression is your ridicule. I'm sorry but it's true."

"That's not fair, Natalia." Eddie tried to get his point in, but she wasn't having it.

Natalia continued, "I guess you can't help me. Nobody can help me, but I did find something that might work. It's a remedy for deep anger and hatred. It's CH."

All roads led to Consciousness Healing and their methods and modalities and other buzzwords that described them. Natalia continued to explain how the founder of CH, as they now called it, was going to be running a seminar in Arizona for all the certified healers. Natalia was completely on top of the seminar, and so would be Eddie's checkbook. She was ready to start her training, and level 1 certification would be taught as the seminar, with a $15,000 cost, not counting hotel rooms and expenses. However, there was the added benefit of meeting the top instructor of them all, the founder of CH. She believed that he was going to solve all her problems and teach her how to pay it forward to others. In reality, however, his teachings centered around recruitment of more CH followers and practitioners, as he was mostly in it for the money. But Natalia couldn't see that truth. She wanted spiritual growth in a holistic, medicinal way. She loved to study, learn, certify, and give meaning to her life.

PUTTING THE DIVORCE discussions on the back burner for the time being, Natalia booked her flight into Scottsdale, Arizona, to spend five days with her godfather of CH. The result was Eddie gaining five free days with just himself and Izzy—an experience worth looking forward to, the despondent man that he had become.

When the day of the trip and Natalia's flight arrived, Eddie dropped her off at the airport, and with Izzy in tow, he headed south—straight to LEGOLAND. Although still technically a baby turning into a toddler, Eddie wanted Izzy to experience the joys way ahead of her time, and this was no different. While Natalia was sipping on orange juice at thirty thousand feet, Izzy would be downing chocolate milk and sampling cheeseburgers. The family had really turned quite opposite of each other; orange juice and healing class versus chocolate milk and amusement parks.

Certain moments in life are so telling. The father-and-daughter trip ended, and on the return home, as they entered one of his favorite spots to eat, who was at the bar—in North County San Diego of all places—but Lisa Manning. She was camped out alone with a glass of red wine in hand.

*Damn! What a coincidence*, Eddie thought as he looked her over, capturing every piece of her. What could this possibly mean? She looked, well, gorgeous to him. She always looked gorgeous to him, but at this particular moment all he could do was stare at her, and ponder the chances they could be at this location, at this time and day. This was either a blessing in disguise, or it could very well be... no, it was good fortune, and he found himself thinking that as signs from above go, this one smacked of pure clarity like running into a wall at lightspeed.

BACK IN ARIZONA, Natalia had landed and was super anxious to get right to the hotel to start her mingling. As she arrived at the Marriott, she noticed that there was nothing but women running around the lobby, putting up all the CH material and advertising. Very few men were present, but she convinced herself it was to be expected, as women tend to be a bit deeper in thought and process than any football-watching, ESPN-junkie guy like her husband. The first night was a meet and greet for all the CH practitioners, and Natalia suffered the discomfort of strolling the grounds and introducing herself to people and making small talk. Being Brazilian hindered her ability to relate well to Americans, as her language and accent always led to questions, which she hated. Plus, she just didn't really care that much about superficial conversation; she wanted to dive deep in to the souls of people.

She decided she would return to her room for a nightcap and study the material handed out her first night of the conference to be absolutely ready for the next morning.

By sunrise, Natalia was in full-fledge CH mode. The other folks couldn't help but notice her in almost every seminar, every class. Her mind was opening to more and more of the CH sustenance they were spoon-feeding her. The awakening experience became exceedingly more important as she became a healer. Plotting a career that would provide inner fulfillment along with outward success, she dreamed of a happier life, never once thinking about money to be made or how it would pay the bills. Those details were for the unenlightened people, not for the likes of her.

That day, the founder of CH invited newer members and trainees to a workshop in the science of CH. Being a pyramid scheme, the more trainers he trained, the more people would sign up, become trainers themselves, and so on, to where he would create an empire.

At completion of the lecture, the founder—Don Thompson, as he was so plainly called—approached her and asked, "Are you Natalia?"

"Yes. How did you know?"

"It says on your name tag there," Don pointed out, thinking that was clever after seeing it in some romantic comedy before. "Anyway, I've seen you throughout the conference. We're a small community here, and you seem to really be enjoying yourself."

"Yes!" She excitedly sighed. "I think I really found my calling!"

"That is wonderful! I am extremely proud of you. I can tell you have a beautiful soul, strong passion, positive energy," he said, lying to her face. "I think you are special and have a real place with us here. Can we meet after the conference for a drink?"

"Definitely! I would love to!" she replied, particularly poor at hiding her enthusiasm for a one-on-one sit-down with Don.

"Okay, then. Let's say 5:30 tonight at the hotel bar?"

"See you then!"

MEANWHILE, AS A table became available for them back in California, Eddie and Izzy sat down for their post-LEGOLAND, unwholesome meal. Eddie had yet to ask Lisa to join them at their table, as he was investigating her situation over at the bar. After all, he didn't want to be a barrier, nor did he even want to be a witness, if Lisa were there meeting another man. But better judgment got the better of him, secretly wanting to disrupt any possible liaison she may have planned.

"Hey, Lisa! What's up? What are you doing in San Diego?"

"Eddie! Oh my God! What are you doing here?"

"I hacked into your calendar. We've been following you around, and now we're going to kidnap you and force you to eat dinner with us!"

"Oh, I knew it! And Izzy is your disguise as a normal father just having a meal with his girl, huh?"

"Well, actually, it was all Izzy's idea. I was just going to let you suffer on your...date...or whatever you have going on here." Eddie spit that last part out a little nervously.

"No date here. I had a meeting earlier around the corner, so now I was just going to let a little stress out through this glass of wine."

"Why don't you come join us for dinner, then? I'm buying!"

The three claimed their positions within the booth. If one didn't know any better, one would have thought the three were one happy family. Food came and went, and so did the drinks. As the cocktails started to empty, Lisa became increasingly inebriated, and Eddie offered her a ride home.

"Lisa, you shouldn't be driving. Why don't I give you lift, and tomorrow, I can drive you back to your car. Cops are everywhere. Last thing you need right now is an accident or a DUI."

"I don't know, Eddie. I might just hang here a bit longer and sober up. Kind of weird if Natalia calls and I'm in the car with you and her baby, don't you think?"

"First off, Natalia won't call. She hasn't called all weekend. She's way too wrapped up in all that shit. Doesn't even matter. Secondly, I could use an adult conversation on the ride home!"

"All right, but you have to promise you'll help me get my car tomorrow!" she said, smiling.

During the car ride home, they continued to talk, laugh, and enjoy themselves. It was plain-old fun for them. No ex-husbands with custody issues or current wives with mothering issues. And although possibly crossing a bit of a line, Eddie wanted to continue the exchange.

"Why don't we stop by my apartment a bit? Izzy needs to go to bed, and we can have a few more drinks and get you home."

"I don't know. Okay. Whatever. But only for a minute."

As they reached the apartment, headed up the stairs, and passed a few neighbors, they received the stares and the sidelong looks of those wondering why he was bringing another woman back to his apartment. But Eddie cared little about his neighbors at this point. He hadn't heard from his wife, and he was pining for continued involvement for who walked in front of him. Lisa had all the attributes that fit his existence—*beautiful* being on the list, and she was a great conversationalist, a kind and sensitive person, but more importantly, the kind of mother every kid should have: fun yet responsible, caring yet not hovering, and a mentor. Eddie was in trouble.

FAST-FORWARD TO NATALIA'S meeting with Don in Arizona. It was something she was fittingly excited about, as she was nearly losing her mind. She sported her nicest dress, doing herself up pretty. She was genuinely excited, not thinking for a moment that anything sexual could ever happen (although the shadow of Padrinho still followed her keeping her quite aware), she just wanted to pick this man's brain. He was aiming to be her mentor, she believed, someone to teach her to be the best CH practitioner out there, where she could continue her dream of being a healer. Natalia strutted into the bar, and Don was sitting and waiting, looking up at her in amazement while congratulating himself about his score.

"Thanks for coming, Natalia. Why don't we sit in a booth over there and chat?"

"Sure," she replied as they headed over to the table and squeezed their way into the seat.

"Natalia, tell me everything about yourself."

As Natalia commenced, she found herself opening up to Don like she was a patient at a psychiatrist's office. *It's really amazing what a noble listener this guy is! Much better than Eddie.* She didn't indulge with all the details, though, but when the topic of her marriage was broached, things got a little intense.

"Natalia, you have a very interesting life, but I see a lot of sadness in your eyes when you speak of Eddie. What's going on there? Let's discover your true soul here."

"Eddie is a great husband. He's a very devoted father, he takes care of us..."

"But?" he asked, prying.

"Well, to be honest, he just doesn't *see* me. You know? He doesn't look deep into my soul and understand who I am. He doesn't look at me like I am the greatest light on the planet. I've tried to share with him my pain, but I can tell he just tunes out and wants to keep the conversation at a certain level."

"Not to be completely up front and blunt, but how is your sex life?" Don asked.

Natalia wasn't really taken aback at this; she was glad to open up. "It's terrible. I'm basically just a warm body for him to *use* whenever he wants. He doesn't connect with me; he just wants to relieve his stress or whatever and go about his day."

"Well, that's very unfortunate," replied Don. "But I have seen this before with young couples, especially those with a baby. The good news is, I have helped these couples regain their magic. Would he be willing to meet with me?"

"Probably not. He really doesn't believe in what we do. I mean, he says he does, but I can tell he's lying."

"But there's something else, Natalia. I see something deeper." Don was really pushing now, and although Natalia shared her biggest secret with very few people, for some reason, Don made her extremely comfortable... and chatty.

"Well, there is one thing. I guess... well, okay... so, I was sexually abused a few years back."

"And how do you think that is affecting you today?"

"Well, I can tell you this: with my husband, I think that is one reason why maybe I don't want to get intimate with him, but I'm not sure. Maybe it's all the fighting we do too. Not sure."

Don decided to lay it all on the line. "Natalia, I did sense something traumatic about your past. I could feel that as we spoke and I performed the process on you yesterday. I felt that energy within you, so I am not surprised, but I am glad you told me. There is a way you can heal internally and at the same time pull your *husband's* energy flow back to align with yours and really try to mend the relationship."

"Okay, please, do tell!" Natalia was happy to discover a possible solution.

"Well, it works in two ways. First, I will prescribe a homeopathic tea for you. I want you to drink it every morning. It helps eliminate the bad chi from your body while repairing your cells and your inner self. Second, and more importantly, and this is a big one. No sex for *six* months. This will be hard for him, but you must stress that you are going through a healing process, and restraining from sex will create connections from your brain to your reproductive organs and, in a biochemical reaction, restore the light within you that will make sex pleasurable again."

MEANWHILE, LISA AND Eddie were having the time of their lives. Music blasting, dancing, cocktails flowing, good old-fashioned American fun. Lisa positioned herself on the couch, glanced at him with a devious look, and said, "Eddie, please don't hold this against me, but we are perfect for each other. I know you feel it too. I don't want to make anything weird; I just feel like you get me, and I get you. I'm sorry for saying it, but I had to."

"I'm so glad you said something! Lisa, I totally agree! It's like we were made for each other! When I look at you, I see a real woman—someone I can share my life with, have more children with, and be a true partner! You don't even know what I want to say to you right now... how beautiful you are, how amazing you are at being a mother, how smart, witty... everything!" Eddie started to raise his hands and shout in the air like he had just won the lottery.

The two looked deeply into each other's eyes, no more than two feet apart, for what seemed like ten seconds. And as they started to close the gap between them...

"Whaaa! Whaaaaa!" It was Izzy, woken up by a bad dream in the other room. Eddie and Lisa immediately snapped out of their gaze.

"Umm... I need to go get Izzy. Be right back," Eddie mumbled, trying to spit out the right words.

Lisa waited ten minutes for him to settle Izzy down, but she started to realize that maybe she was making a mistake, as he was technically still married. She creeped down the hallway to Izzy's room, and seemingly every single foot of the floor creaked with every step. Peeking around the corner of the door, she whispered, "Hey. I'm going to leave now. I'll just grab a taxi."

"Wait! Don't leave yet!" Eddie nearly half shouted while trying to rock Izzy back to sleep. He laid his daughter gently on the bed and put the covers over her. "I'll be right out. Just wait one minute."

Eddie reentered the quiet living room where Lisa was sitting in complete contemplation, and she looked up at him. "I'm so sorry, Eddie. Please forget everything! I'm drunk; you're married! Tomorrow, we won't even remember. *Please* forget I said anything! In fact, I'm going to deny anything if you bring it up!"

This caught him off guard, but he didn't want to appear desperate. "Yeah, I guess. But I meant what I said, Lisa... just for you to know that. You are right, though, and I can't cheat on my wife, even if, in my mind, she is no longer truly my wife."

"Well, the *truly* part is the problem. So for now, we're going to have to be friends," Lisa replied, making complete sense.

# 13

THE NIGHT NATALIA returned home from Arizona was quite an unforgettable increase of frustration for Eddie. Four days without seeing his wife, in addition to the multitude of no-sex days previous to her trip because of their constant bickering, plus the oh-so-close night with Lisa firing up his testosterone levels, equaled Eddie ready to rip every shred of clothes off her. As she walked through the door, he made sure to time Izzy's nap so they could have at least an hour of alone time.

"You won't believe the trip I had," she started with. "I found myself—so amazing! I know how to heal!"

The smart move would have been to listen to her attentively and be completely understanding. However, Eddie could not contain his desires and made a detrimental mistake.

"Yeah, yeah, great. Now get naked," is what he wanted to say, but he instead went with "That's great, honey. Glad you fulfilled everything you wanted to. Let's definitely talk about it, but first, you know that I put Izzy down, so we have like... fifty-five minutes to ourselves to catch up."

"Well about that..." Then she began to explain the new healing situation she was taking on. She began with the tea she needed to drink every day, but Eddie's attention was still not quite at full capacity. But then those words went across her lips: "No sex for *six* months." They rolled out of her mouth like a knife chopping off his manhood. Now this sobered up his attention immediately.

"Come again? Sorry, I thought you just said..."

And she replied, "I did. I'm serious. If I am to really heal from my past and present situation, to have a future, I need to do this."

Yes, this was a sacrifice most husbands could make for their wives to heal. But to Eddie, of course, *if* a qualified MD gave her that prescription. He wasn't going to give up so easily, seeing how this particular prescription came from a CH expert rather than an aforementioned qualified professional.

"Natalia, I think I understand you, but maybe what you don't understand is the natural state of a man. You see, a man needs sex; a man needs to release, to unwind, if you will. A woman's physiological anatomy might be different; I'm not sure, but a man cannot just 'talk it out' so easily, or any of that. We need to have sex with our wives—it is what it is. When a woman tells you—"

"It wasn't a woman who told me," Natalia jumped in. "It was the founder of CH, who is a distinguished, extremely knowledgably man. And healer. He knows what he's talking about!"

"So, some guy tells you no sex will improve our marriage? What a crock of shit! What if I told you that you can't cry for six months, no matter how sad you are?"

"It's not the same thing, Eddie."

"Oh yes it is! By the way, don't be so gullible! I guarantee you that guy knows exactly what he's doing; he is trying to drive an even deeper wedge between us!"

"Why would he do that? He's there to help us! To improve our marriage!"

"Right, and professional wrestling is real too, right? And cats and dogs can fly all over town! And—"

"What the hell are you talking about?"

"I don't even know! See, my brain is all clouded... and confused. I am stressed! But I know what his plan is: maybe this founder thinks I'll get so frustrated that I'll eventually cheat, or maybe we will end up fighting all the time. I don't know, but that crafty little shit is good. He's trying to jump between us!"

"You're being absolutely ridiculous... and selfish, might I add!"

NEEDLESS TO SAY, the weeks and months dragged on from that point forward. Eddie was extremely on edge, and every time Natalia wanted to talk about biophysics or how the universe feeds you signs, he was unwilling to listen. Plus, he was getting bored, really bored. Then it happened. Izzy woke up one night around 2:00 a.m., screaming her little head off. They tried everything to calm her down and get her back to sleep. She was approaching two years old, so sleeping through the night was not generally a problem for her; therefore, they knew something was wrong. After the sun rose and nothing changed, Eddie suggested they take her to the urgent care center. Natalia refused, saying they were just going to pump her full of drugs. She had a point, but on the other hand, Eddie believed drugs were supposed to help you feel better. There's a reason polio was eradicated.

Eddie reluctantly agreed to let Natalia do some of her CH sessions on Izzy; however, her condition did not improve. "It takes a while to realign and for the body to heal itself," she explained. But the next night, it was worse. Up all night again, screaming in obvious pain, Eddie couldn't bear it any longer, though for Natalia's part, she refused to budge. "No doctors," she repeated.

As the second morning came, he took matters into his own hands. "Maybe you're right, Natalia. Maybe it just takes a little bit of time. I think if I take Izzy out for a nice long walk in her stroller, maybe the fresh air and sunshine will help."

"Absolutely!" she proclaimed excitedly. "Natural sunlight will feed her body with much-needed vitamins!"

He packed up Izzy's walking-bag items and headed out the door. Contrary to his suggestion, he wasn't about to go for a walk in the park. Instead, he jumped in the car and headed straight to the urgent care center. It turned out Izzy had an ear infection, and the doctor prescribed antibiotic eardrops, along with some children's pain syrup to help her through it. But Eddie never conveyed any of this to his wife. That night, Izzy slept well, only waking up a few times in pain. Over the next couple of days, he continued to sneak the medication to her, and of course, her health improved until she was back to her old self.

Natalia was so proud of herself, as in parallel to the secret antibiotic attack Eddie and the doctors performed, she was busy running CH therapy on the girl. "You see, Eddie? You are so against Consciousness Healing and it works! How can you doubt it?"

"Wow. I just don't know, Natalia. Now remember, even if it is helping now, it can't heal everything, and we don't want to be those parents who go to jail because we don't take our kid to the hospital when she needs it."

"What are you talking about? How can you say that? We don't need doctors when I'm a healer. You see it right there!"

"Sure, but I'm just trying to tell you that you have to be open to modern medicine too," he countered, trying to reason with her.

"There you go again, never believing in anything I do, even when there is proof staring you right in the eye!"

Trying to stay calm, but already agitated by the whole situation, Eddie arrived at the point where walking away would be the smart choice. Their relationship had now declined to where the slightest argument might set one another off, so he concluded that was the best course of action.

"Okay, Natalia, you're right. You're always right, and I don't know shit. I'm taking Izzy for a ride."

"Don't walk away from me! And no, you're not taking Izzy anywhere!"

"What do you mean, I'm not taking Izzy anywhere? I'm her father—I can take her wherever the hell I want. You're trying to pick a fight with me, and I'm trying to walk away. Let it go!"

"You just don't get it." She started to cry. "Every time I try to prove to you what I was put here on earth to do, you blow me off. Why can't you just be a man and support me in what I do?"

Eddie's pissed-off level upgraded to extreme. "Support you? Are you serious? You have a college degree and are running around in a cult! You don't work. You might have made $300 this year on CH clients while spending thousands of dollars on training with the money I earn for us! I let you do whatever you want, whenever you want. You don't clean the house, you want to have a nanny and a maid, you don't even perform your duties as a wife anymore! And I'm not even going to go there with your mothering skills. Don't support you... you're like another child!"

"Fuck you!" she yelled. "I do everything for Izzy, I am building a career, in another country, where I have no friends. All you want to do is hang out with Izzy and watch sports. You don't even care about me or see me in what I want to do!"

"You're right!" he shouted. "Maybe I'd want to hang out with you if you acted like a real wife and mother! Maybe if we had sex like at least once a week, or maybe if you read to Izzy or got involved in her life! You know what? I'm fucking out of here. I'm over this shit. I don't even like you anymore. You're boring, and you only want to talk about deep, nonsense bullshit. You used to be fun, but you changed, and now we can't even enjoy being husband and wife because of some idiot who wants to sleep with you told you not to have sex with me. There are plenty of girls who would think I'm a great husband, a great supporter, and a great father."

"Fine!" she yelled. "I want a divorce! It's not working, and I'm through with you!"

"Okay by me!" he screamed. "One more thing: Izzy got better because I secretly took her to the doctor and got her antibiotics, you crazy woman! You're not a *healer*. That shit doesn't work! Wake the fuck up!"

Running into the room to grab Izzy, seeing that she was fast asleep, he leaned down and nudged her quietly. "Izzy, wake up, sweetie. You're going for a ride with Daddy."

Natalia was having none of this. She wasn't even concerned with keeping Izzy; she was just concentrating on *winning*, and that meant inflicting pain on him. The best way would be through his beloved daughter. "You are not taking Izzy!"

"Damn right I am!"

"I swear if you touch her, I will have the police over here in two seconds and tell them you have been hitting me."

"You wouldn't dare! I'm your daughter's father! How could you be so damn cruel?"

"Try me, Eddie!"

Eddie had a big decision to make. He definitely didn't want to strand his daughter with her, but he knew she was capable of somehow sending him to jail, no matter the lie. What good was he to Izzy from a prison cell? Scared beyond belief that she could disappear again, as she has a history of that, he was stuck.

"Natalia, do you want me to leave, really?"

"Yes, I do! You are a dick to me! You don't *get* me! I am evolving, and you are returning to childhood. Eddie, we are not good for each other right now!"

"Then please, let me take Izzy. Please, you know she is everything in my life!"

"Absolutely not!"

"Then you know what? I am canceling your credit cards and bank account, and you will be sitting in the house all day with nothing but darkness! No electricity paid, nothing!"

"Oh, and you would do that to Izzy? Great parenting you hypocrite! Anyway, I can find somewhere for us to stay. Trust me!"

Now it was backfiring on Eddie. He'd just shot himself in the foot while trying to unholster his gun. He couldn't have her taking his daughter and ending up somewhere he would be oblivious to.

"Okay, okay. Fine, Natalia. I'll make you a deal. You stay here with Izzy, and I get to see her whenever, wherever I want. If you agree to that, I'll continue to pay whatever you need paid until you can support yourself."

"Deal. Now just get the hell out of here!"

EDDIE CHECKED HIMSELF into the nearest place to his ex-family he could find—a bachelor pad—but it was too expensive to stay there for any considerable length of time. But he wasn't thinking about that right now, having more pressing things on his mind. Overlooking the mess that was a suitcase and clothes strewn about the bed, he felt too overwhelmed to begin to organize himself. Instead, he reached into his pocket, pulled out his phone, and dialed a number. "Hello, Lisa. It's Eddie. What are you doing right now?"

ALTHOUGH HE HAD moved out of his family apartment and into a hotel and he'd made his first call to his hot coworker, he wasn't the only one reaching for immediate companionship. As Eddie was on the phone with Lisa, recovering, repairing, and building the frame of what he hoped to become the solid structure of another relationship, Natalia was immediately on the phone with Don, tearing down everything she had built with her husband. And of course, as one could imagine, Don wasn't surprised at all. In fact, his plan was working to perfection, and he was ready to pounce.

"Natalia, get someone to watch Izzy, and let's meet when I get to town so we can walk through the next phase of your life," he instructed. Having no babysitting options, and without her husband—who she always counted on to be able to leave Izzy with on a whim—Natalia ended up dragging Izzy along with her to visit Ed. She never questioned why Don could so quickly and conveniently get to Southern California, leaving his house in Arizona in no time at all. She didn't realize that the idea he planted was bearing fruit even faster than he'd planned, so when she made the call he had been waiting for, Don was on a plane and in a hotel that night.

When Natalia arrived at Don's place, he of course welcomed her with open arms. "So sorry to hear what happened, Natalia. You are such a shining light in this world. How could Eddie be such a fool?" He rambled on and on to make her feel like it wasn't her fault. "Is this your wonderful daughter you told me about? She's beautiful, and she has that sunshine about her, just like her mom." Natalia ate it up... all of it. And before long, when Izzy was napping on the bland hotel-brand couch where thousands of others had slept before her, Natalia found herself in bed with Don, doing things with him that he prescribed her not to do with her own husband.

MEANWHILE, IN EDDIE'S more upscale but no-less-used hotel room across town, he had convinced Lisa to come over for a chat.

"You know, Eddie... you know in your heart that this was coming for such a long time. You can't be surprised by any of this. No disrespect, but your wife is crazy!"

"I know, Lisa, and the ugly, sad thing about it is I'm not even sad. I don't feel the need to cry; in fact, I'm a little bit excited! I *will* have my daughter, believe me, and a new life ahead of me free from the crazies of the world that I had to live in before!"

"That's great you feel that way. You know I've been there, and honestly, it's better for Izzy to see you happy rather than grow up in a house with parents who don't even like each other."

"Yes, for sure," he agreed, "and that's what I guess kept me in that marriage for so long. I really didn't like her, let alone love her, but I wanted the best for my little girl. Anyway, let's go downstairs and grab a drink, yes?"

"I don't know, Eddie. Things are kind of weird between us. I don't know if it's a good idea for us to get drunk together. I really don't want to make a mistake, seeing how you just left your wife."

"But, Lisa, it wasn't a mistake!" he explained. "We're good now. I agree with everything you said that night—we are perfect for each other, we understand each other, and we can be a great couple!" He started to inch his way closer to her, reaching out to grab her hand.

"I don't think so, Eddie. In fact, it's probably best I leave. Last thing I want is to be some rebound chick. You should wait for your divorce to actually happen and go out and date as many girls as possible. Maybe down the road there can be something between us, but not now, not today."

"But, Lisa—"

"No, Eddie. I should go." Lisa knew exactly what she was doing. She couldn't give in to Eddie just like that. Although the desire was there and the timing was lining up, she had to play a little hard to get with him, not wanting to be there for his comfort alone. But what she failed to grasp at the time was that Eddie's intentions were quite honorable. He was falling for Lisa; he knew she was the right person for him. In every way possible, from her attitude, actions, and positive personality, she was the one for him. Even without years of dating, he knew her well. Understanding what kind of mother she could be to his little girl and what kind of partner she could be for him, he wasn't looking for one-night stands and online dating; rather, he wanted a real family. And for him, Lisa was that missing element.

Not able to muster the right words to make her stay, Eddie watched her walk out that door, wondering if the sure thing she was would ever materialize. Was his chance now leaving forever? Could he convince her of his true intentions? This time, this night, he just didn't have the energy to deal with another relationship problem straight away, so instead, he visited the hotel bar and indulged himself.

That night was not unlike the next six months of his life: drinking to a limit, back to his room, and passing out on first available space—bed, couch, or floor. Good times, right?

NATALIA, ON THE other hand, was quite enjoying her freedom. She was full-steam ahead with her new man, perfectly playing the part of the hot young girlfriend for the rich older man. Eddie didn't mind, however, and was almost happy for her. He was able to see Izzy whenever he liked, as previously agreed to. He figured that he could forever close this marriage chapter of his Life Book and not have to revisit it or at least find a way to not have to include her in his future writing. Optimistic, Eddie settled on a new target, a new mission. He needed Lisa by his side, and he made up his mind to win her over—even being used goods, baby in one hand, the rest of his baggage dragged by the other.

## 14

EDDIE REALIZED VERY quickly what kind of an ex-wife Natalia was going to be; working and providing were low priorities, Izzy played second fiddle to hanging out and partying with Don, and CH dominated all aspects of her life. To Eddie, it was not unlike having a college-age child, just another mouth to feed and her bills to pay. He was stuck in neutral for the time being, assuming at some point that Natalia and Don would get married, so Eddie could move on with his life and not carry her burden both financially and emotionally. For now, there was no use fighting over every dime or every extra day with Izzy, so he swallowed his anger and wrote the checks.

Natalia persisted in her drive to be the best CH healer on the market, even while she continued to dream of a life back in Brazil. Sure, she loved her child, and sure, she appreciated her life in the States, but she quickly realized that the market in the States for CH wasn't quite what Don and his followers had promised.

Brazil had a much more open-minded sort of folk willing to part ways with cash for natural, holistic cures. On the contrary, the typical American loved his Western-based medicine, and CH was just another fad to them.

Eddie made peace with the fact that Natalia would continue to strive for her naturistic goals that provided no quality income, funded by his generosity. As long as he had his daughter whenever he wished, the money could be made back later in life. His eyes were set on working hard, providing for his daughter, and winning over Lisa. But less money in his pocket meant less to impress Lisa. This was a high-class Southern Californian woman used to guys with Bentleys, while he could barely afford the lease on his Ford Explorer. That didn't stop him from the hunt.

Understanding that Lisa also valued family more than anything else, he planned to capture her heart via the family life, through her boys, through Izzy; the more time they could spend together as a complete bunch, the more they would grow on each other. Although Lisa's boys were a bit older and tended to be off doing what they wanted to do, Eddie felt it was important for Lisa to spend more time with Izzy. Maybe she would fall in love with the whole package deal.

Workdays with her in a confined office allowed Eddie some consistency in his approach. For months, she had pushed against any sort of relationship, wanting Eddie to get out and date as much as possible. She was busy enough and didn't want to bother with the heartache that went with a rebound relationship, but she was starting to witness a truth about him. Small offices allow rumors to run wild, and everyone was interested in Eddie's new single life, but never once did she hear any stories, any tales about him out on the town. Was this all the best cover-up job in the history? Or maybe, just maybe, this guy really did want something significant with her.

The Friday afternoon of a particularly dull week had arrived, and Eddie decided to give his best shot. "Lisa, how's life today in the world of being beautiful?" he asked as he meandered into her office.

"Good one. You're going to keep trying, aren't you?"

"You know I am! C'mon, Lisa, let's have dinner tonight. I can prove to you my good intentions!"

"Eddie, you know I believe something's there. I just want to make sure you sow all your wild oats before I dive in. What if I build this relationship with you and your daughter, and it disappears? Let alone my boys. I can't be introducing you, then you're out of my life a month later."

"Well, don't you think I have the same concerns?" he countered. "My daughter is my world! I promise you, I would never bring *anybody* into her life who I didn't believe could be a long-term player in our lives! By the way, I'm not calling you a *player*, just a football analogy!"

"Yes, I got that, Eddie."

"Okay, so... dinner tonight?"

"Okay, but you'd better not make me regret this!"

DINNER CAME AND passed nicely. Actually, it went fantastically for them. Spending more and more time together was fun, but Lisa still held on to her hesitations. She refused to let anything get too serious, even if deep down inside, her heart felt quite the opposite.

Days turned into weeks, and after a few months had passed, the frustration was sitting heavily on Eddie. "Lisa, haven't you been having a great time?"

"Yes, Eddie. I definitely care about you...a lot. But you complain about Natalia, and at the same time, you want this relationship with me. Why so quickly?"

Eddie thought about it awhile. Yes, he could easily date and party, but he knew what he knew; and the fact was, a girl like Lisa didn't just come along every day. She was a once-in-a-lifetime girl to him. She was such good wife and mom material that he knew he had to grab ahold of her, especially given his experience with Natalia. But he also genuinely loved Lisa, so why waste time out at the bars looking for what he had right in front of him?

Putting it not so articulately, he tried with, "Lisa, you are prime meat. Why would I go out looking for burgers when I have a filet here? You are the cow I want! Oh, shit. Wait...let me retract that. It sounded so much better in my head."

"You'd better try something new right now, Eddie!"

"What I am saying is, you are everything I want, so all I would be doing out and about is finding the lesser versions of you."

"You suck at telling someone what they mean to you, Eddie. You know that, right?"

"I know. Shit."

Lisa decided, though, to carry on with him and to invite him to dinner with her father, who was visiting in town. She would just have to see where this went.

Lisa's father came to town from some rural, hard-core biker spot somewhere out of *Sons of Anarchy*. Lisa had warned Eddie that her dad was a big Jack Daniel's drinker, and from what he saw in pictures, Eddie knew the dude had about a hundred pounds on him. Thinking he could use her father as another move in his scheme, Eddie cut a deal with her. "Lisa, if I can go head-to-head with your dad drinking Jack, then you and I will really discuss progressing this relationship. You will give it a shot, yes?"

"That's totally fine, because there is no way you can compete with my dad in a drinking contest!" Lisa said quite confidently.

Entering the room, handlebar mustache, 280 pounds of Jack-absorbing poundage... Eddie knew he was in deep shit.

"Nice to meet you, Eddie," Lisa's dad proclaimed quite loudly. "I heard you're a Jack drinker, so I got you a present." And with that, he went to his car and pulled out a Jack Daniel's–themed cooler and lugged it into the house. Weighing about forty-five pounds, the cooler could only mean trouble for Eddie. Placing it nicely on the kitchen floor, they opened the cooler to find no less than ten handles of Jack, or 1.75-liter bottles, and a few random outliers of beer.

"Lisa called me on the way down here and told me about your little bet. I respect a man who makes a bet about my daughter over drinking Jack. Actually, shut the hell up. That's the worst thing I have ever heard! She's not a prize. You need to win her over with love and friendship and compassion."

"Well, with all due respect, sir, I've tried all of that, so this is my Hail Mary! I know it looks bad, but what the hell. I had to give something a shot! Your daughter wasn't falling for all the tricks in the book I desperately deployed!"

"Eddie, I like your honesty. That makes you a good dude in my book. You could have lied and bullshitted me. I get it; Lisa is a pain in the ass and quite stubborn. I hope you do win her over, but there's no way you're outdrinking me!"

Lisa chimed in, "I could probably take both of you down at the rate we're going here. I can't wait to see this! Let's get going!"

And the first shots were poured. No dinner, no getting to know each other. Tour of the apartment? Nothing. Just start drinking.

WAKING UP IN a hospital with needles in your arm is never a fun experience. All Eddie could see were bright lights shining down, a nurse and doctor prodded like he was already a corpse receiving his complete autopsy.

"He's awake. Make sure the electrolyte drip continues for another hour. Mr. Watters, we had to pump your stomach. You might have a concussion, as you fell off a wall. Not sure how or why you were on a wall, but you fell. You were quite inebriated. You will feel terrible today but should recover completely. By the way, don't try to drink a whole 1.75 liters of Jack Daniel's by yourself ever again."

"Fuck, is that how much? What the..." Eddie was hurting... bad. And while someone pushed him into some room, lights still blaring everywhere, he witnessed a divine figure approach and eclipse the glare. Lisa bent down over him, whispering into his ear, "I'm so sorry. You're going to be okay, I promise," and so on, Eddie could only comprehend a few words here and there. But he could sense her worry, mixed with the relief at seeing him recovering.

"You scared the shit out of me, Eddie. You were a maniac last night! After about eighteen shots, you were incoherent. You ran to the pool and jumped in fully clothed. Then you climbed the pool wall and yelled how much you loved me! But then you fell right off on your head. I'm sitting here in the hospital thinking the worst of the worst."

"Sorry, Lisa. Shit, my head hurts," was all he could muster.

But Lisa had some good news for him too. "You know, seeing you out cold like that really shook me up. You scared the living shit out of me!" She looked at Eddie, into his hazed-over eyes, and began to tear up a bit. "I knew that you were and are always right. All I could think of was what would happen if I lost you. I *do* need you in my life, with my boys and your little girl. I can't ever lose you!" As she leaned farther over his body, they touched lips softly, careful to not get his disgusting throw-up mouth and tongue all over her. Eddie reached up, pulling her on top of him, wrapping the IV cord around their bodies like a spiderweb. It didn't matter about his atrocious appearance or smell; they were going for it—full-on making out on the gurney. The puzzle pieces that were once scattered across the murky floor of their lives were now starting to come together, presenting a now beautiful family portrait.

NATALIA BEGAN TO feel unhappy with the way life was working out for Eddie. She and Don, once happy, were now beginning to fight constantly after she witnessed him pulling the same "mentoring" moves on no fewer than five other girls. But it wasn't just that. Natalia found it quite odd that Don could be extremely flirtatious while at the same time having an extreme jealous streak. One night while at dinner, a waiter happened to be a little more into Natalia than just serving food and drink.

"What the fuck, Natalia? That guy is all over you, and you don't shut it down."

"What are you talking about? He wants a bigger tip!"

"And I bet you want a bigger 'tip' too, huh?"

"Classy, Don. Please stop talking."

The night actually ended something like this:

- Don continuously confronted the waiter
- Waiter was completely confused but had had it with Don's insults
- Natalia did nothing
- Don stood up and got in waiter's face
- Waiter told him to "sit down and shut the fuck up"
- Natalia did nothing
- Don punched waiter and ran out of the restaurant
- Natalia did nothing

But even now with both a jealous streak and a violent side, Natalia clung to Don because he was the CH guru, and to her, that was the most important attribute in this world.

Meanwhile, Natalia started to take her frustrations out on Eddie. Continuously playing the blame game, she blamed him for Izzy wanting to spend more time at his house than with her; she blamed him for not being able to buy an apartment on her own; she even blamed him for Izzy now being three years old and unable to understand a lick of Portuguese. Natalia was living through a big dose of "the grass is always greener."

Meanwhile, Lisa and Eddie were gaining steam. Izzy spent more time with Lisa, and Eddie believed Lisa to be a much better mother than Natalia. And having found the right woman who was more compatible with him than Natalia ever was and knowing Natalia felt regret and vengefulness, he sensed she was up to something.

The pair had planned a little couple's getaway so that they could experience some alone time, free of the outside stress and pressure that followed them like a crazed dog. This was a long-overdue vacation, and although Eddie was apprehensive about leaving Izzy for an extended time, he believed that maybe Natalia would see that her ex-husband was serious about moving on with a life of his own. But Natalia, being who she was, decided to throw a little curveball into the fray of life, right as Eddie and Lisa were turning that corner.

"Eddie, I've decided that I want Izzy every night now going forward. It's too hard to pick up, drop off, and schedule everything," Natalia complained to him one afternoon. "She's my daughter, and she needs to be with me."

Eddie knew this was a blatant lie. Natalia was growing jealous of the relationship he had built with his daughter, and even though she wasn't perfect mother material, she also didn't want to be left out in the cold as her daughter started to mature. With Izzy, she wasn't totally alone in the States. In fact, she was the *only* reason Natalia stayed.

"Natalia," Eddie replied, "this is divorce. This is what it looks like. This is what you chose. Like it or not now, you have to deal with it. We have fifty-fifty custody. You can't change it just because you are inconvenienced."

"I can, and I will. You can expect to hear from my lawyer if you don't agree!"

"Well, fuck off, Natalia! I'm sick of paying you to do nothing. You don't help at all with her activities, her extracurriculars… nothing! You just cash checks. I buy her nice clothes; you go and buy cheap crap. You're being a terrible mother, and you're using our daughter to get money. That makes you an evil person!"

She immediately hung up the phone, driving Eddie absolutely insane. Every day was a similar conflict, and Eddie was reaching his boiling point.

"*Fuck!* I am so sick of dealing with this crazy nutjob!" he screamed to Lisa. "We're going on vacation tomorrow, and now I have to worry about what is going to happen with Izzy when I get back. I just wanted to have a good trip, drink a couple of cocktails, whatever. Now I have to worry about a frickin' court appearance and paying a lawyer. This is why people drink, isn't it?"

"Calm down, Eddie," said Lisa quite steadily. "She always pulls this shit on you, getting you all worked up, then nothing changes."

The following day, they hopped on a flight. Eddie was stressed, and Lisa provided the calming effect. Deciding to leave his problems in California, Eddie planned to focus the week on Lisa, but he couldn't shake that strange feeling that something was off. Maybe it was the margaritas and bad Mexican food, but something in the universe was unsettled.

For Natalia, struggling with her life in the States even with Don by her side, it was time to do something drastic. Forget the ramifications, the feelings of others, and any common sense. She made up her mind, and that was a decision for her own happiness. Even if it meant disaster for everyone else in the entire world, once she made up her mind, even the Holy Father himself couldn't dissuade her.

EDDIE MUST HAVE left ten messages on Natalia's phone and also called her friends, the divorced moms and man-haters, not expecting or receiving much from them. He attempted to reach her family in Brazil, sending e-mails, but still nothing. Wearisome and worried, he continuously expressed to Lisa that something wasn't right, and she started to believe he was being overly paranoid.

They chalked it up to a bad case of missing Izzy, since he had never spent this much time separated from her.

Now Eddie was not a big social media user, but it can be a useful tool for investigation, discovery, and, well,... messaging. "Lisa, what if we try contacting Natalia on one of her pages? Maybe she turned off her cell phone? The cellular waves can be too toxic to the brain or some shit. Worth a shot, don't you think?"

"I still think you're being paranoid. Leave it alone! Let's enjoy the rest of the week!"

Eddie knew she had a point, but he was going to throw one last piece of bait out there to see if anything bit.

He clicked through some of her pictures attentively, leaning over the computer like a thirteen-year-old boy who had just downloaded the latest video game. There were a few random posts about the Brazilian political nonsense, a few likes... nothing. Wait, there was a picture of Natalia at her mother's apartment. He could see Izzy in the far background!

"What the fuck! Is this new?" he shouted, dissecting the next picture of Natalia holding hands with Izzy. "When the fuck was this taken? How old is this picture?"

A rush of fear swept over him as he looked at the post. It had been uploaded two days earlier in Brasília, Brazil. Two days! He'd always known she might be capable of this. He started to shake, becoming extremely tense. His worst fear crashing in on him.

"Holy shit! Lisa, come quick!" Rage started to overtake him as the realization was apparent. "Natalia didn't say anything to me about a vacation to Brazil, especially with Izzy!"

"What are you talking about, Eddie?" Lisa hurried over for a glance.

"Fuck! I knew Natalia wasn't happy in the States, and she's even more pissed off and jealous of you and me... and Izzy. Her family is always pressuring her to make Izzy more *Brazilian*, but no, there's no way Natalia could do what I think she just did!"

"What do you mean. What are you saying?"

"*That fucking woman just kidnapped my daughter and took her to a third-world country!*"

Eddie wasn't being crazy, knowing the traits Natalia possessed. There was no reason for her to hide this trip from him unless it was permanent.

"No, there's no way she would do that to you, Eddie. She's breaking the law, first of all. Second—"

Eddie interrupted softly, "Talk about the valley of all valleys, the lows of the lows." He raised his voice. "I'm not some chump. This is going to be war! I'm going to make this a frickin' international incident! She'd better understand what the fuck she just did, what she has in store for her!"

His spine was tense, his bones ached with hate, and he could taste revenge with every gasp of air he took in. He was ready to unleash hell on Natalia and her entire country and citizenry.

"What are we going to do, Eddie?" asked Lisa, complete shocked.

"I'll tell you what I'm going to do! I'm going to do whatever it takes to get my little girl back! Izzy will be returned!" Eddie looked up at Lisa and began gathering all his belongings. He headed straight to the airport, right into the headwinds of the hurricane that had become his life.

# PART II

# 15

WHAT LENGTHS WOULD you go to, when you lose the single-most important person in your life, to exact revenge on those who stole her from you and to safely return her to the sanctuary of your embrace? For Eddie, that is to the depths of hell. But this time it really was going to be hell, the hell he now found himself. Freshly back from their trip, he didn't know where to turn. He didn't know where to go, who to go to, when to do it, other than to try to do everything right that instance—right now. But how?

"Why would she do this to me? Why would she take her away from me? Why would she take me away from her?" For Eddie, Natalia was turning out to be much more insane than first imagined. And now she had stolen the world from him, and she was going to pay for it, no doubt about that. "I just need to focus. Security of Izzy first, Revenge later."

The story of his past had been written. Life Book part 1 complete. Everything he had ever accomplished, every action and step taken, had now led to this point. As Eddie stood there, the warmth of the California sun radiating his every cell, filling him with the power of the heavens, his anxiety shot through the roof. He was soaking everything up. Every detail of every sound... his senses completely awoke. When rage enslaves you, the body becomes intensely aware of its surroundings, probably because of the expected fight to come. Eddie was ready for attack. But these were modern days; he couldn't just ride his horse across enemy lines and kill everyone in sight, rescue their hostage, and ride off to the fort. He needed help, and it had to come from people everywhere, folks who had zero stake in the game, so why should they fight to the death? Eddie could only hope that community existed—those who could only imagine being in his circumstance, who were willing to do whatever it took to right the wrong committed.

He had to make sure that Natalia wasn't being her stubborn self, protesting her life, her misery, and taking it out on him. He picked up the phone, wondering if there was a chance in hell she would respond.

"Natalia, it's Eddie again. Please call me. I know what you did. I know where you are. Please, asking as a father, I need to know if Izzy is okay." To that, there was no answer. So, he persisted. "Natalia, please, *por favor, liga pra mim!*" Thinking that her native tongue might tug on her heartstrings a bit more heavily than the English she now seemed to revolt against. But still nothing. And on and on for a week he tried—every digital avenue and platform, and anything else he could think of. He called her cousins, her father, her brother. Nobody had yet to reach out. Even out of common courtesy for a suffering father, somebody could have at least given word.

Late into the night on a Saturday, it was early in the morning in Brasília. Eddie was drinking heavily; he couldn't sleep and was extremely anxious and nervous. Lisa headed over early that day to comfort him. As even she fell asleep after trying her best, Eddie sat there on the couch, watching, staring. Usually she was an extremely light sleeper; even the light of the moon at night could wake her if the blinds weren't completely shut. But this morning, she'd passed out. She had been up with him those past weeks, worrying and not resting either. She was his best friend, and he felt sorry for bringing her into this bullshit.

Suddenly, Eddie felt the vibration of his cell phone. He knew right away who it was. It had to be them, because who else would be calling at this hour?

"Hi, Daddy. It's me, Izzy!"

He immediately started bawling, but choking it in as to not upset Izzy.

"Hey, baby girl! I've missed you so much! How are you?"

"I sat by the window on the plane, Daddy—"

"That's enough," interrupted Natalia. "Eddie, you need to leave us alone now. I need my space, my time to build a life here now. It will be a good thing for Izzy. She will learn a new culture, a new language, and in time, you can talk to her every night on the phone—maybe even visit."

"Are you fucking nuts? You kidnapped our daughter, Natalia! You stole her from me! She needs her father more than she needs to learn a new fucking language!"

"That's why I didn't tell you I was bringing her here. I knew you would react like that and wouldn't give it a chance. This is your new reality. You're going to have to deal with it."

"You fucking broke the law, Natalia! You know what I'm going to—"

And with that, she hung up on him.

"Lisa, what do I do? I need your help!" Eddie asked, shaking Lisa awake.

"Huh? Was that her?" Lisa was rising out of her slumber.

"Yes! I need to get on a plane now!"

"Eddie, you need to turn your thoughts around," she explained, rubbing her eyes. "You can't just be an enraged madman. You are an American citizen in need of some help from your government. We need to go into research mode. Start with if this has happened before, and to whom, and if it was specifically Brazil. Check the State Department website. We should have been on top of this weeks ago, but your anger and your anxiety are only telling you to run off to Brazil."

But they learned quickly that opening the State Department website was not very encouraging. The simple post provided by the government was vague at best, leaving the two to wonder if they really could provide help or not.

> It is important for parents to understand that, although a left behind parent in the United States may have custody or visitation rights pursuant to a valid custody order, if the parent attempts to gain access to the child, the parent's actions may be illegal in the country where the child is physically present and may ultimately delay the child's return and even result in the parent's detention. To understand the legal effect of a U.S. order in a foreign country, a parent should consult with a local attorney. For

> information about hiring an attorney abroad, see our section on Retaining a Foreign Attorney. Although we cannot recommend an attorney to you, most U.S. Embassies have lists of attorneys available online. Please visit the local U.S. Embassy or Consulate website for a full listing. The U.S. government cannot legally interfere with the judicial system of another sovereign nation.

This just pissed off Eddie even more. "Seriously? Are they basically saying, 'Don't take matters into your own hands'? and if that is the case, they aren't really offering much beyond saying that you *need* to take matters into your own hands!"

However, as they dug deeper, they realized the one positive about this situation and Natalia's current residence: Brazil was a signatory country and party to The Hague Abduction Convention. What that means is that through this international treaty, Brazil is supposed to honor any California court order giving fifty-fifty physical custody. The result: Izzy should be returned to California.

"Well, that's good news, right?" Lisa asked, trying to shed a positive light.

"Right. Good luck with that. I'm sure the Brazilian government, with an extreme left-leaning party in power who are friends with the Bolivias, Venezuelas, Irans, and Cubas of the world, are just going to say, 'Oh, sure. We will take a Brazilian citizen away from her Brazilian mother and send her back to America because some gringo court says so.' This shit is turning out sour!"

But Eddie realized he needed to continue down this path; it was really his only hope. Apparently, this type of situation happens more than anyone ever hears about on any American news outlet, regardless of political leaning. While American kids are kidnapped left and right, there is no mention of it—the news is more worried about who Leonardo DiCaprio's current model girlfriend is or who in Congress is lying, or whatever topic of day. All this while children were being taken away from their parents!

"You know what, Lisa?" Eddie continued with his rant. "Why the hell are there no exit controls at US airports? Any old dipshit can take any kid they want onto an international flight, no questions asked. There's so much talk about immigrants and refugees coming in—what about children going out? We are one of the few civilized countries who don't give a damn about who's leaving the country!"

But since this does happen, there happens to be a special unit within the State Department that deals with this specifically. And their number was finally right there for the two to see—amazingly enough without having to click on seventeen different links.

They had spent hours getting to the point of a phone number. Because it was late morning on the West Coast, Eddie dialed the 800 number and prepared himself for some robotic answering service to reroute him a hundred times before he spent the next thirty minutes of his life trying to explain the situation. But to his surprise, he heard, "Hello, this is the Office of Children's Issues with the Department of State. How may I help you?"

"Holy crap! I mean, sorry, I'm just surprised I reached someone right away."

"Yes, sir. We take this very seriously. What can I do for you?"

"Yes, I am an American citizen whose crazy ex-wife is also an American citizen but is from Brazil, so she is a dual national. I have a daughter who also holds both American and Brazilian citizenship. She's crazy you know? She has my daughter. She stole her. She kidnapped her, and she is in Brazil! I need help!"

"Well, sir, I'm going to get all of your information, but did you allow her to get a passport? Did you apply for the Children's Passport Issuance Alert Program?" she asked like he was an idiot. Evidently, this was the first step if you suspected an incident like this to occur—it alerts the authorities if someone applies for a passport for that specified child. But this lady didn't follow the situation, as he just told her his daughter held a Brazilian passport. How was preventing her from getting an American passport helping this situation?

"No. How was I supposed to know she was going to kidnap her own kid? She doesn't even like having a child. She's a terrible mother. I assumed she might move back home by herself and leave my daughter with me. I don't know if it's just to piss me off or what! I read through all the steps, and I need to call my lawyer and put an emergency court order in, call the police and all of that, but am I too late?" He was getting frantic.

"Unfortunately, you might be too late, although I will forward you to our division that deals with the post-abduction process. So you know, though, once you are in the situation you are in, it will be an extremely long, sometimes difficult process. But let me—"

"Are kidding me right now?" he screamed. "How can this be? You just let kids leave the country, stolen from their fathers, and all you can do is tell me it's a long process with limited results? What the hell is this? This is the United States of America! Surely we have some weight to pull!"

"Unfortunately, sir, like I said, I can forward you—"

"Fuck this! I want the FBI, or Homeland Security, or the goddamn fifth fleet to sail their asses to Brazil and start a war! This is *my* daughter I'm talking about!"

"Sir, I realize you are under extreme stress, but yelling at me won't help. There are diplomatic steps we can take, but I need to get you to the right person for help."

"You can forward me to the goddamn ambassador to Brazil is what you can do!"

"Sir, once again, try to remain calm. It doesn't help the situation to raise your voice."

"Fuck that! You try losing your daughter and have your government say jack shit. Fine. Please forward me!" He was completely out of his head. As they sent him to some other robot, he was giving his best effort to keep calm but was still ready to lose it.

"Sir, let me tell you how this is going to work." He heard this new State Department employee talking, but he was not really listening. "The steps we are going to take are as follows: We will notify the US embassy in Brasília of your situation and initiate conversations with the local authorities. This will be the first step in the negotiation process. Next, you need to hire an attorney who specializes in these types of cases. Make sure they speak the local language of Spanish and have knowledge of the interworking of the country."

"Is this a joke?" he snapped. "You know they speak Portuguese in Brazil, not Spanish. Are you the right qualified person to be—"

"Yes, sorry about that, sir. I'm not a Brazilian specialist. I'm here to instruct you on the process post-abduction."

"Well, I'm sorry too, but what you're telling me is that we need to call lawyers and embassies and whatnot. That doesn't sound like a short-term solution. I need my daughter back tomorrow!"

"Well, you need to have the right expectations on this. A case like this, even if Brazil is part of The Hague Treaty, can take months or, more likely, years to settle. Are you sure there is no reasoning with your ex-wife?"

"Reasoning? She fucking kidnapped my daughter! She is obviously not reasonable!"

"Anyway, sir, we can provide you with a list of attorneys who specialize in Brazil, but I am assuming they will be in Miami, where most lawyers who deal with Latin America reside. On top of that, you need to get a court order in place in the jurisdiction where your divorce and custody were settled, then call the police and explain the situation, so we have everything documented. Furthermore, they will have your daughter on their radar in case she does return without notice."

As the expert kept instructing, Eddie wanted no part of his line of reasoning. Lawyers, cops, ambassadors—he wasn't going to see Izzy again until she turned sixteen years old!

He decided the best way to deal with the immediate problem was to go into his TV stand, which also doubled as his liquor cabinet, and down five straight shots of Jack. As he stared at his piece-of-crap TV stand with bottles of liquor on it, another thought crossed his mind, and he mumbled, "I don't even have money to buy a proper liquor cabinet, let alone a nice room to house said cabinet, let alone a condo to fit said room. And now lawyers, and Brazil, and time off work to deal with this shit? Financially, I am fucked."

"What are you saying, honey?" Lisa asked from the other room, not witness to the alcohol he'd consumed to damper his anxiety.

The Jack was starting to warm his body, but at the same time, it was fueling his anger.

"I said ... you know what, Lisa? Here's something: I remember there was a time when I loved Brazil, even thought of it as my home. Now I want to blow the entire place off the map of the world, so when you Google Brazil, all that will be there is a giant crater, with Natalia underneath it, along with her whole damn family. I need to go for a walk, clear my head, and get my thinking straight." Eddie downed two more shots. At this point, they had skipped breakfast, and with an empty stomach, this meant it was going to be a long walk by a very drunk man.

Outside the apartment, he decided to head toward the mall to maybe see if he could be distracted with the early hustle and bustle of the crowd there. He was about a mile into his walk, but his mind was not settling. In fact, the reverse was occurring. He was becoming even more pissed the more he thought of little Izzy down there, wondering why her dad wouldn't see her anymore. The thoughts started to enter his mind like a flood. *I wonder if Izzy will think it's my fault as she grows up without a dad? Who knows what lies Natalia will feed her? Izzy might be thinking I don't want to be a part of her life. I can't even get on the phone with her and tell her how much I love and miss her, how I'm trying my best to get to her.* His rage and anxiety were just steaming more and more. Feeling like an oil well recently drilled, he was ready to burst with pure hate.

Close to the mall, he realized a huge mistake was about to fall upon him, but he didn't care. What did he see? None other than Natalia and his favorite *churrascaria*, or Brazilian BBQ / steak house that they used to love to visit on date nights. He couldn't believe that he would accidentally wander right past this place!

"I swear I could stab anyone or anything I see that has yellow or green on it, or anything that resembles Brazil!" he slurred in his drunken stupor.

Inching closer and closer to the *churrascaria*, an oversized Brazilian flag waved at him, swaying in the wind back and forth, taunting him, teasing him, saying, "We screwed you, Eddie! We own you, and there isn't anything you can do about it!"

Leading up to the door was a long pathway straddled by nice arrangements of flowers and rocks. The flowers were quite beautiful, actually. Another day and another time, Eddie might have appreciated the artistry of the landscaper who'd majestically designed and created the walkway. But not now. Not today. All he saw were beautiful weapons of destruction: the rocks.

First order of business was to destroy the outside of the restaurant. He picked up the biggest rocks he could find and began his assault, throwing stone after stone. Acting like a center fielder as the runner rounded third base, he chucked those rocks like a bullet from a gun. *Smash!* One window shattered to pieces. *Crash!* There went another. And on and on he went, until he had destroyed every window on the face of the restaurant. Next was the door. He heaved stones at the nicely designed logo hung nicely for all to see.

"Fuck you, Brazil!" he screamed while terrorizing the place.

Luckily for him, there weren't any customers present, just a couple of employees. They were scattering around, startled to death, witnessing the demolishing of their livelihood, so they decided to put an end to it.

As part of their routine, churrascaria waiters floated from table to table, using large knives to slice pieces of meat onto the plates of famished customers. In other words, these waiters had no shortage of extremely sharp knives. And they were now after Eddie, about ten pissed-off dudes, all geared up with sharp utensils in both hands. It was a full-on rush, out the restaurant, straight toward the drunk idiot. Eddie's first inclination was to say, "Whatever," stand there, and allow them to kill him. At least his suffering would be relieved. But he also realized that he couldn't leave the planet; he couldn't let Izzy grow up with her crazy mom and wild family down in Brazil. He must live to fight another day.

Eddie spun around and made it into a full yet stumbling sprint, out of the parking lot and down the street. He felt the wind blowing through his hair, thinking he was moving faster than a cheetah. Ten yards, twenty yards—he was racing now as he heard yelling and cursing in Portuguese from behind. Thirty yards, forty... *boom*! A blindside tackle from someone flanking his right side. The hit forced him, sliding, across the parking lot, with his face pushed into the ground, used as a brake, as they came to a stop. Who could have caught up to him that fast? He lifted his head, ready to go guerilla warfare on the guy, but no, staring right back at him was not one but no fewer than three policemen.

Elbows into his neck, knees pressed against his legs so he couldn't move, he felt them pinning his hands behind his back and slapping some on the ice-cold handcuffs, listening to them respond on their handhelds that they had now apprehended the maniac as he was fleeing the scene.

*Dang. What was I thinking?* Eddie thought as he immediately sobered up. *I let my rage engulf me, take over my mind and body. That wasn't even me; it was some shell of me. This can't help my case.*

As he sat in the cell, the clarity of it all sank in. He needed to play the game. He needed to stop acting like a victim, put the pads back on, as it were, and return to the field. Yes, he carried the impulse to grab a direct flight straight to Brasília, run Natalia down, and grab his daughter. Every fiber inside him told him this, but he knew that wouldn't work. He couldn't reverse-kidnap his daughter. Brazil has exit controls, where both parents need to sign forms to agree to let a child out of the country, unlike America. He couldn't just sneak her across to Argentina or Uruguay or wherever. Wait... could he? No, no—The Hague Convention laws were set up just for this purpose. So, he would play the game. The diplomatic game. First things first, however; he needed to get out of jail, and money was a necessity.

Eddie was a hard worker. There were no complaints from David, and other than breaking a few company rules by dating a coworker, he was a pretty stable contributor. He thought his only angle was to lean on David for maybe a little sympathy.

"Hey, David. It's Eddie. How are you?"

"Eddie, why am I getting a collect call from the Orange County jail? And where the hell have you been? You go on vacation, send me an e-mail about your daughter, which I am deeply disturbed and sorry about, but I haven't heard from you since. Is everything okay?"

"Sorry, but I've been struggling big time. I appreciate you hanging in there with me and letting me take this time off."

"No problem. Obviously, anything I can do to help—and take as much time as you need."

That was the advantage of a start-up. If he had been stuck in some giant corporation, they would have fired his ass by now.

"David, listen, I've lost my mind these past couple of weeks. I'm getting a lot of pushback trying to have Izzy returned, and honestly, I've hit a breaking point. But I'm clearheaded now and I'm ready to fight... the right way, the legal way."

"That's great, Eddie. How can I... *we* help you?"

"I tried to get ahold of Lisa. Can you please send her down to the jail? Secondly, and not really related to why I am here now, but I am going to need a lawyer who specializes in these types of situations. It's going to be expensive. I know this is a big ask, but I need you to consider vesting forward all my stock options."

Silence.

"Eddie, yes, I will call Lisa and get her down there, but there are so many legal issues there, and HR issues..."

"Please, David, put yourself in my shoes. Only money will help me now."

"Okay. Get your ass out of jail and come visit me. We can talk."

David's company was killing it. The stock options were paying off. Eddie being an early employee, having a few years under his belt, meant a significant chuck of change. But most of it was still unvested, meaning David would have to do him a huge favor.

As Lisa marched into the visitation room, Eddie looked up, staring deeply at the girl. He watched her every step, still thinking about her beauty, even in his stressed-out state. *I'm going to need her more than ever now, but how can I convince her of this?* he wondered.

"Hey, baby. Sorry I haven't called in a little while, but as you can see, this is a no-conjugal-visit jail, ha-ha!" He was pathetically trying to break the awkward heaviness of the situation.

"Eddie, what the hell? I thought you had killed yourself. Are you okay? What did you do?"

"It's an embarrassing story, and I'll tell you everything, but first, I really need a favor. It's a big ask, but I need it."

"Anything you need. What is it?"

"I need you to call your ex-husband. I know, it's bad to ask, but I need to get out of here without lawyers, judges, and all that shit. I can't have a blemish on my record as I go to war with what I think is going to be the government of Brazil. Tom's a sheriff now. He's worked here in the jails. I need him to pull some strings and release me. Anything you can trade for that?"

"Eddie, I've been fighting him for years. He's going to want me to drop every complaint and let him do whatever he wants from here on out!"

"I know, Lisa, and I wouldn't even ask. Listen, don't worry about him, because you tell him if he does this, you won't ask for another dime, you'll stick to fifty-fifty custody, all that. You won't need his money anymore. I'm working a deal with David. Please trust me on this."

Truthfully, even Eddie realized this was a complete long shot, but that's the funny thing about life and real love. Good people in this world do exist. Lisa was one of them, and he just hoped he was lucky enough for her to really jump on board, 100 percent together. But her elongated silence was worrisome, so he had to push through.

"Lisa, I promise you, we won't need money. We don't need anything or anyone but each other. We'll get married; we'll live happily ever after. We just need to get through this right here and right now!"

Asking her to give up possibly more custody for her kids, plus child support, was a huge favor, to say the least. Who could ask a mother for that? But Eddie knew her ex-husband. He didn't care how much time the boys spent with her or with him. For that man, it was all about money and not having to pay her any alimony or child support. Giving his best to explain to Lisa that she would have the boys as much as she wanted, she just had to give up the money part, was actually not so hard. She got it. He just needed her to understand that they were still winning. Furthermore, what she really desired was the commitment and to recognize that Eddie was trustworthy in his proposal.

"Lisa, we can support the family between the two of us. We will be all right, I promise. Honestly, I'm not so sure how much money I'll have left, or if I'll have any... but I *will* make it work some way or another!"

"Eddie, this is too much to ask of me."

"Please, Lisa. I'm begging you. Please."

Lisa left without giving an answer. He waited three days for the news to come in. Three days in a tiny cell shared with some sketchy, drug-addict loser. The cell was shrinking each day, yet the window was growing. He was left there with only his thoughts and that window.

*I need to get out of here. I need to continue the fight. Please let this happen. Please let Lisa trust me enough to make a good case to her ex. Starting now, I will stop the pointless drinking, rioting, and all that shit. One hundred percent focus on Izzy*, he prayed and hoped it would be received.

"Eddie Watters?" the guard snapped as the door to his concrete block of a cell rolled open with a gust of nasty jail air swooshing in, air that never felt so good to him.

"Yes, that's me."

"Rise up. You're being processed out."

# 16

It was becoming quite clear that Eddie had a tough time controlling his emotions, his temper, his rage. From his first fight in grade school up to losing Izzy, he has steadily declined in that aspect of his life. Spending time in jail for such a loose-cannon reaction was supposed to shake this temper thing, maybe even force him to see the ways of his actions. But, of course, as he continued to be bailed out of situations (this time, quite literally), he was learning the opposite.

He didn't know how Lisa convinced her ex-husband to go to bat for him, but he sure did appreciate what she'd done. What was she giving up to release his sorry-ass from jail? As he wandered out the door of the county jail and made his way down the stairs, he glanced ahead to see his angel. Lisa was waiting for him, arms folded across her chest and right foot tapping, like she was ready to dish out a scolding.

Eddie began with, "First off, Lisa, I'm sorry! I don't know how you did it, but I owe you big!"

"You owe me big? Do you even know what I had to give up to get you out? I had to go to that asshole and basically drop any custody filings I had against him. I could have just lost more time and money because of *you*!"

Eddie was appreciative, to say the least. The two seemed to be really growing in love, and Lisa really put it all on the line for him. "Lisa, you know if the roles were reversed, I would do the same."

"Don't give me that BS! You would never give up more time with Izzy for me!"

"Well, I think you're wrong," he countered.

"And guess what?" she continued. "I actually only did it because I knew I wasn't going to win more custody anyway."

"What do you mean?"

"My son told me the other day that his father, that asshole, notified him that if we went to court for custody, if he sat in front of the judge, being old enough to do so, and told the judge he wanted to live full-time with his father that he would buy him a car when he turned sixteen—only two years away! So you see, this way, that cheap-ass now gets off scot-free—he doesn't have to buy anyone a car, and he gets what he wants. Either way, I was going to lose, so at least I got you out as part of the deal."

"What a chump!" Eddie said, although he was completely relieved that he didn't totally screw things up with Lisa. "But still, Lisa, I don't know how to thank you. Since I've met you, all you've done is take care of me, help me, support me. The word *happy* doesn't even describe how I am feeling with us. You are everything I will ever want in my life! Lisa, I love you!"

Lisa had heard him say this before, but looking at Eddie, at this time and place, she knew that he really meant it. "I love you too, Eddie!" They moved closer and gave each other a tight embrace. "But you smell like sweaty disgustingness. We need to get you home and showered!"

"Oh yeah. That's actually my cellmate's sweat. You might not want to hug me too closely till I get a penicillin shot, ha-ha!"

"Disgusting."

Having the Lisa situation sorted out, Eddie knew the next phase was to secure his stock by somehow convincing his boss it would be a good return on his investment. Luckily for Eddie, the company was growing at an even more exceptional rate than initially perceived, and David 1) liked Eddie's work, 2) liked Lisa's work, 3) knew he was helping both of them at this point, 4) had a soft spot for kids and dads who got screwed, and finally, most importantly, 5) knew he could lock Eddie into employment forever. The deal was this: Vesting forward his stock was fine, but Eddie would work ten years under contract for the company upon his return. Furthermore, he would be granted no further shares until that ten years was up. Had this little situation not occurred, he would have received stock grants every year, and with the growth trajectory of the company, the possibility of millions would have been realistic. Receiving a good chunk of change was worth it at this point, as Eddie was looking at lawyer fees, travel, and general living costs as he was taking a leave from work to battle for his daughter. The net of it all: soon he would be flat broke and working as an indentured servant for the next ten years.

Eddie had successfully rallied the troops, as it were. He received support from Lisa, who'd agreed to take a few weeks off work herself to help in any way she could; David had offered financial support; and now his brand-new Miami-based lawyer would help navigate through the mess.

Javier Gonzales had all the credentials one could desire—a law degree from Harvard, years of experience in international cases, a Latin American name and family, and, most important, friends. Referred by the State Department, Javier appeared to be well connected. Although mostly coming from the business world, he had spent the previous two years getting into this family law racket, mostly dealing with immigration cases and reuniting families who might otherwise be split by deportation. A noble lawyer, he was, but what Eddie really needed was his connections in Brasília in the Itamaraty Palace—the Brazilian department of state—and the local courts.

Lisa and Eddie found themselves on a flight to Miami, and as Eddie stared out the window, he couldn't help but think about how much he missed Izzy. She was such a good kid, very playful, athletic, smart, and cute as a button. He used to hate being away from her for even a day or two as he traveled on business trips, never wanting to neglect even one hour of her childhood, because growing up was a guarantee, and he knew one day she would leave and have her own life. He loved her so much. The pain was unbearable. He'd already missed weeks of her childhood, not days. Soon it would be months, maybe years before he saw her again. Natalia had stolen Izzy's childhood away from him, and Izzy's father away from her. Eddie was a damn good father; Izzy somehow grasped that at a young age. He hoped to the heavens that she knew he didn't abandoned her, that he was coming for her, because he would never leave her or let her out of his sight again.

"Eddie, are you okay?" asked Lisa. But she knew the answer. She had known the answer, and she also realized it wasn't a smart question to be asking, but he did his best not to snap back.

"I'm holding up, thanks. Just nervous to meet this guy. I hope he is solid and has some good news for us."

"Make sure you have everything written down and you cover all the bases."

Frustration was setting in.

"Lisa, I know. I stayed up till 2:00 a.m. and woke up at 6:00 a.m. thinking of everything. Please, I've got it."

"Don't be a dick. Eddie. I'm here to help you!" she snapped, irritated.

"I know. Lisa. Sorry I'm just tired, pissed, and everything else. I didn't mean to snap." Eddie wanted to say, "If you wanted to help, you could get on a plane, go to Brazil, shoot Natalia in the head, and...," but of course, he kept that little psychotic rant to himself.

"Ladies and gentlemen, as we prepare for our final descent, please have your trays closed and seats in the upright position," interrupted the flight attendant on the speakers.

Eddie's evil and pissed-off thoughts were saved by a sixty-year-old flight attendant. "Who the hell are they kidding?" Eddie turned to Lisa and asked. "This woman couldn't operate one of those exit doors or carry out an injured kid if they ever needed her to. What the hell is wrong with the airlines these days?"

"What are you talking about, Eddie?"

Eddie sat quietly and didn't respond, just thinking, *Damn, I'm going nuts... haven't slept, can't think straight. Shit, I feel claustrophobic on this plane. It's so small and enclosed. Keep it together. Keep it all together...*

"Eddie, did you hear me?" Lisa tapped him on the shoulder.
"Yes, sorry, sorry. Are we there? Let's get on with this."

ARRIVING AT THE lawyer's office, Eddie and team felt a great sense of hope for the first time since the beginning of this battle.
"Mr. Watters, *bem-vindo* to Miami, sir. Welcome to my office, and thanks for making the trip. These meetings are much more productive in person, at least initially!" exclaimed Javier, much more jovially than they would expect a lawyer to be in a kidnapping case. Javier was a sight to look at, probably weighing in at three hundred pounds, with the Latin flare they picked up on right away. It didn't escape Eddie either that he continuously peeked over at Lisa, checking her out. Probably not a lot of girls like her made their way into his office.
"Thanks, Javier. This is my girlfriend, Lisa. She's here to help, and we can discuss anything in front of her."
"Very good, then, sir. Let's get down to business. I know you gave me the basics on the phone, but now I need the details. Every single detail. The key to winning this case is in the details. We need to make a strong enough case to the Brazilian government, backed up by all the court rulings here in the States, that it would set an extremely negative precedent for them to go against us, so much so that we would hit them with media, news outlets, and such, plus the strong arm of Uncle Sam. The US government needs to know that you've done everything right and that it would be unwise for them not support you. Together, with the combination of bad publicity to both the Brazilian government and the United States, we will win. Brazil needs the US tourism industry. They don't want us painting them as a extremist, unfriendly country

to foreigners, especially when their marketing to the whole world is *jeitinho brasileiro*"—the very friendly and open Brazilian lifestyle—"and the last thing the US government needs is bad press for not going to bat for one of their own."

"Great! I love it! How do we begin?" Eddie asked, starting to get excited.

"I know it's complicated, but again, we start with the details," Javier responded. "There is one very strange and possible coincidence I noticed here. You said your ex-wife's name is Natalia Pacheco, and she's from Brasília, yes?"

"Yes, that's right."

"By any chance, is her father's name *José*? As in José Pacheco, the artist?"

"Shit, you know the family, don't you? It's like every damn place I go where there is a Brazilian, someone knows this family! How did I not get millions divorcing her?"

Javier reacted in a way that made Eddie know immediately not to trust him. "Yes, I know José and his father from the days when Brazil was a dictatorship. I provided a lot of services for his family that I'm not at liberty to discuss at this moment. But don't worry! I am on your side, completely impartial to my history."

Eddie called bullshit. But what was he supposed to do? This guy could either keep his word and help, despite his connection to Natalia, or they could find a less qualified lawyer—which would be very difficult, being a specialty field, with not a lot of expertise running around—and take their chances.

"I don't know, Javier. If we're to continue this, I'm going to need some sort of assurances. This is not sitting well with me. What about my payment plan to you, tied to certain small victories, like 1) getting us in front of a judge, 2) visitation, 3) final victory, or something along those lines? This is all the money I have in the world, for the most important fight of my life. I want tangible assurances you're going to be on this 100 percent."

"Mr. Watters, I can tell you that I will be dedicated—"

"I don't care what you tell me, Javier. I need you in my corner, and I need to be able to trust you."

"Okay, Mr. Watters. I'll run it through my contracts if you demand so, and I'll come up with something."

*Damn straight.*

FOURTH OF JULY in Brasília isn't quite the same as back in the States. With the US embassy fortified within the city, however, the folks in residence do know how to put on a nice show. Izzy had now been an officially kidnapped expat for close to six months, and Natalia could see that she was missing her father like crazy, but she didn't care. She believed it was more important for her to reside in Brazil, with her family, speaking Portuguese (which she was adopting nicely) than to be in the Great Satan of the United States with her biological dad. And this time, there was a wrinkle.

Unbeknownst to Eddie, even after the thousands of times he'd attempted to contact Izzy, there was a new man in Izzy's and Natalia's lives. Well, not exactly *new*, but new to the whole family thing. Natalia and Don (of Consciousness Healing fame) had advanced their love further, but also their disdain for each other. Their love seemed to be winning out, leading to Don spending a lot more time in Brazil than his visa should have allowed.

But Natalia couldn't let him go, even to the detriment of Izzy and her own mind-set. It was quite the irony: Don was the

CH guru, who was teaching Natalia how to heal, yet his presence in her life was responsible for more damage that would require further healing. Maybe this guy was a smart one and had it all figured out with this cycle of hurt and heal.

The damage he was applying came off quite strangely. Every couple argues, and with Natalia, there would be fights. She was drama and could drive any guy crazy trying to deal with her. But Don was just off, more so than you would think of a guy who'd invented a ridiculous scam to lure women. Yet he was loving his life in Brazil. The money poured in from all over the world while he slept, without lifting a finger, funneled from the pyramid scheme of training the trainers, who then went and trained others. It was a gold mine now, which allowed him to spend time with Natalia in her home country.

Natalia was turning out to be much less of a mother as Izzy grew and grew. She and Don loved to leave Izzy at home while they went out for nights on the town, treating themselves to nice dinners and drinks afterward within an upscale bar or club or whatever else adults in Brasília liked to do. The problem was, they went out every night, and this new Natalia was enjoying flashing her money around—along with her body—to really attract the attention of the male Brazilian species, much to Don's dismay. But he hid his jealous anger well, because he knew it could lead him into dark places, and he'd visited these places more than enough.

"Natalia, it's almost 8:00! When are we going to get dinner?" Don asked as if he hadn't eaten in a year.

"Don, how many times do I have to tell you? Brazilian Saturday nights! Nobody sits down for dinner until at least 10:00 p.m. Have another beer with my dad, or go ask the maid for a snack. I still need to get ready in here."

"Fine, but please hurry. Izzy is out there crying again about you leaving her home. Plus, I'm hungry, and your dad is starting to ask more questions again about leaving Izzy another night with him."

"She's fine," Natalia explained. "This is Brazil. She needs to learn that children are lower priorities than adults here. She was spoiled by her dad. Now she needs to understand her place."

Standard line from Natalia. Even Don thought that statement was a bit messed up, yet he didn't care—he had his hot little Brazilian chick and his money rolling in. The kid wasn't his, so Natalia could raise her daughter any way she pleased.

As Natalia and Don pulled up to the chic, new, and popular restaurant, the number of younger and older Brazilians out and about was staggering. Who knew this many residents stayed in the nation's capital on the weekend? Most of the city dwellers headed back to their base camps on Friday nights, only using Brasília as a place of employment throughout the workweek. But the city was growing every year, flooded with folks looking to escape the overcrowded megalopolises like Rio and São Paulo.

Immediately as Natalia exited the vehicle, she flashed a little leg to get all the young guys staring. In Brazil, the guys don't bother about their surroundings. They are chauvinistic for the most part, and they have no qualms about checking out all the women, no matter who is accompanying them.

Don didn't like this one bit, as one could imagine. To him, Natalia was all *his*, and that should have been respected. So, as they made their way through the opening of the bar and restaurant, he could feel his blood boil with every glance at Natalia's bouncing behind. He flashed the stare right back at the disrespectful gawkers. He normally couldn't back it up in a physical confrontation, but he didn't worry about that. He was more concerned about respect and accomplishment, and he deserved the respect for the accomplishments he'd made in life, including landing Natalia.

Drinking beer in Brazil was a spectacle. Patrons received a card at the door with the numbers one through one hundred on it, and the bartender would mark the next number, therefore tallying how many beers were consumed throughout the night. Don and Natalia hadn't even assembled for dinner yet, and Don was already at number eight. As the minutes passed and Don continued indulging, mainly to cure his hunger, the empty stomach plus multiple drinks were starting to catch up.

Don could see the sharks starting to circle. Maybe it was his imagination, but more than likely, it was the skin Natalia was flashing and the overbearing Brazilians who kept inching their way closer to her. One particular shark was having an unusually delightful chat with Natalia. Don had had his eye on him since the bartender marked off beer number five on his card.

*What the hell is this guy doing?* he thought. *That's my girl! Does he have no shame?* As Don directed himself over to the one-on-one his girlfriend and this random guy were having, he felt the blood start to boil and the adrenaline rush. Don housed this demon full of anger that lived deep within him, and when the demon had woken, it had cost him several relationships. But after beer number ten went down, he didn't care.

"Don, this is my friend Marcelo. We grew up together, and I haven't seen him in years!" Natalia exclaimed a little too excitedly for Don, because he wasn't even listening to what Natalia had to say; he was just watching this Marcelo dude be a little too handsy with his girlfriend.

"So, do you let all your friends grope you and flirt with you when I'm not here too?' asked Don like a total possessive dick.

"What the hell, Don?" Natalia snapped, and she turned to Marcelo: *"Desculpe, ele esta muito bêbado,"* she told him, warning Marcelo that Don was drunk.

"Fuck this guy, Natalia, or have you?" asked Don sarcastically.

"You're so inappropriate, Don. Get the hell out of my face!" she yelled, becoming exceedingly pissed.

"Sorry, I no mean trouble, Don; Natalia is really good friend I know," Marcelo explained in broken English, which just annoyed Don even more.

"Well, you have disrespected me, you loser. Get the hell out of here!"

Marcelo looked at Natalia quite perplexed and asked, *"Que isso,* Natalia?"

At that moment, he felt the weight of Don's shoulder driving him toward the ground, with fists thrown all over the back of his head, as Don was now on top of Marcelo from the sucker punching, whaling away.

Now one might think that this was an overreaction to a few good friends catching up, but Don thought differently. He understood what Natalia was capable of in the cheating world. Hell, it had been pretty easy to lure her away from her husband, so in his mind, he wasn't taking any chances with someone else doing the same to him.

"Get off him, Don! Somebody help, please!" As Natalia screamed and arms were swinging, Brazilians from all around grabbed Don to pull him off the surprised and now bloodied Marcelo. But it wasn't stopping there. The Brazilians decided to take the frustrations of *their* lives out now on this cornered animal. And what better way to do so than to beat the shit out of some American jackass?

When all was said and done, Don's jealous rage cost him a broken nose, broken ribs, and, most of all, broken trust with Natalia. Could Natalia stay with such a man? Did she really need to deal with this now? She realized that she was quite flirtatious; but what was the point to live this way? Why deal with such jealousy? Oh yes, Don made a lot of money.

# 17

J AVIER WAS APPARENTLY sticking to his word, although truth be told, neither Eddie nor Lisa really knew what was happening behind the scenes. But the point was, they now had a plane ticket to Brazil, with Javier in tow, for a court date aiming toward a goal of visitation. The question was, though, was it all going to be for nothing? Did Eddie really have a shot through the Brazilian court system? Was he just wasting more time and money? He hadn't seen or even spoken to Izzy in such a long time; although he was perhaps being melodramatic, he wasn't sure she would even recognize him if they did manage a get-together.

Finding himself on another plane, his wandering mind once again reared its ugly head. *Why did I choose Natalia to begin with? It was such a hasty move. I know the robbery thing made it feel like destiny, but how could I have been so wrong? I mean, she seemed like a nice, semi-fun girl when I met her. But she changed completely, and that's the thing about it. You're not supposed to change that much! I haven't changed—I'm still the same ol' Eddie. Natalia, on the other hand, she did a complete 180-degree turn on me with the CH crap. What the hell? I should have vetted her more. But then there's Izzy. Without that crazy person in my life, I never would have had Izzy in the first place. So, I need to move past this. I need to reconcile the fact that, yes, I am in a crap situation, but it will be all worth it when I get Izzy back. I'll spoil her rotten, like nobody has seen before—and fuck everyone who will judge me.*

While the flights and the time alone in an enclosed metal tube hurtling through space always got his mind racing, they also presented Lisa in a whole new light. Eddie couldn't help but turn his thoughts toward her. *She has given up so much for Izzy and me: money, security, time with her own kids. What else does she need to prove for me to see that she is in this for the long run? Maybe I should ask her to marry me. Would that be too soon? Do I really want to get married again? I guess she does understand where I'm coming from and hopefully isn't expecting too much, but I really don't want to lose her. She's beautiful, smart, loyal, and isn't a foreigner who would kidnap my child! Maybe this is what I really needed all along?*

It's always hard flying to South America, for it's an overnight flight, and if one isn't able to sleep on the plane, then good luck the next day. Luckily for Eddie, yes, he could sleep... and the best thing about this international destination is that the time zone wasn't too harsh on the body. When it's winter in Brazil and summer back in the States, it is only a one-hour time difference from eastern standard time. There's no losing a whole day and crossing the international date line, causing extreme jet lag. Just sleep a little en route, deplane, and pass immigration and customs, then start the day like any other.

But that could be easier said than done. As Lisa and Eddie waited in the immigration line to stamp their passports, Eddie caught Javier entering the Brazilian citizens' queue.

"That dick. He's a little bit more well connected than I thought," Eddie whispered to Lisa.

The two Americans approached hand in hand, and as Eddie handed over his passport to the officer, the guy was noticeably taking his time. The officer waved over to his supervisor and mouthed something Eddie couldn't quite make out. Eddie's Portuguese skills had diminished significantly, but they were purposefully whispering like they knew he could understand them.

"What the heck is going on? I've been to this country too many times to know this isn't right," Eddie wondered aloud.

"Mr. Watters? Ms. Manning? Please come with us," the officer said, with no fewer than three other suited-up guys with him.

As they entered the back office, Eddie detected out of the corner of his eye Javier zipping his way out of immigration into the customs area. He wasn't even waiting for his clients.

"Javier!" Eddie yelled out, with no response.

"Please, have a seat," demanded the officer.

"*Que isso, senhor?*" Eddie tried to smooth them over in Portuguese.

"We will speak English, sir, so everyone in the room can understand," he explained as he glanced over at Lisa. He continued on, delivering the news, "I'm sorry to say, but your passports have been denied."

"What are you talking about? I have Brazilian permanent residency, I don't even need a passport technically. And Lisa's visa is new!"

"Yes, that's the problem sir. Your residency has expired since you don't live here anymore, and Ms. Manning was granted a visa by mistake."

"The hell!" Eddie shouted. "I'm allowed to be out of the country for up to two years at a time. And how can you 'grant a visa by mistake'? That's the whole point of going to the embassy and getting a visa."

"I'm sorry, Mr. Watters, but we have the power to see when someone is abusing the residency system, and that's exactly what's going on. And as for Ms. Manning, the order to revoke her visa came from my boss. I'm sorry."

Eddie knew exactly what was going on. Javier must have tipped off Natalia's family—they'd pulled some serious weight to keep them out.

"These corrupt motherfuckers. I prepaid that asshole lawyer half his fees with the rest upon my contingencies. He must have been hooked up with even more cash from Natalia and company. Damn, I knew not to trust that shady piece of dirt." Eddie was steaming.

Now if there is one almost certainty in Brazil, it is that you will run into some situation where you get screwed, but there's always an avenue to buy your way out of it. Case in point: these corrupt immigration officials were obviously paid by Natalia, which showed they were for sale. And if they could be bought by Natalia, then they could also be bought by two Americans who knew how to work the system. It's simple economics—their service is in demand, so they will go with the higher dollar amount.

"Okay, *senhor*, I totally understand. But let me ask you a question. Does your wife love jewelry as much as my girlfriend here?" Eddie asked quite blatantly.

"I don't understand, Mr. Watters. What does that have to do—?"

"Because you see that Cartier watch she has on? That, alongside the necklace she wears, is worth about $10,000 US. I bet that's about $35,000 Brazilian reals, isn't it?" In the hustle and confusion of all that was going on, Eddie forgot to tell Lisa that you never wear expensive jewelry in Brazil. It's just not worth possibly getting mugged. But keeping her in the dark had now worked out to their advantage.

Lisa shot Eddie the evil eye. "Why don't you give them something of yours?"

"Add it to the list, Lisa. I'll pay you back... with interest. Plus, my watch is only worth $500."

"We'll take that too," demanded the officers.

"Fuck."

Back to their mission, Lisa and Eddie headed to the hotel, minus two watches and one necklace, but with clean papers.

"If I see that little squirm, Javier, I just might murder him. But I too have connections in Brasília: I have the US government on my side. We need to shower and get ready as quickly as possible and head straight for the US embassy," Eddie instructed Lisa.

But as they flew through the streets of Brasília, winding through the crazy, curving turnouts and ramps to other roads, Eddie couldn't help but feel a bit nostalgic about a life once lived. He did experience some good times in this city, albeit with someone who he now despised, but nevertheless, it had been enjoyable for him living there, drinking, eating, and hanging out. Now a dark cloud loomed steady over this once second home of his.

As they continued down the road, Eddie grew a little indecisive. *Should I just skip this whole court thing, go straight to Natalia's father's house, and grab my little girl? But no doubt if Javier tipped them off, Izzy won't be there. Or they'll be surrounded by security. Damn it. No way around it*, he thought.

"Lisa, let's try to hurry. It can be a long wait at the embassy," Eddie explained, becoming quite nervous. Generally on time for everything, Eddie knew there was a chance the appointment at the embassy was never even set up by Javier, but he still wanted to get there and initiate the proceedings.

"I'm going as fast as I can! I just got off a long flight and provided an unwanted donation to the Brazilian government. The least I can do is take a shower and get cleaned up."

"Sorry, baby. I'm just getting worked up."

The US embassy in Brasília is like a fortress. Many of the other country's embassies don't look like anything more than big, private residences. Of course, some of the larger South American countries that have importance in Brazil are set up well, like the Argentinas of the world, but the US embassy is quite imposing. It sits on a large piece of land; the blockade and security just to get into that piece of land is like trying to enter the White House. Quite ironic, because Brazilians wouldn't dare do anything to the United States, their diplomats, or their property. Take aside the ramifications from the tourist industry, or trade, or any of that... Brazilians, by nature, aren't those people. When was the last time you heard of Brazil going to war with anyone? Oh yes, because it's never happened, ever. Yes, they sent a few troops to World War II, in the ballpark of like five hundred soldiers, but that's it. These folks weren't fighters, they were lovers, and only liked to fight within themselves.

FIRST THING ON their list when they cleared the security entrance was to bypass the outrageous line of Brazilians waiting to apply for US visas. Never a shortage of residents trying to make their way to America. Then there was Natalia, who was opposing the norm by taking an American girl back home... quite backward in Eddie's opinion. And as they stepped into the embassy to check in, who did they see but their hired lawyer, Javier?

"You asshole, Javier! You have some balls showing up here! You're lucky there are marines here, or I would drag you out into the street and beat you silly!" Eddie shouted for almost everyone to hear.

"Eddie, I don't know what you're talking about. I saw you get detained, so I left, thinking you were trying to smuggle something in or who knows what? I can't get caught up in any of that!" He grinned when he lied.

"Fuck you, Javier! You set that up. Don't you lie to me anymore! I want my money back, you corrupt piece of shit!"

"Eddie, I provided you a service. I got you this far, and you want your money back? Don't even worry about paying me the rest of the money you owe!"

"The money I owe? I am doing this on my own! I don't even know if I have an appointment here because... wait a minute. If you thought we were detained and had to leave the country, what the fuck are you doing here during my appointment time?"

"No, Eddie, see? I don't lie. I made this appointment, so I'm here—"

"You dick! You're here for *her*, aren't you? You made an appointment, all right! For Natalia!" And wouldn't you know it, as if on cue, in through the door walked Natalia, and holding her hand was Eddie's little girl. Izzy was dancing around, looking cute as he remembered her. He hadn't seen her in so many months, he couldn't imagine how much she'd grown.

As she heard his voice cry out, she looked up, sprinted out of her mother's grasp and effort to try to pull her back, and ran straight toward her father. Eddie reached his hands out the farthest he could while she jumped at a forty-five-degree angle right into his arms. It was the sweetest hug he had ever received in his life. He squeezed her so hard she almost lost her breath. Eddie was crying like a newborn baby by this time, as Izzy had the biggest smile on her face. It had been a long-waited reunion, Izzy closer to four years old and Eddie's stress aging him like he was seventy.

"Daddy! Daddy! Where have you been? You missed so much, Daddy! Grandpa lives here! Me and Mom and Don are here! Are you going to stay with us?"

"I'm here, Izzy! I'm here!"

DON LAY AWAKE in his newly rented hotel room, wondering what the hell to do now. He didn't know whether he should even continue trying to contact Natalia, who wasn't returning his calls, let alone answering her phone. He knew he'd screwed up, and this time pretty bad. But was he wrong for what he did? In the end, he was protecting his girlfriend, right? How could she be upset about that? One little fight.

Figuring he would make an in-person trip down to the house, attempting to make peace, could be his only route. After all, what other option did he have? He couldn't just sit around a hotel room in Brasília, where he knew nobody, didn't speak the language, and had no idea where to even start. But he thanked his lucky stars knowing his business allowed the money to roll right into his bank account, no matter where in the world he might sit.

But getting up the nerve to go have a showdown with Natalia, which might mean her father also, was turning out to be a little bit more difficult than he'd first suspected. *Shit, I need a drink.* The thought of alcohol curing his demons was flawed at best. He drank to calm his anger, and it worked up to a certain point, but if he stumbled past that point, the drinking turned the anger into rage, which then, of course, was counter to what he was trying to accomplish. It was a vicious cycle.

But you only live once, and he was aware that there might only be one last chance to win Natalia and her trust back. Making his way to the hotel bar, he decided on his libation. It was nearing 3:00 p.m. local time, just the right time for a caipirinha. The old creeper drink. It happened to almost every tourist that visited Brazil for the first time. The drink was made with just four ingredients—Brazilian rum, sugar, limes, and ice—a great cocktail that is nearly nothing but liquor, but very sweet and tasty. Drinking three or four felt great, like a nice little buzz hitting. But somewhere between thirty minutes and an hour, the knockout was hard. It's a drunken metaphor of starting off crawling, to a full-on sprint very quickly. No walking or jogging—direct drunkenness!

Don wasn't quite aware of this, since he had mostly been drinking Brazil's other favorite indulgence, Johnnie Walker whiskey. As Don began his caipirinha cycle, ending badly was the likely outcome. About four drinks down, Don figured the sugar was too sweet to drink many more and ordered a beer. Sitting at the bar, lonely and depressed, the creeper went to work.

"Holy crap, I feel great!" he proclaimed as he stood up to stretch out. "I think that's it for me, sir. I've got important business to take care of!" he informed the bartender. Don paid his tab and made his way to the front of the hotel to catch a taxi.

The creeper raised up further as Don was dealing with some issues getting a taxi. It seemed Uber was illegal in Brazil, due to the taxi unions and all, and one had to be very careful what taxi one hired, as some are regulated and some are not. The hotels, of course, want to utilize their hired drivers, so there's a lot going on just trying to get a cab. At this point, Don was not prepared for any of it. He was too wasted to negotiate, so he agreed to a price the concierge sold him (and, honestly, he didn't quite understand) for the hotel's car, and off he went.

"*Fala Inglês?*" Don asked the driver.

"Yes, sir, I speak English. Where would you like to go? The hotel told me Lago Sul neighborhood, yes?"

"Yes, I have the address right here in my phone."

Arriving at the house, Don's head was spinning. *Man, did I get roofied or what?* he wondered. *Fuck it. I'm going in.*

Don buzzed the gate, and Natalia's dad, José, and brother, João, exited out the front door toward him. He was in it now. Not only did he have to deal with the dad but the crazy brother too. He should have stayed at the hotel and drunk away his sorrow, woken up hungover, and taken the next plane back to Arizona. But something about Natalia kept him in the game. She *got* him, and he really was enjoying their time together—even more their continuous spiritual conversations. The CH in him sometimes outweighed his manipulative ways.

"I just need one minute of Natalia's time, please."

"Don, you get the fuck out now. Go home to America. You are mean. You are bad person," said Natalia's brother in his best pissed-off English.

But by now, Don's head was spinning. Becoming extremely upset, he couldn't seem to gather his thoughts enough for a cohesive sentence in any language.

Unwisely, he began with "You fucking Brazilians! You ass-backward mother... mother... motherfuckers!"

Not very elegant, to say the least, but the xenophobic outburst did its job. It flipped that little switch in Natalia's wound-too-tightly brother, João, all right. So as Don started to see the sky circle around him clockwise, but looking down the ground was turning the other way counterclockwise, likely from the caipirinha creepers, João came at him, and he came at him hard. All it took was one good punch to Don's left cheek to knock him out. The same result could have been accomplished without the help of alcohol; but with the levels in Don's blood, that was all too easy for João, and he was feeling quite proud of himself.

João smiled down, standing over Don like he was Mike Tyson, proud of his conquest. That should teach this gringo a lesson.

# 18

THE MARINES WHO protect the US embassy in Brasília are a unique bunch. Like all marines, they are always alert, always on the lookout and ready to jump into action at a moment's notice. And just like those marines back in the day when Eddie first met Natalia, these guys were no different. They saw the Lisa-Eddie couple and, frankly, were happy to be at the service of other Americans.

With both Natalia and Eddie finally in the same room together, along with the sleazy Mr. Javier, the marines could sense trouble. And they certainly knew where their allegiances lay. As Eddie stayed fixated, kneeling down with Izzy in his arms, in the welcoming room of the US embassy, the only thought that crossing his mind was, *Do not let go... ever!* But then Natalia ran over, pulling on Izzy's arms.

"Stop, Mommy, stop!" she yelled as Eddie used his right foot to block Natalia's body while simultaneously swatting at her arms that were pulling Izzy's out of their sockets. "Get the hell away from us, Natalia!" he warned as she began screaming to let her go and to stop hitting her. As one could imagine, the scene created there was something the US government didn't like to present, in a country where they had sometimes good, sometimes sketchy relations.

"Natalia, get away from us—*now*! You are a criminal! Kidnap her from me? You're lucky you're not in jail right now!"

"This is my daughter! You lost the right to be her father when you stopped caring about her mother. I'm sure Lisa here wasn't a part of that either, was she?" said Natalia.

All this time, Lisa just stayed at Eddie's side, never wavering. She was an incredible woman to him. Eddie knew what she had to deal with. And now, she found herself running to a tug-of-war between two parents and their very confused daughter.

"Eddie, not here, not here, baby. We have her now; her mom isn't going anywhere with her. You're scaring little Izzy," she calmly whispered into his ear while he continued to shield Izzy from Natalia, turning his back and covering Izzy, staying at every angle between Natalia's approaches and Izzy.

But Eddie was not giving up this fight. This little girl was staying in his arms no matter how logical Lisa sounded or how scared to death Izzy was becoming. He realized it was a selfish move; however, the pain he held overruled that objection. And as all this was going down, five US Marines ran over, along with US embassy staffers to involve themselves.

"Please! Everybody please stop fighting! What is going on here?" yelled one of the diplomats.

"This guy is crazy!" shouted Javier to the staffer.

Eddie replied, "This is my daughter, who was kidnapped by her mom! I'm not letting go! I came down here to get her—that's the woman who took her!"

"This is the Brazilian mother I made the appointment with your staff about—Natalia Pacheco; she's here to finalize her physical custody of her daughter with your government," explained Javier while the wrestling continued.

"Physical custody, my ass! This girl was taken from me without my permission from that criminal! Take her to jail immediately, right now! Please! I am an American citizen, and she is a kidnapper!"

"Please, please, everyone, calm down... for the girl's sake! Let the marines take the girl, and we can go settle this together!" Javier continued.

This was the right option for Eddie, but he wasn't about to let a stranger take Izzy out of his sight.

"They can take her, as long as they are right next to me the whole time, away from the crazy criminal woman!" he protested.

"This is why I am asking for custody. Do you all see this? He is violent and aggressive!" Natalia wailed.

"Sir, what is your name?" asked one of the marines.

"Eddie Watters. I'm came to find and bring home my daughter. Please!"

"Sir, I promise, let me hold her hand, and we won't leave your side," the marine explained with a wink. Maybe some good luck was coming his way, after all. They realized he was an American, putting them on the same team.

"Daddy, Daddy!" cried Izzy as the marine pulled her away.

Eddie struggled to let go, reaching out and holding her arm. He told her, "It's okay, little Izzy. I'm here. I'm here."

The staffers and the five marines led the two opposing parties through an incredible security apparatus and process, but everyone understood; this was an embassy after all. Nothing bad was going to go down there that day.

Entering a large conference room, completely white with only the glass doors, Eddie shot a glance at Lisa, with her returning a warming grin. There were pictures of the American flag on the wall, the Statue of Liberty, and a copy of the US Declaration of Independence. On the opposing wall were photographs of the Christ the Redeemer statue and a few others of varying postcard-type shots of different Brazilian cities, most likely where the satellite US consulates were located.

Taking their seats, the diplomat asked if anyone would like water or anything to eat. After a resounding no from the party, the man, who was a witness to all the wrestling, began to speak. "Everybody, I am Frank James, I am the senior diplomatic affairs officer here in the embassy. I am well aware from Ms. Pacheco's lawyer why she is here."

"He's actually my lawyer," Eddie interrupted. "But apparently, he is playing both sides." Javier shot back a look.

"That is not exactly true," Javier began to explain. "You see, when I found out who Mr. Watters was referring to in his case, I thought it was best to be a mediator in the effort to resolve this peacefully from both sides. I think Mr. Watters doesn't see the value in that."

"That's total bullshit!" Lisa blurted out.

"Okay, okay, the matter of lawyers can be discussed later. What I want to know is, why are you here, Mr. Watters?" asked Mr. James.

"Why am I here? I'm here to get my daughter back, legally, from her mother, who kidnapped her and escaped to Brazil."

"I understand you have begun to work through the legal system here in country, correct?"

"I thought I did, but who knows now with my lawyer. He could have done absolutely nothing as far as I know."

"Well, we can check into that and help you through the process. And I'm sure you are aware of The Hague laws, so doing so legally is the right course of action," explained Mr. James.

"That's fine, but I want to know why *she* is here, at the US embassy?" Eddie inquired, pointing at his ex-wife.

"Ms. Pacheco has requested an audience with the US government to give her side of the story as the case works its way through the legal channels," responded Javier. "It's very important that both sides follow the process to a T, and this is just part of it."

"Yes, that is correct," replied Mr. James. "And as you can imagine, this can be an extremely long process, Mr. Watters. So, I am not sure you being here right now is the best use of your time. Legally, we cannot force Ms. Pacheco to give up her daughter; that has to be the Brazilian courts. I'm not sure how else I can help you other than continue to advise you on the matter, whether you are here in country or back home."

"Oh no... oh no." Eddie was beginning to heat up. As his heartbeat raced and the adrenaline began to pump, this was normally when his uncontrollable rage crept up. "I am not leaving here today without my daughter. You don't know what that woman there is capable of. She could be in Argentina by 5:00 tomorrow if you let here leave this embassy with my daughter."

"I would never!" Natalia yelled. "I will be fair about this! Don't try to paint me as a bad person!"

"A bad person? You kidnapped our daughter without telling me! You aren't bad... you are coldhearted and pure evil!"

"Okay, Mr. Watters, let's cool off," Mr. James said calmly.

At the same time, Lisa leaned over and rubbed his leg a little bit, knowing she needed to keep him relaxed. She'd witnessed his off-the-deep-end episodes enough already.

"Listen, this is technically American soil here," Eddie attempted, "so why can't I just stay here with my daughter? She is a US citizen, and we are here in *America*. The minute you let her out the door with her mother, all bets are off!"

"Mr. Watters, that's not how it works. I'm sorry, but we have to let this run its course. You will see that in the end it is best for both parties and both countries." Mr. James said it like he didn't give a rat's ass.

Eddie's blood boiled further. "I can't believe what the hell is happening here. She stole my daughter, and I'm going to have to let her go after I finally tracked down? Oh, hell no! Not on my watch, not today, not ever!"

So right as Mr. James was spewing his next piece of "advice," Eddie unwisely and without thinking clearly decided to take matters into his own hands. He was looking at a losing hand, so all things considered, he felt it was his only option. Looking around, he caught a glance of Izzy right outside the conference room doors, holding the hand of one of the marines. This was it.

Jumping out of the chair, he walked rapidly toward the conference room exit. Swinging open the door and nodding to the marines, he grabbed Izzy by the hand and he ran. He ran like a deer being chased by lions, not even hearing the shouting and screaming coming from the commotion behind him as he was practically dragging Izzy down the same corridor they'd entered while in a full sprint, only stopping to throw his daughter up into his arms. And as the end neared, the secured exit was in full sight, but as he tried to charge through the door, it hit him like the wall it was. Crashing into the door over and over with his shoulder, he tried to open the damn thing, but it must have been on lockdown. As he continued trying to push his way out, all while searching frantically for another exit, he felt the arms of several marines wrap around his body.

"I'm an American! I'm an American!" Eddie screamed as he went tumbling to the ground. Lisa was beelining it straight to the turmoil. She shouted words, but Eddie couldn't make out what they were. Izzy was stripped from his grasp as he felt the pressure of several bodies on top of him, which now seemed to be a regular occurrence for him.

Eddie looked up through the arms around him to see a smattering of the ceiling above him. Only one thought was sparked in his head: *Damn, I'm going to lose her again.*

HE FOUND HIMSELF once again in a holding cell. This same routine was becoming a constant event with the only difference being physical location. He was alone, in this little cell, in the US embassy in Brazil, and still without his daughter. He couldn't just get a win.

"What do I have to do to get people to realize the pain and suffering this has placed on Izzy and me? Did the US government really just side with a Brazilian? How can that be? Their sole purpose of having an embassy down here is to protect the rights of Americans abroad and to serve our best interests. My best interest is not to be in an embassy holding cell while Natalia is free to leave with Izzy again. It just doesn't make sense." Eddie was having a conversation with the window.

He had no idea what time it was or how long he'd been there, wondering where the hell Lisa was, but knowing she was surely doing her very best to get him out of there. With nothing else but time and thoughts, his sense and sanity began to leave him as he stared at the ceiling and wondered, *Why the hell do they have a holding cell in the US embassy? Who has actually been in this cell before me? Political foes to the US government? Protestors? Drunk staff members? Why is this here?* But then footsteps came toward him. Thank God for that, as he needed to breathe.

It was the disloyal diplomat Frank James.

"Mr. Watters? I'm sorry we had to do this to you. Please come with me. I'm sure we can sort this whole mess and misunderstanding out."

"Sure thing, Mr. James. I'm sure you will. And believe me, if you let my daughter leave these grounds, I'm writing to every media outlet in the States. You'll have CNN and Fox News down here so fast you won't know what to do. In fact, why didn't I think of that before?"

"I don't think that's a good idea, Mr. Watters. Let me explain when we get to where we are going."

Looking around at the walls of that place, with every step he took, the corridor grew longer. How could that be? It was the typical story of his Life Book. Every time he put one foot in front of the other, with a destination ahead, the goal seemed to move further and further away. He'd finally made strides in getting his daughter returned, but now she was further away than ever. It was the evil, hypocrisy of life, told many times over. Keep doing the right thing, they say. Keep within the laws of the land, they say. Everything will work out in the end, they say. *Fuck them.*

"Mr. Watters, why don't you sit down here next to Bobby. He's one of the marines on my staff who will be escorting you while you are here," said Frank, like Eddie was a standard criminal.

"Nice to meet you, Bobby." Eddie scowled. "I'm sure you're really going to have your hands full with me. Now, Mr. James, can you please tell me where you took Lisa? I haven't seen her. Is she still here too?"

"She's been escorted back to your hotel. You'll be free to go as soon as we are finished here."

"Oh, goodie. Free to go. Go where? Back to the hotel? Back to California? Without my daughter, whom you let right out the front door of the USA?" He was starting to get heated again. Not good.

"Well, Mr. Watters, I don't know how much you read about international relations or current events. Do you study anything of that nature?"

"Not too much recently," he said, stating the obvious. "I'm busy with my own international-relations situation to frankly give a shit about the rest of the world."

Mr. James leaned in. "I know the whole story here. You have a very, let's say, excitable ex-wife, whose life in California wasn't panning out the way she'd hoped. Maybe she became upset that you moved on to bigger and better things and she was left behind, all while thinking that she would be the one to ditch you in the dirt. Then she decided to put a real knife in your back, taking the most important thing in this world away from you, all while serving another purpose of getting her back to her home country, where she wouldn't have the strains of being a pretender in a foreign land. And just like that… *poof!* She takes your daughter, moves back home to Brazil, and you're left with the shitty end of the stick. Does that about sum it up?"

This took Eddie by surprise. *How could this man understand the situation so clearly and still let her win?* He decided to stick with that route of questioning with Mr. James. "Then tell me, how the hell do you understand my situation so clearly and still let her walk out that door with my daughter?"

"Listen, I have a family and kids too. I can only imagine what it would be like to be in your shoes. In fact, I don't know what I'd do. But you have to understand, there are much bigger fish to fry for the United States government than Eddie Watters. Now I know that sounds like a raw deal, and I know you want to go to the press and make a scene, but trust me, we have ways of dealing with the press. We employ a team here whose sole function is to spin stories to our advantage. Sometimes it doesn't work in our favor, but you would be going up against a trillion dollar–plus machine. Do you really want to do that? Do you really want to be on the US government's radar? Do you really want us looking into your affairs? I'm sure you would like to continue your life, not being audited by the IRS, and so on and so forth."

"Mr. James," Eddie said surprisingly calmly, "I also understand that you have a wider scale you're dealing with, but I will never give up trying to get my daughter back, even if it lands me in prison. My life is an eighteen-year sentence without being able to father my own child."

"Be smart, Mr. Watters. I never asked you to stop trying, but there are ways to do it without raising red flags and sounding alarm bells all over the place. As I said before, we are dealing with much bigger issues."

It was starting to make sense. Eddie was just a pawn in a giant, global chess game, not an important piece at all, rather a crappy little wasteful decoy to be used as collateral damage to advance the needs—not the wants—of these people.

"Mr. James, I'll make you a deal right here and now. You tell me what it is that I am screwing up for you. Blocking some deal? Support of some new candidate? Whatever. I am just curious at this point. You tell me why feathers cannot be ruffled down here, and I promise you that you will not see me making a fuss. I will go about my business and legally try to get my daughter back."

Mr. James thought about it, but truthfully, he was already prepared to dish and was just playing Eddie up for a fool pretty well. But Eddie also felt he could act just as surprised, so he played along like a good citizen.

"Okay, Mr. Watters, but you have to swear to secrecy, and I'm only letting you know because it will put your mind at ease."

"Deal," he responded gently, "but let me tell you one thing. If I get screwed over by the Brazilian courts, it is going to be extremely difficult not to come here and ask for your help once this *thing* is over."

"That's fair," Frank said as he continued with the game. "You see, the United States government has built and operated aircraft carriers since around World War II, but new technology arrives, and we retire the old boats, like you do when you buy a car. Trouble is, these carriers, and the weaponry and intellectual property that come with it, cost a hell of a lot of money to just throw in a scrapyard. So, you see, we have a surplus of aircraft carriers from several generations, all the way up to the eighties. Let me ask you a question, Mr. Watters. How many aircraft carriers do you think Brazil has in its arsenal?"

"No clue," he responded, being completely honest. Then again, when would anybody ever think about aircraft carriers and Brazil?

"Well, I'll tell you how many. The answer is one. Yes, one aircraft carrier for a country with two hundred million people and a whole hell of a lot of coastline to protect. They will never be ahead of us with new technology in the military space, but they really don't mind being just one step behind either. So that positions us in a nice supply-and-demand situation with our aircraft carriers. And believe me, for us to sell a few carriers to a country like Brazil is a lot different from selling it to a Middle Eastern country, if you can imagine."

"Yes, I would imagine so."

"Now France, the UK, they're all thinking the same thing. Therefore, we have to be ahead of the curve here. You see, aircraft carrier sales then become other weaponry transactions—planes, tanks, munitions and so on. There is a huge windfall for us to sell military equipment to a country who would rather buy than build. You get my drift?"

Eddie was not shocked. It actually did make a lot of sense. "Well, Mr. James, I get it, and what I get is that it is all about money, as usual. But what does that have to do with me?"

"When is it not the money, Mr. Watters? You see, we can't start a war with the Brazilian courts, the Brazilian government, over some child-custody battle, right when we are in the middle of this agreement. We need to all be good friends right now, as harsh as that sounds."

"You sound like my kindergarten teacher here. This is complete crap, as usual. But you know what? I am actually pretty smart, and I understand. I don't have to agree with it, because I am the one getting screwed over, as always." Eddie knew it was a pointless argument, and he was never going to abide by any rules placed on him anyway. This was his life, his daughter. *Screw them all.*

"Bobby." Mr. James turns to the marine escort. "Will you take Mr. Watters out the diplomatic entrance and make sure he gets a ride back to his hotel?"

"Yes, sir."

Back in the windowless, soulless corridor they went, this time heading closer to another physical destination, yet farther and farther from the real place Eddie wanted to be—and that was home in California with Izzy, Lisa, and her boys. But first things first. How the heck was he supposed to get back to the hotel? Where was Lisa?

"Sir, I can let you use an embassy phone if you want to call your wife to pick you up. Seems she took your cell phone with her." Of course.

"That would be great, um, Bobby, right?"

"That's right, sir."

"Well, thanks, Bobby. Do you have a gun I can shoot myself with too, while we're at it?"

Eddie saw a look cross Bobby's face as if he were holding something in. It was that shifty look, like when your stomach hurts and you're really uncomfortable. Or maybe it was the other end of the spectrum; maybe it was more when you're holding in a laugh. Either way, Eddie knew this guy had something to say.

"Sir, I really don't want to get involved in your affairs, *but* not sure if you noticed that I was there during that entire conversation. Also, I was present earlier in the day when you created that scene. Sir, if you don't mind me saying, you are getting screwed big time. And wait... before you get upset, I really would like to tell you something."

"What is it, Bobby? More great news or what?" Eddie was now expecting the when-it-rains-it-pours thing to happen.

"Sir, I think I know someone who can help. He works, shall we say, part-time down here for our staff. Well, not down here, but all over, uh, down here, you know?"

"I'm not getting your drift."

"You know the Navy SEALs, correct?"

"Yes."

"Well, when Navy SEALs retire, they still tend to have a specific skill set that is really overqualified for working at Walmart. Therefore, they tend to operate in different parts of the world—for hire, I guess you could say."

# 19

EDDIE HAD SUCH a nice, or even *fantastic*, conversation with Bobby the marine at the embassy that he couldn't wait to see Lisa and tell her all about it. Plus, he really missed her. He had developed an even greater dependency on Lisa; they had made their way through his marriage, dating false-start and getting back on again, and now this nightmare situation leading them to Brazil. Eddie was really becoming attached to her, and she was feeling the same. Trauma can bring couples closer as they work their way through it—but then again, it's been known to drive a wedge and split them up, though the pair truly believed they were going to be an example of the former. For Eddie, she was just 100 percent woman—beautiful and smart—and as he picked up the phone to call her, he heard the most magnificent sounds to cross his ears in a while. Not just her voice—that, of course, was great—but she had also been up to something big.

Bobby had procured a driver to drop Eddie back off at the hotel, and Eddie was bursting with anxiousness to hear Lisa's story. On the phone, she basically described her actions as comparable to those of an evil genius. Knocking on the door, it was hard for him to contain his excitement for what she had in store.

"Eddie! Baby! I know I should be pissed at you! But seriously, I don't care right now that I was left to fend for myself in some country where I don't speak the language or know anybody."

He detected some sarcasm from Lisa.

"I know, babe, I'm sorry, but I'm getting so pissed that nothing is going our way. You saw it! I had Izzy! I had her! Then the damn embassy people let her get away. I know why too, and it comes down to the military, money, and not wanting to stir the pot with any political-dividing child-custody case. Why the hell not, I suppose, but this is *my* daughter we're talking about!"

"Don't get worked up, babe. You can tell me all about that later. But guess what I did?" She smiled and giggled as she continued, "I had a nice conversation with who else but Natalia's American boyfriend! I got the whole frickin' scoop from him. And maybe, just maybe, I planted a little seed with him... just to screw her over."

"Tell me more, tell me more, please!"

Lisa narrated the entire story of how now they were to be twisted up with Natalia and her boyfriend. To give the short version, it went something like this: When Eddie was locked up in the embassy holding cell, they sent Lisa home to the hotel to wait for him to be released. The driver dropped Lisa off at the hotel entrance, and as she was heading toward the elevators, she decided to go have a drink in the bar to blow off a little steam. As she walked up to the bar, a few stools down sat some guy, obviously a gringo, who was plastered out of his mind and maybe even a little physically abused. Someone really beat the shit out of this dude, and he was not in good shape. Anyway, Lisa and he got to talking, and when he mentioned the magic words *My Brazilian girlfriend, who I am down here with because she took custody of her half-American daughter*, Lisa quickly put two and two together.

"My name is Don, by the way. Nice to have a conversation with someone who speaks some native English. I'm getting so sick of the Brazilian accent down here," he proclaimed while the bartender shot him a dirty look.

"Hi, I'm Lisa. Nice to meet you too. If you don't mind me asking, what happened to you?"

"Well, to be honest, I have a little jealousy problem with my girlfriend, and that doesn't pair well with her problem, which is to flirt with every guy who takes a look at her. So, we got in a little fight, and when I went to go sort it out with her, I might have mixed it up a bit with her dad and brother, maybe the neighbors—hell, I don't even know. Worst part is, I give that girl and her daughter everything! I pay for every single thing they have! Her family is losing money, and all she has is me to fund her!"

Lisa's mind started racing. *How could we use this to our advantage?* And the idea entered her brain.

"Don, you know, I feel your pain. Really, I do, because I am experiencing it firsthand myself. I really would like to chat more, but maybe during a time when you'll remember. Can we have coffee tomorrow? I think you'll want to hear what I have to say."

Back in their room, Eddie looked at Lisa, and he still didn't understand. He was shocked, yes, that they were at the same hotel as Natalia's boyfriend, who Natalia was obviously not that into anymore and was seemingly just using as a money tree. But what was the excitement of all this?

"Well," Lisa explained, "I figure if I can produce a story of how you and I are down here to get Izzy, and maybe play up to his jealousy, we can really fuck with them."

"How do you mean?"

"What would Don do if he found out that you came all the way down to Brazil to not only chase Izzy but also make amends with Natalia? And maybe when reconnecting... you two possibly found that old spark? You see, the way I figure it, this Don guy is truly unbalanced if he's got a jealousy issue so hard that he's fighting everyone, including her family. Why not use that to our advantage? If he ever got wind that you and Natalia were hooking back up—and of course, I'm the victim too, which is why I am telling Don this—well, Don would be done with her and would be on a flight back home, along with all his *money*. Then what would Natalia do? No money, no boyfriend, nothing. Maybe she would be a bit more apt to negotiate with you, no?"

"Diabolical, Lisa! Truly, that is great! This is why I love you! Always pulling me out of the depths of darkness to show me there is a way!"

"Thank you very much!" she said, smiling and taking a bow.

"By the way, Lisa, I have a little story of my own that we can use as a backup."

"Do tell."

"It seems, for a small fortune—the only downside—I have a friend who can maybe help with a little reverse-kidnapping. There are ex–Navy SEALs who operate in this kind of shadiness who have connections, who can help me with a little snatch and grab, and smuggle us out of the country. This marine I met at the embassy is going to try to have someone call me tomorrow. Think it's worth the conversation, right?"

"Shit. That sounds dangerous. Are we really at that point?"

"I don't even know anymore what point I am at. This whole situation is surreal. I'm talking to marines about kidnapping and smuggling. You're crafting schemes and lies. What the heck is happening?"

"This is a mess, Eddie. I'm just here to visit Brazil, ha-ha! Just kidding, babe. You know I am 100 percent in now, so you'd better get your daughter back and not screw this up."

"I know. Damn. But I just want to say thank you, Lisa, and I love you." Eddie was really falling even deeper for her.

"But back to the plan, or now *plans*. I guess it never hurts to have a few irons in the stove, or the fire, or whatever the hell that saying is," Eddie continued, trying to focus.

"Then what do you want to do?"

"I don't care how much this Navy SEAL guy is going to cost, or if your plan with Don holds any merit, or if there is even a third avenue out of this mess. One way or another, we will get Izzy back, we will be on a plane with her back home, we will be safe and sound at home with my family again, and Natalia will be left to figure it out. Let's continue with both for now. Worst-case scenario is I find my way back to some other jail cell once again... and out of money. Maybe I can tell my story on *Locked Up Abroad*. At least I'll be the most famous American guy to get raped and beaten by some Brazilian prison gang. But best case... well, I think it's obvious, isn't it?"

As Eddie woke up the next day in his posh hotel in Brasília, or at least as posh as a hotel in Brasília can be, he couldn't help but continue to ponder his previous life spent there. He *had* gone to Brazil on his own to search out something different, something exotic. He'd lived there and experienced so much in such a short amount of time as an expat. How crazy was the whacked-out robbery scheme where he'd met Natalia? And Natalia wasn't always that bad. She was a pretty, young girl who liked to have fun. How could he foresee her going nuts with this CH crap? And he did get Izzy out of the whole ordeal.

But Eddie knew that time was ticking, and one of these plans had to bear fruit quickly. He prayed to the Almighty that Izzy didn't inherit the crazy side residing in Natalia's genes. He needed to retrieve her before she learned too much of how not to be a woman, how not to treat others. Izzy needed a mother like Lisa in her life. Eddie couldn't do it alone, especially with his own temper problems, but Lisa provided stability and sense. Yes, the time was now. Time to go.

"Bobby, it's me, Eddie Watters, the American from yesterday. Listen, can I meet your Navy SEAL friend today as proposed? I am ready, and I need to do this immediately!"

Bobby seemed as about excited as could be. The smart money said Bobby would receive a kickback out of all this, since there really wasn't a whole lot of action going on in Brasília for a marine. So, Bobby continued to communicate when and where to meet, instructing Eddie to go alone. It worked out for Eddie anyway, as he sent Lisa into action with her parallel plan for Don. Best option was to see if they could get through this in a nonviolent way first, assuming this Navy SEAL might bring with him a little bit of a heavy hand.

Of all places in a populous city to meet this guy, this warrior, they chose the McDonald's in Asa Sul. Or in other words, a strangely nice restaurant in a high-class neighborhood, where it wouldn't be weird to see two Americans chatting it up. McDonald's in Brazil are very well-liked restaurants. The typical Brazilian eats rice, beans, and some type of protein and salad for almost every meal, making cheeseburgers quite a tasty alternative. But McDonald's isn't cheap there. Visiting a place like McDonald's is a nice night out for a Brazilian. The best part, however, is the burgers themselves. Although very similar to those in the States, the difference is in the quality of the beef. The McDonald's Corporation in Brazil buys Brazilian beef, which is usually free from hormones, antibiotics, and all that other crap, and it just seems to have a better flavor. So, add all that up to the traditional McDonald's recipe, and you have yourself a wonderful little burger, even if it did cost a pretty penny!

As Eddie so rudely chowed down, not waiting for his party to show up, he made sure to glance around the restaurant to see if he noticed anything out of the ordinary. After all, he'd frequented enough movies in his life and had experienced enough betrayal that, even being an American, he couldn't initially trust this guy. Bobby could have been paid off by Natalia's family, after all. This whole thing could have been a trap. Eddie needed to be extra careful.

Then as he saw Rocco, the ex–Navy SEAL, walk through the door, all his worries were out the window. This man was about six foot two, 235 pounds of solid, farm-boy muscle. He was what men strove to be when they hit the weights in the gym. And he wore a jacket with a huge American flag on the back and what seemed to be military patches up and down the sleeves. No hiding anything there! It was a pretty ballsy move to sport that kind of representation of what a lot of locals believed was an imperialistic nation, but obviously, this guy Rocco didn't give a shit about any of that.

"Mr. Watters?" Rocco said as he moved close enough to where nobody else could hear him.

"Yes, that's me. You are a friend of Bobby's, correct?"

"That I am," he stated, staring Eddie right in the eye. "You can call me Rocco."

"Nice to meet you. Please call me Eddie. I want to get down to business. Here's the story—"

"Not here, Eddie," Rocco interrupted. "Please finish your burger, and we'll take a drive."

Typical American, military or government, or anything not Brazilian, they jumped into Rocco's SUV and drove. Brazilian cars are smaller than those found in most countries. Most folks drive a Volkswagen Golf or something similar, or some miniature Chevy or Ford if they could get their hands on one. Only the expats or extremely wealthy Brazilians drive the SUVs. Guess Rocco was really not trying to hide anything there.

"Rocco, not to question anything you do here, but shouldn't we be a bit more discreet? I mean, it's pretty obvious if anyone is watching that I am going around with some military dude." Eddie didn't mean any disrespect, but he had to ask.

"Well, Eddie, sometimes it's good for someone in your predicament to show a little muscle. We don't want the opposing team to think they can continuously bully you around, now do we? Even with the options I will present you, it won't make a damn of a difference if they know what's coming. Trust me on this. All it will do is make them tighten up, which increases the risk of mistakes. But enough about that. We'll get to that piece much later. Now, tell me the whole story, from the very beginning."

They seemed to have driven around Brasília for an hour while Eddie told Rocco everything, from how he'd met Natalia to the present and even Lisa and her support. Eddie spilled his whole life to this stranger, even tearing up during the interview. Eddie had always given pieces of the story, but never in as much detail as he gave Rocco. He probably needed that release, if anything. And at the same time, Rocco must have really understood the importance of the situation he was now involved in and that Eddie would do whatever it took to get his family back.

With Rocco not having children himself, Eddie wondered if he could genuinely understand the predicament. But Rocco discussed his nephews and how he saw them as kids of his own in that protective way. Rocco described how he started his career in the US Navy flight school and obtained various licenses but wanted an even bigger challenge—hence the SEAL thing. Now he desired to use his skill set to help folks, not just follow the orders of a ranking officer. He wanted to make a difference in real people's lives, and Eddie was the perfect client.

After their drive around the city, Eddie looked straight into Rocco's eyes to judge the depths of his passion for the project, and the result delighted him. Eddie knew he had a great hammer in his tool bag of tricks to reunite him with his daughter.

As they parked the SUV, Rocco leaned forward with a booklet full of pictures and other documents. "Eddie, I already went to work on phase one of the plan, which is surveillance. I am going to track every movement of your ex-wife and daughter to identify the soft spots in their schedule. I know you're anxious, but we need this to be surgical. We'll watch them and determine when the best time to make the snatch. That will be phase two. That detail has yet to be determined. Phase three will be getting out of the country, and I will tell you that's no laughing matter. It will include a rigorous travel to the south of the country to try to cross the border. There might be outside circumstances we'll run into—the local police, the unfriendly outdoor environment, and of course Natalia's family coming at us hard. But if you, your daughter, and your girlfriend can handle the demands, we'll get it done."

"We can handle it," Eddie said quite confidently. "Believe me, there's nothing the Brazilians can throw at us that we can't deal with. You've seen what I've been through, which means what I'll go through in the future isn't shit compared to that."

"Well, you might think differently as it happens," Rocco replied, trying to present to his client the ramifications of this type of work.

"Yes, I know. Before we continue, though, I need to tell you about a plan B we have involving Natalia's American boyfriend. I think we can use it to our advantage," Eddie admitted.

Rocco wasn't happy about that little nugget. "Let me say this, Eddie. Don't waste my time here. If I'm to do this, I'm going to go at 100 percent. I don't need the extracurriculars fucking anything up. You are going to pay a price for my services, and I am not cheap. Don't go rocking the boat on your dime."

"Got it." Although Eddie understood, he still wanted Lisa to move forward with the plan for Don. He told himself that he could agree with his mouth but not with his heart. He thought, quite contrary to his agreement, *I need to cover all my bases because this is my daughter we're talking about. Nobody will truly understand that unless it happens to him or her. So yes, I understand, Rocco, but I will try all angles here, so too bad for you, my man.*

LISA KNEW WHILE the military attack against Natalia was in motion, she needed to go to work on the diplomatic front. Well, at least what most diplomats do to get what they want: lie and manipulate the situation. When Don agreed to meet with her to swap sob stories, she went to work.

Surprisingly, to a lot of people, Brazil is quite advanced, technologically speaking. Most people have an idea of what Brazil is, and they think of this idea of the Amazon—women running around naked on the beaches of Rio with monkeys on their shoulders (portrayed in several movies, actually) and of a backward-ass country where they still ride around in horse and carriage. While yes, they are a backwards country in many ways, they have put a large investment in their technology. Brazil even rivals India as a big offshore country where the United States can obtain cheaper information technology resources.

This trivia about Brazil was now coming in extremely handy for the plan they had for Don. They were able to download some old pictures from when Natalia and Eddie were married. Very nice ones too—pictures of the couple at dinners, toasting how wonderful life can be, pictures taken in Brazil, no less, hugging, kissing, like there were no worries in the world, except where to go for dinner.

Lisa was able to take these pictures and find some expert techy guys right out of the Craigslist of Brazil. These people could work wonders with the pictures, inserting Izzy in the background, along with pictures of Natalia's folks' house, current cars, and so on. It was very high-quality imaging, enough that Lisa used her HR influence and promised these tech guys some work when she went back to her employment in California. This was to be the damning evidence Lisa would use in her master plan, and quite damning it looked indeed!

As Lisa approached the open room, bar to the left side and tables of the restaurant on the right, she quickly scanned the quite dull and blatant room clockwise to see if Don had arrived yet. Quite nervous, she moved her left hand down to the side pocket of her cargo pants and squeezed the pictures gently just to make sure they were still there. She recognized this could be a make-or-break meeting. After all, the other option included using a Navy SEAL and kidnapping, so she was going to have to give the best Hollywood-born acting job of her life to avoid that one if possible.

Don strolled in looking like he'd been on a two-week bender, and the hangover from fourteen days of drinking had compounded all to this very day. But as he caught sight of Lisa, the day brightened up a bit for the struggling man.

"Hey, Lisa!" He half blurted out his words, coughing. "Sorry. I feel like shit today, but a few beers, and I'll be back to my old self."

"No problem. We've all been there!" she responded, leaning over and giving Don a hug. This surprised him a little bit, but to Lisa, it was all part of the performance. The more she could be his confidante, the closer they could become, and the higher the likelihood he'd buy what she was selling.

"Lisa, let's sit over at that table by the window. I feel like I need a little sunshine, and the weather is calling for rain for like, I dunno, the next two weeks. Plus, sunshine is excellent for one's inner core. I don't know if you know much about it, but the sunlight can actually provide your skin with nutrients, which then turn into energy within your body. That energy can be moved to a positive aura if you know how to harness it."

Lisa couldn't believe it. They hadn't even reached the table yet, and Don already started in with his CH-based healing method nonsense she'd been warned about. As the conversation was falling right into place, she realized he'd be eating out of her palm.

"Wow, Don, that's amazing! Eddie had told me a little bit about what you do... but, of course, he always was so negative about it. I'm actually quite interested, because, as you know, I need some positive energy in my life right now!"

"Well, I am definitely your guy! And forget about Eddie. We can get to that situation later. I want to hear all about it, believe me. But first, I want to focus on what brought you and me together. Nothing ever happens by chance, you know. It's quantum physics! It's the universe doing its thing! It's magical, believe me!"

Lisa started to feel the room spin a little. She was not the target audience here, not that girl to fall for this sort of thing. She didn't even believe in yoga or vitamins! She was old-school and a girl who grew up knowing how to take care of her body the old-fashioned way: eat healthy and fewer calories than you exert, and exercise every day. If you have a problem with the mind, then you have a few cocktails and work it out. No Consciousness Healing would ever make its way into her vocabulary, let alone in practice.

"That sounds wonderful... err, not wonderful, but I mean it sounds like you know how to handle situations, Don, right?"

"I know how to prepare the body to respond to emotions, either positive or negative. We as humans need to take everything that is thrown at us and use our bodies to transform that crap... and that's what it is most of the time—crap! We need to turn that crap into a wave of energy that will benefit us and those connected to us. I know that sounds like a lot, but this is the way of the universally connected. Tell me if you need me to slow down."

*Oh, wow. Eddie is going to owe me so much*, Lisa thought. It was hard enough to pull off this scam, but she didn't realize she was going to have to sit through a whole psychiatric/metaphysical/emotional balancing from this dude.

"See, Lisa, I've been off track lately. I have my own issues, as you can see. I am an extremely possessive person. When I say that, I don't mean that I own anybody. I mean that I have such a deep connection to those I love that I *hate* to see those bonds break, especially from people, mostly men, who want to come in and destroy those bonds with something so shallow, such as sex. So, when I have a girlfriend, I do my very best to protect our bubble, because I know the connection we make, if strengthened and kept intact, can positively benefit the universe, making everything around us boundless. Does that make sense at all to you?" Don was smiling, grinning, and flirting all at once.

The problem with Don's game was that he didn't practice what he preached. He spouted all this vocabulary, but in the end, he was no different from most men. It was upsetting when a guy hit on his girl, so he tried to fight his way out of it. How was that benefiting the universe? But Lisa continued to play along nicely, and she was as effective as a pro.

"Don, I *totally* get you! I mean, here I am, I find the man of my dreams in Eddie, who I think I'm going to spend the rest of my life with, and suddenly, it's a complete lie! Here's what I'm talking about. You see, I know you are aware with what's going on regarding Natalia and Eddie's daughter. You are here with them, after all. And I get it. In fact, I get both sides. I am a mother too, so I see what Natalia is doing. But I too felt a universal connection with Eddie, so I followed him to this foreign land just to support him. I paid for his plane ticket. I'm footing the bill of the hotel. Everything! What do I get in return? Complete betrayal!" Lisa's eyes welled up as she mouthed the last couple of lines. She'd practiced it earlier in the hotel room, and now it was all coming together.

"I know, I know. I've been there, Lisa. I've been betrayed! I've been to the depths, and I've made mistakes, but I have fought my way back. I can help you with your problems. Tell me more about your relationship with him. Tell me about your love life, your conversations, everything."

"Wait a minute, Don. I know you are trying to help here, but before you dive into healing me, you're going to want to hear the rest of what I have to say."

"Well, of course, then. Please continue." Don's attention was successfully captured.

"You see, I brought you here to tell you about something that affects both of us. I struggled with if I should or not, but I saw immediately how sincere you are and how you are hurting, and I don't want to see you suffer anymore. Likewise, I don't want to be in pain anymore."

"Lisa, what do you mean? I can take it. What is it?"

Lisa reached back into the pocket of her cargo pants and fished out the doctored pictures of Natalia and Eddie getting cozy.

"You see, Don, the betrayal I am talking about is with Natalia and Eddie. I don't know if they had been speaking to each other previously or if they reconciled and he didn't have the balls to tell me or what. But for the last couple of days, Eddie would leave for hours at a time, day and night. After it happened twice, I paid a taxi driver to shuttle me around and follow that dickhead first to a bar, then back to a house. The house is Natalia's father's house."

"Wait, are you telling me that Eddie and Natalia have been meeting up secretly? Is that a good thing or a bad thing? Are they trying to work out the Isabella situation?"

"Don, take a look for yourself."

As Don reached out his hands to take ahold of the pictures, Lisa could see the tremors that made his fingers shake like a tweaker. Witnessing his hands fumble around with the photos, Lisa couldn't quite make out if it was the nerves causing the tremble or if he just hadn't had his first drink of the day. But she glared into his stone-cold gaze and witnessed as Don then developed a look on his face that was half sickening, half raging. He was examining every detail in each picture. And it was apparent to Lisa that he wouldn't be offering anymore CH teachings this day.

"How could I be so stupid? All this time, I'm worried about the one-time kisses that the Brazilians give or the idiot friendships with guys that Natalia might get involved with or even less. But this? This is not only a physical violation of our relationship; this is emotional. Do you get this, Lisa? These two were *married*! That means they have a bond that was as strong as the galaxies at one time, which makes this affair much more dangerous. This is the ultimate act of betrayal!"

"I know, Don!" Lisa now broke out in full tears. "Fuck some girl you met at a bar! I can get over that! But rekindle with your ex-wife, after everything we've been through, that they've been through! I hate his fucking guts!" Lisa was in full Oscar-nominee mode.

"No, no... this can't be," Don repeated over and over. "Natalia and I are soul mates. I know she is flirtatious, but this violates every single natural nuptial we've established together. This is a damn spear to the core of all my being! We spoke about raising Izzy together and more kids to come. I was going to move down here to Brazil permanently with her. We were going to lecture and educate on Consciousness Healing as a team, as a family. We were going to spend our lives together in this life and in eternity! Now it's all washed away like cleaning some piece of dog shit off the bottom of your shoe! *Fuck!*"

Don jumped up from the table, almost knocking over waiter, who not-so-smartly approached to interrupt the duo in the middle of this conversation. Don circled the restaurant probably no fewer than five times, mumbling to himself over and over. He yelled to the bartender to bring him a Johnnie Walker double and a beer, all while snapping his hands downward like he was jumping rope without the rope. In other words, he was losing his dang mind.

As Lisa watched this spectacle continue, a feeling of guilt trickled up and washed over her. But Eddie had warned that Don was a psychopath; he might go unhinged, so if anything got out of control, she would leave the situation entirely. As Don slammed a beer, she decided to make a move.

"Don, I am crushed by all of this too. You have to understand that."

"No, no. I know. I'm sorry, but what Natalia and I promised each other... she owes me her enlightenment, her healing ability. Oh, and she is *nothing* without me financially. Trust me, I know her family's in dire straits."

And there was the opening.

"Don, I understand. Trust me, I do. I think the best thing to do is to just get on a plane and go home. I'm going to do that. I'm getting the heck out of here. Not to overstep my boundaries here, but why don't you just cut her off, forget all about her, and move on with your life back in the States?" There went the cast; now she waited for him to take the bait.

"*Awww!*" Don screamed, still walking around in circles. "Shit, you're right! I'm outta here! Screw this! I have the nerve to confront her immediately, but you're right! It will hurt her deeper to just... well, to just leave!" And he turned to Lisa. "Lisa, you have been an angel, opening my eyes to truth in this world. Please keep driving toward your truth, and never let the evils of life engulf your consciousness and bring you down. Love to you!" Off he stormed, right out the front door and down the road, leaving Lisa there with her guilt and the bill.

The meeting was a success. Who would have thought that he would go as nuts about it as he had? But Lisa admitted to it being about as close to 100 percent as one could bet on. And if all it cost was a whiskey and a few beers, well, then, they could call it a total victory. Now all they had to do was wait. They would wait for Natalia to get the news that Don had skipped out on her, and then negotiations could begin. She would have to be smart enough to know that affording Izzy on her own was impossible. And the sooner she came to that realization, the sooner she would crawl to the bargaining table, where Eddie would be sitting, holding all the big chips to use against her dwindling pile. Sweet victory was in his grasp.

# 20

**P**ICTURE THIS: EVERYTHING was finally falling into place for their extraction plan. Actually, for both extraction plans, which Eddie was now calling:

1. The Rocco Plan
2. The Don Plan

Indeed, not very original, but he didn't care.

All that was left to do was wait, but the waiting for each avenue to come to fruition led to frustration, creeping in each day heavier than the last, while they sat there in that Brasília hotel room, wondering what the hell was going on. The room had been converted to their home away from home for what had now been over a month. Scanning around the room, as nice as it was, the dreariness of the rainy season in Brasília was starting to leak into both the room and into Eddie's life once again. The same old routine for the past couple of weeks: wake up, eat, wait for surveillance reports from Rocco, and, in parallel, wait for news that Don had returned to the States, rinse and repeat. To be honest, they were getting bored, and the money was running out quickly.

Regarding the Rocco Plan, Eddie had yet to admit to Rocco that he and Lisa were running another approach to this whole thing, because he didn't want to lose their ace in the hole. Moving forward with Rocco's phased approach to smuggle Izzy back to the States was still their primary option it seemed. The first thing Rocco wanted to accomplish, as a detailed and professional military man, was increased surveillance. Two weeks of spying on every Natalia movement might lead to any habits, or potential mistakes and, therefore, openings for them to execute the subsequent phases. So far, the reports from the surveillance had been as expected.

Natalia's daily routine was insignificantly repetitive. She was enjoying life without responsibility. Her father's maid basically took care of Izzy, giving her the freedom to work out, practice yoga, have lunches with friends, and enjoy the occasional beer at night. What Eddie learned through the surveillance, though, was quite spectacular. Two weeks earlier, Lisa had told Don about Eddie and Natalia's reconciliation, and Rocco hadn't reported any Don sightings with Natalia since. Maybe the Don Plan had potential? Was it developing as desired? But based on her daily activities, one could conclude that Natalia didn't seem to give a shit that Don had disappeared.

Having another key piece of usable news that had come from the whole reconnaissance program, though, gave them something to exploit. It seemed that Izzy, as a normal young girl, did not enjoy being cooped up in her grandfather's house all day every day. Natalia (on occasion when it suited her), or the maid, or the grandfather, or somebody in that house liked to take her out once a day, to get some fresh air at the very least.

It appeared the best place they decided to frequent was the only real happening location in all Brasília—the same Pontão spot where Don had his previous scene with Natalia. It might have seemed a little strange to an outsider why one would bring a little girl to a spot full of bars, but this place was much more than that. If you can imagine, Brasília surrounds a giant man-made lake, with the housing, wings, and government buildings built up around it. The large lake has a couple of bridges that vary in size, with the biggest of them a beautiful piece of architecture, spanning its white paint over the center of the water much like the new Leonard P. Zakim Bunker Hill Memorial Bridge in Boston, Massachusetts. It's claimed that this Brazilian bridge is the most expensive one of its kind to ever be constructed in the world, per square foot. The reason for that is pretty obvious given the corruption in Brazil. Out of one hundred dollars for a project component, ninety-five of those dollars might find their way into local officials' pockets, streaming downward like a reverse pyramid scheme.

But back to Pontão. Traversing across the lake toward the southern edge is a crossing via a much smaller and older bridge. The local municipality realized they needed that popular spot where families could enjoy lunch during the day, letting their children play in one of the little playgrounds located there, or the physical fitness folks could frequent to pursue the sculpting of their bodies with an outdoor workout. This whole complex sits lakeside, and one, if so inclined, can wander from restaurant to restaurant or playground to playground alongside the lake and docks that stretch their shape out into the water.

It's actually magnificently constructed, and Brazilians gather their families to spend all afternoon on the weekends there, while the younger crowd loiters and drinks at night. The best place to have lunch is the local surf shop, called Mormaii, where one can shop for board shorts, then savor the local, favorite afternoon snack, açaí, or taste on delicious sandwiches and even sushi. And Izzy loved her açaí. Americans are just now learning of this superfruit, once reserved for Brazilian surfers as a way to provide themselves with important nutrients, which they would consume as a natural energy booster either before or after paddling out in the waves all day. Izzy ate it up like nobody's business, and, of course, due to all the health benefits, both parents were happy about that Brazilian piece of influence.

Most afternoons, Izzy and her guardian of the day took a trip to Pontão, running around the playground with some of the other local youngsters, then making their way over for an açaí bowl for a nice snack. Sometimes they stayed long enough to catch the sun starting to make its way across the lake, reflecting off the surface into the bars and restaurants in an array of colors like someone dropped armfuls of paint cans of colors across the rainbow spectrum. Usually, they left before the sun completely set, but it all depended upon the day of the week and whether or not Natalia joined them after one of her own routine outings of the day.

Although Pontão can be crowded throughout the day, there are certain times when you can be there almost alone, minus some rented security officer who is asleep at the front entrance. This is where Rocco had found his weak point. Brazilians are notorious for not keeping a close eye on their kids when they are out and about. Eddie argued with Natalia repeatedly about it all the time. Her family would take Izzy to the mall or some other crowded area and go about their shopping like they had no worry in the world. Meanwhile, Izzy would be one hundred feet away, running wild. When he would become extremely upset at them, it was usually followed by everyone laughing at him over the whole scenario. But who was laughing now? Rocco noticed that this lack of awareness when Izzy went to the playgrounds of Pontão could be exploited. With Natalia, or whoever, was occupied by his or her phone staring out into the lake or doing anything except keeping a close eye on this little American-looking girl, Rocco would strike. That would be phase two of his master plan: the snatch.

The Don Plan: As seen from Rocco's surveillance, Don had not been heard from for weeks. Lisa and Eddie were fairly confident that he had flipped out, packed up his belongings, and headed back to Arizona. But the question remained: Had Natalia taken the bait? She couldn't support herself, nor could her immediate family provide for both her and Izzy for the long term. Nor did Natalia want that, one would have thought. So why hadn't she followed suit and trailed Don back to the States? Maybe she believed the struggling, single-mom life in Brasília was a risk worth taking. Strange indeed, but it could quite possibly provide Eddie the bargaining power he so desired.

Eddie decided there was a need to investigate this just a bit deeper. Surely there was someone at the US embassy or within Brazilian customs who had a record of Don's departure. Unlike the American's ass-backward policy of letting anyone leave the country with whomever they'd like, the Brazilians have exit control procedures in place, meaning this whole situation could have been avoided if the United States did that. But that's a topic for some law professor, or at the very least the political science department.

Lisa and Eddie threw on some weeks-old clothes (nicer digs at that) to head back to the US embassy. They'd been down there so long now that they had recycled articles of clothing multiple times. Eddie kept reminding himself that they needed to take some time out of the day, maybe hit the hotel gym, do some laundry, and reset a little, but there just hadn't been the time, or maybe they just didn't have the energy. Every spare second Eddie was speaking to Rocco on the whereabouts of his daughter or trying to dream up how this whole thing was going to play out.

Going through security at the US embassy was always a nightmare, but Eddie looked forward to it because he loved seeing the US Marines, fellow countrymen, and it made him feel at home. The United States is so blessed to have the resources to staff Americans around the world, even if they were sometimes less help than desired in a situation. At the very least, when you find yourself in a foreign world, having someone there with you provides hope that your back is covered.

Lisa and Eddie received the *all clear* from the gate security set of marines, then moved to the actual building once they lowered the series of roadblocks and the circular steel gates. Inching toward the parking lot, the line seemed a lot shorter than usual. Maybe it was the day where just the lawyers were allowed to go for their clients to apply or argue cases for various types of US visas.

The pair grabbed the closest parking spot and made their way to the door reserved for US citizens. Two giant metal detector systems were still situated just inside the opening, but only one was functioning, which was fine by them, as they happened to be one of the few sets of Americans going through the gate at that moment anyway.

"Weirdly light crowd," Lisa whispered as she leaned over to him.

"Yeah, I noticed. But good for us!" Eddie responded.

Working their way toward the window in the waiting room, Eddie noticed a few marines guarding various corners of the room. Approaching one of them, he gave it a shot.

"Hey, man, have you seen Bobby? I think he is usually working here, right?"

"Yes, sir. He is in the back on break. Would you like me to get him, sir?"

"That would be excellent!" he responded, trying not to sound like that movie with Bill and Ted, but still with a slight smile.

"One second, sir. I'll be right back."

Bobby appeared from the back door, the one Eddie remembered so well from just a few weeks back, the same one where he entered and then reemerged with a whole different set of respect for the diplomats down there—and not in a positive sense.

"Mr. Watters, sir! Welcome back!" Bobby was pretty fired up to see them.

Eddie wondered if Rocco had looped him in at all, what with him being the guy who had put this whole thing together. Maybe he received that finder's fee from Rocco. Maybe Rocco had put the word out and Bobby had been the only one who actually came through with a real client?

"Hey, Bobby! What's up, man? Been a few weeks!"

"Yes, it sure has. I would take you in the back, but I'm not really permitted that clearance. Plus, I'm on my break. Would you like to sit down and just chat here?"

"Sure thing, man. It's going to be very quick. Sorry I didn't call ahead, but I didn't want to raise any alarms. By the way, you remember my girlfriend, Lisa?"

"Of course I do. Nice to see you again, Lisa."

"Nice to see you too." Lisa smiled giving the room a sense of immediate calm.

"So listen, Bobby," Eddie interrupted the serenity. "There is an American who is critical to our situation. I need to know if he's left Brazil. Do you have any contacts in the Brazilian customs office or anything like that? I wouldn't ask if I really didn't need this info."

"Well, Mr. Watters." Bobby leaned in very close. "If Rocco needs something, he has plenty of resources to find out."

Eddie leaned in even closer. "Bobby, this is outside of the Rocco umbrella. This is something Lisa and I need to know. Oh yeah, and you can't say anything to Rocco."

Bobby's smile suddenly washed clean of his face, and he looked a bit perplexed. He was trying to find the right words to say so to not offend the couple.

"Mr. Watters, I'm sorry, but I don't have any way to do that. Plus, just a little piece of advice from me to you: I wouldn't do anything outside of Rocco's 'umbrella,' especially without him knowing about it. Rocco is a pretty particular guy. He likes to do things in a very, shall we say, *specific* way. Please, Mr. Watters, just listen to him and all will be fine. You're in good hands with him, I promise you that."

Eddie glanced over at Lisa, and she turned her head and shot back a look that said, *What have you gotten us into?* But she then jumped in so as not to allow Eddie to go any further down a rat hole.

"Thanks, Bobby. We appreciate your help. Eddie, let's go and leave Bobby to finish his break in peace."

Eddie threw himself back in. "But wait. Don't you have any other friends who may know—?"

"Eddie!" Lisa gritted her teeth, pushing the words out, urging him to shut up. "He said he doesn't. Time to leave now!"

Eddie got the picture. Reason would prevail that day. And as they bid Bobby adieu, Eddie couldn't help but decide to put the nail in the coffin on this one. There was no sign of Don; there was no sign that Natalia was upset that Don even left. And there was definitely no sign that any of this would help him get Izzy back. How long could he wait for Natalia to come crying for support? It just didn't seem like that would be the case. Coupled with the possibility of pissing off the ex–Navy SEAL helping them out, Eddie had a decision to make: that just might be the end of the Don Plan.

# 21

THE PHONE HAD been ringing off the hook, or so Lisa informed her boyfriend. But every time she answered it, the there was nothing but dead air on the other end. Not having been involved in international espionage before, she didn't quite understand it, so Eddie did his best explain it to her—but really, what did he know?

"You see, Lisa, Rocco will only deal with me. He doesn't want any other spiders in his web. This is his operation, and the fewer the variables, the greater the chance of success."

Lisa thought and pondered. The seriousness of what had befallen her only now started to come crashing down. "Eddie, what the fuck are we doing here? We've hired a Navy SEAL to kidnap your daughter! We can't just take kids and smuggle them out of the country! There has to be another way!"

"Right. Another way." Eddie retorted sarcastically. "I've only tried lawyers, the embassy, crazy boyfriends of Natalia's. What else do you want from me? We've spent so much money, extended a leave from our jobs, left your boys. I'm sick of this shit. We've come to the end of the line. I'm done with everything else."

Lisa still couldn't understand why he hadn't come to his senses. "Eddie, do you realize if we get caught, we're going to jail... in Brazil?"

"Nobody's going to jail. You heard it yourself from that diplomat. They will do whatever it takes to avoid any issue between Americans and Brazilians. I have to believe this is going to work out, even if something gets all fucked up." Eddie knew he was lying, but he needed Lisa, his rock, more than ever. But he also realized he was putting her right in the crosshairs of danger. "Anyway, Lisa, if you want to go home now, you can."

Lisa thought about it long and hard, but in the end, she also understood that Eddie somehow was going to screw everything up. And like the many times before, she would need to be there for him to keep him out of trouble or at least bail him out if she couldn't. Lisa had now become a main character in Eddie's Life Book. And she wasn't going anywhere. Not today. Not ever.

Early-morning rain clouds formed over the city as it had been nearly the whole couple of months they'd been down there. But finally, there was a break from the spattering of drops from the sky, banging against the roof and dripping ever so slowly down the window. The phone began to chirp, but this time, to avoid any hang-ups, Eddie was there to answer it.

"Eddie, it's me. We're a go." Rocco's voice was direct, low, and anxiously serious.

Everything had been building up to this moment. The chance meeting with Natalia, the marriage, the healer she became, the divorce, Lisa, the kidnapping, the Don Plan, and now, the next phase of the Rocco Plan. Was this phase three? Was that the phase for the snatch? But what about the escape? Lisa was right, and he didn't mention phase four. Or were they still in phase two, and phase three was getting out of Brazil? Eddie was so mentally drained at this point, he just couldn't keep up. He hit the wall. Mentally, physically, emotionally—not knowing how much more fight and energy he could provide. But hearing those words *we're a go* was like an immediate shot of adrenaline.

"Let's do this," he said.

They decided that Pontão would be the location to take back Izzy... and take back their lives. From Rocco's surveillance, it seemed Natalia had Wednesdays, when there were no happenings for her to run off to. She usually took Izzy on a few errands, visited friends, and then headed to the parks in Pontão. Furthermore, Eddie forced the point to Rocco that he wanted Natalia to be there when they took Izzy—no nanny, no grandfather, but Natalia. He wanted her to see him and feel the same hurt and pain he'd been experiencing for so long. Maybe it wasn't a nice thing to do. Maybe he should have been more benevolent. But even the kindhearted soul he believed he exuded, deep down inside, wanted her to hurt just a little bit. So be it. He had become a bit of an asshole.

It was Monday, but unlike the rest of the world, Lisa and Eddie weren't getting up and going to work. They were preparing for what was to come in just two short days, which meant two days to rehearse the whole ordeal. Eddie loathed that part. He hated the mundaneness of rehearsing, of going through every detail. His hair-trigger personality told him to just show up and do it, but he appreciated the benefits of practice, so he agreed to go along with the expert. And Rocco was *the* expert, having spent hours at Pontão, scoping out exits and assessing possibilities for risk, security situations, everything. What were all the alterable components? What if Izzy didn't want to leave her mom? No way; it did not matter. They were doing this, and they were doing this Wednesday.

After the day's rehearsal, Lisa and Eddie were allowed a little bit of downtime back at the hotel. He desired to express his appreciation for her constant support and her companionship, but most of all, he wanted to thank her. Thank her for sticking through this with him. Thank her again for spending her money and her time, being away from her own boys for such a long duration. He had truly witnessed her care and sacrifices, and he knew deep down inside that she was there... forever.

"Lisa, I thought a bit today about what you said. I know you are scared out of your mind. I can't imagine how you have been able to keep going with me. I mean, talk about baggage!"

"I do love you, Eddie. And I know how much your daughter means to you. I can't stand seeing you without her; in fact, I can't live with you that way. But with her, when you are sane and straight, I want to spend every day with you, and us, as a family!"

"I do too, Lisa. When we get back, I'm going to make everything right for us: a home, a family, the whole shebang. Your kids are older, I get it, but we will have them in our lives just as much as Izzy. I want all of them... all of us. I truly see our lives together forever. I love you so much."

As Lisa leaned over for a hug, he whispered in her ear, "I want to marry you!"

"Are you serious?" Lisa jumped out of the bed, a smile splashed across her face. "I mean... you know what the answer is!"

Eddie once again was being spontaneous. He *did* want to marry her, obviously, but right when he said it, he thought, *You have no ring, you idiot!*

Deciding that was going to have come later, he jumped right into the moment. Flying off the bed with Lisa, he shouted, "Yes! Yes! Wait... you did say *yes*, right?"

"Of course I did!" Then Lisa looked down at her hand, and back up to Eddie, and back down at her hand. This went on for what seemed to be ten minutes, though it was likely only for ten seconds.

Eddie had to jump in to stop her thoughts from hitting the wall too. "I know, I know. The ring! Listen... I'm not giving you some crap ring here on the fly. When we get home, we'll hit every store. You will try on as many as you'd like. It will be perfect." He didn't care that his ring money was now in Rocco's pocket; he would have to figure that out later.

But Lisa was happy enough. "Nothing can ever be normal with you, Eddie. But you know what... abnormality is *our* normal!"

TUESDAY MORNING CAME quickly, and that meant another couple of run-throughs with Rocco. He was completely and utterly professional, to a T. There wasn't one situation unaccounted for—nor should there have been given what his services cost, which was close to six figures for a month or so of his expertise, but Eddie learned to live with that. He also grew more confident with his soldier every day. Let's face it: Rocco was used to fighting terrorists and big, thuggish men. All Eddie was asking for was to deal with a little Brazilian mother and her half-American toddler. Eddie was secure knowing he'd handle it, all right.

"One final question, Rocco. I understand the plan. I know you are in charge. I get the escape route and how we're getting out of Brazil. But then what about you? What's your next job?

"Where do you go from here?" Eddie was quite curious of this guy's life, and honestly, Rocco enjoyed the inquisition.

"Well, Eddie, it'll obviously have to be off to a new job in a new country. Probably don't want to hang around Brazil too long after this. But to be honest, I'm over this fucking rain, the dirtiness of it all, the poverty of a third-world country. I just want to go somewhere clean, where I don't see dead homeless people lying on the sidewalk. I'm tired of looking over my shoulder, waiting for some punk little teen ready to stab me with his rusty old knife just to rob me for ten dollars. I'm thinking a nice little farm town in middle America. Yeah, that sounds nice."

"I get it," Eddie replied. He had only been back down there for a few months and was obviously under a lot of stress, but he was also ready to walk around in a city where it too was unpolluted, where everything *worked*. No potholes, no uncertified construction where a building might fall over on itself. "I want to go home too."

The big day neared, and Eddie found himself with a bad case of insomnia. Everything was building up to the next morning, and he couldn't contain his anxiety. *What the fuck am I doing? I've hired a Navy SEAL to kidnap my daughter and get us out of the country. How did it get to this point? How did my life end up here?* His mind refused to take a breath. He just wanted morning to come. Lying in bed, he stared at the clock and painfully watched the sleep-hours dwindle, that little back-and-forth dance with almost getting the rest, but then a new thought popping right in the mind like a dagger. *C'mon, Earth, rotate!* Eddie thought as he moved his head over the pillow and gazed upon Lisa. At least she was getting some sleep, and that made him happy. It reassured him that one of them would be 100 percent and thinking with complete clarity.

Eddie stared out the window over the city of Brasília, early as hell in the morning, and believed he was witnessing the future. He couldn't tell if the foreign, planetlike buildings were to be the reality in a hundred years or just some peculiar architecture from a genius. The city was both beautiful and disagreeable all at the same time, and he could not wait to get the hell out of there. He was sick of the rain, the roads that wound all over the place with no traffic lights, and the plain ol' drudgery of it all. *Get my daughter, and get me out of this depression*, was replaying like a broken record in his head. *I've hit a crossroads; will I be brave enough to follow through? Will I actually have the courage to look her in the eye? Will Izzy be completely screwed up over another conflict? She is older, but will she understand?"* Ticktock, ticktock.

"Lisa, it's time to get up," he whispered, shaking her gently.

They had already packed their bags and left them at the pre-designated pickup spot identified by Rocco. They kept nothing in their possession but old toothbrushes and the comfortable clothes they had gone to bed in. Lisa had on yoga pants and a sweatshirt, with Eddie looking like a teenager from 1990, wearing cargo shorts, a T-shirt, and a hoodie. Who cared, anyway?

Lisa and Eddie didn't say a word while brushing their teeth, but they continuously caught each other's eyes and smiled. It was all so very bizarre, realizing what was in store.

Eddie broke the silence. "I can't believe this is happening. I feel so much anxiety, like little doses of adrenaline that are just enough to make me tweak out but not enough to give me that superhuman strength. I'm sure that will come later!"

"I know, Eddie. Me too."

"Right now, it just sucks because I can't figure out if I'm hungry or sick to my stomach. What about you? You look super cool and chill over there. Lisa, are you ready for this?" Eddie asked a bit sheepishly, trying to show courage but not hiding the fact that he was freaking the heck out.

"It's going to be great, Eddie. You'll see, it will all work out. Rocco is a professional. We have everything in place. We've rehearsed it a dozen times. We're good. Today, you get your daughter back, and we get our lives back!"

"Well said."

Heading out the door into the featureless hallway and down the elevator to the lobby of the hotel, Eddie's eyes couldn't resist the urge to dart around and try to pick up on any irregularities. He was having a bit of the cold-feet syndrome, thinking, *What if this is all a trap? I don't know this Rocco guy or Bobby the marine or any of them. Or what if Natalia doesn't show with Izzy today? I can't go through another sleepless night and all this stress. If Natalia taught me anything, it was that positive thinking brings positive energy, so that's exactly what I'll do. Think good thoughts. Everything will work out perfectly, just like Lisa said.*

First stop was to meet up with Rocco to check on the condition of their getaway plans and ensure all the pieces were still in place. They drove around Brasília for two hours, checking and rechecking, everyone totally cool with the walk-through. Accounting for every detail equaled no screwups. Eddie asked Rocco the same questions over and over, and although Rocco looked and acted annoyed, Eddie knew deep down he appreciated the attention to detail. "So, Rocco, what if this?" and "What if that?" and so on. "What's the backup plan for $x$?" Rocco loved the focus, and Eddie knew it.

The last stop before the action ensued was a local bakery for a quick sandwich. Rocco reminded everyone to eat enough so that it might last a while on the run, but not enough to make them sick from all the nerves. Eddie ordered the standard fare: turkey and cheese sandwich and a bag of chips. Lisa, the same. As they parked themselves down to eat, Eddie was reminded of the first time he and Rocco met at McDonald's.

Rocco noticed the reminiscing Eddie and placed his hand upon his shoulder, saying, "This is all for you and your daughter, Eddie. You are doing nothing wrong at all. She stole Izzy from you; it is your right to get her back. Be strong. Clear eyes, clear thoughts. No fuckups. Do you understand?"

"Abso-fucking-lutely."

Rocco, Lisa, and Eddie rolled toward Pontão in an old, dusty pickup truck. Dirt was kicking up on the trash-filled side road that led up to the entry of the main road into Pontão. As they approached the front gates, the plan kicked into action. In front of the entrance were all kinds of security apparatuses, but in typical Brazilian style, none of it was functional. But there was a security guard. The team crept closer and closer to the guard. And as they pulled to a stop, he approached and in Portuguese informed them, "*A mulher está aqui com a menina*," meaning, "The girl is here with her daughter." Rocco leaned over, gave a nod, and handed the security guard an envelope, not a very thick one either; he was likely buying off this guy for no more than $1,000 in US currency—a good haul for the guy, probably more than four months' salary, just for a little piece of information and turning a blind eye. So far so good.

Rocco drove all the way along the edge of the parking lot, while Lisa and Eddie ducked their heads just to be sure in case any of Natalia's family members were around to recognize them. They parked far enough away from the restaurants and playgrounds, but close enough so they wouldn't have to walk too far, exposed to any onlookers. The passenger door gave a big *squeal* when it opened, loudly enough for Eddie to shoot worried looks over his shoulders a few times.

"C'mon, man, don't lose it," Rocco instructed.

The best way to get to the playground was to split up, diminishing the unusual sight of three Americans walking around together, one of them a massive soldier. Lisa and Eddie headed straight to Mormaii, where they planned to cut through the store and restaurant, out the door, alongside the lake, then up to the playground. Rocco would take his own route there from the other side of the large parking area, away from the restaurant crowd, and meet them at the same playground.

Lisa and Eddie entered Mormaii and immediately began to inspect clothes, acting like tourists who were just shopping and wasting away the day, not making too much eye contact with anyone. They ignored the überaggressive store employees who immediately tried to pounce on the potential buyers. Politely saying, "No, thank you," they departed out the back exit, nearest to the lakeshore. Hugging the beach side, they stooped over and strolled up the walk to where the playground was in sight. And as if the stars aligned and finally something in his life went right, Eddie saw exactly what he hoped to see. From that distance, he could make out Izzy on the swing set, plus Natalia and what looked like her crazy brother, chatting it up no more than ten feet away from her. But that was it. No other family members or friends, and no other random children or families were at the park. The way the plan was unfolding was almost too perfect.

The idea was for Lisa and Eddie to approach Natalia, assuming she would immediately start an argument. And as they distracted Natalia in that potential shouting match, Rocco would sneak in to grab Izzy, and they would be on their way. Simple. The possibility of a family member being there had been accounted for, which Rocco would also take care of (but, of course, in a professional, not-too-violent way). That would leave Lisa and Eddie to fend off Natalia, which they were very capable of doing. No problem.

As they inched closer, Eddie looked at Lisa and smiled. "Love you, babe. Let's do this."

Lisa shot back a tense wink. She was ready too.

"Natalia!" Eddie yelled. "I need to talk to you right now!"

Natalia was completely stunned as the couple ran onto the sand of the playground. "What the hell are you doing here, Eddie? Get away from us!" Natalia turned toward her brother, who sprinted over to step in between them.

"I need to talk, Natalia!" Eddie responded.

"Daddy, Daddy!" Izzy shouted as she jumped off the swing and ran toward Eddie.

"Shit. Where's Rocco?" Lisa muttered, becoming increasingly nervous about the whole ordeal.

Natalia's brother turned and shot over to Izzy, swooping her up in his arms. "Get out of here, Eddie!" he shouted, then leaned over to Izzy, saying, "It's all right."

"Put my daughter down, João!" Eddie yelled. Then turning to Natalia, he said, "I just want to talk. Please let me tell you something."

Natalia completely lost it. "You need leave us now, Eddie! Take your girlfriend and go!" Turning her body, she looked to gather her brother and Izzy and run away. Eddie wanted to grab her by the arm and pulled her toward him, as if to move her out of the way so he too could reach Izzy, but knew not to be too forceful. *Where the fuck is Rocco?* he thought. The situation was unwinding.

Lisa then jumped for Izzy, but João fended her off, shoving her away as best he could. Eddie was now trying to rush past Natalia to get to their daughter, while Natalia was pushing him and flailing her arms all over the place, ensuring there wouldn't be any contact with Izzy and her father. She gave Eddie one final shove to put about three feet of distance between them, simultaneously screaming, "I'm gonna get the police! You're gonna be—"

*BANG! BANG!*

The first bullet screamed by them with a powerful hiss. The second bullet, however, hit its target, although only slightly off its trajectory. The sibilant sounding connection that entered through the back of Natalia's forearm, exploded upon its exit from the front of it. Natalia immediately cried out in pain, grabbed her now blood-covered and injured arm, and fell onto the sandy ground below her, changing the landscape red.

*What the fuck is Rocco doing!?* But he was not there. Then Eddie heard a different voice.

"I followed that bitch all the way here, and I knew you would be here too, you motherfucker!" Don's words exited his mouth while he shifted his arms and pointed his gun at Eddie. *What? Don? What is he doing here? He never left? This crazy-ass dude just blew my ex-wife's arm off!* The words raced across Eddie's mind in complete panic.

João covered Izzy's head with his coat. At least he was a good enough uncle to try to shield her from whatever the hell had just happened. At the very least, Izzy was too busy struggling in her uncle's arms to actually see what had just gone down with her mom.

Lisa immediately jumped in front of Eddie. "Don, *nooo!*" she screamed. "Please! His daughter is here! She will have no father! Please Don!"

"Step aside, Lisa! He stole everything from me!" Don was now focused on Eddie, not realizing that Natalia hadn't been fatally wounded.

*BANG! BANG!*

Now Don's body blasted about four feet to its right, like some kind of ghost had come out of nowhere and lowered a driving boom. A bullet had entered him from his left chest through to the right side. Blood shot out from just behind his shoulder blade, and his lifeless body landed in the grass, arms spread wide, gun still in hand.

"You! With the little girl. Let her the fuck go. Right now!" Rocco came sprinting up the small hill with his gun still aimed, warm and smoking from the bullets fired at Don.

Completely dismayed, Eddie jerked his head over to João. "Let her go, dude! This is getting out of control! *Por favor! Sai daqui! Agora!*" Eddie needed to tell him to get the heck out of there. He didn't want or need more injuries or dead bodies. This was Izzy's family, after all, and her mother was on the ground in a pool of her own blood while her one time potential stepfather was now nothing but a lifeless body, his soul gone to the heavens for the rest of time.

Natalia tried to manage a whimper, reaching her hand up towards Izzy and João, but was in too much shock herself to be able to adjust her bearings.

"Don't shoot! Don't shoot!" Eddie yelled at Rocco.

"Tell him to grab the mom and get the fuck out of here now without the girl, or he dies." Rocco aimed his gun at João's head.

João got the point, put Izzy on the ground, and ran to Natalia, wrapping his warm body around her like a shield. Izzy tried to struggle to throw the coat off her head that was preventing her from seeing any of this shit happening, and Eddie reached down to immediately put a stop to that.

"Izzy, it's me, baby... Daddy. Keep this coat over your head, baby. You're safe with me."

"Where's Mommy?" she squeaked out underneath the coat.

"Izzy!" Natalia whispered in a panic, but too soft for her daughter to hear.

"Don't worry, honey. She's going to drive home with Uncle João. She's scared of the fireworks they're letting off here!"

Eddie glanced over at Lisa, who was about to throw up. Eddie grabbed her by the hand and pulled her into his body. "Lisa... fuck! I know, I know! Let's keep it together... just for right now!"

Lisa was trembling uncontrollably. She looked up into Eddie's eyes, ready to faint.

"We need to get the fuck out of here, guys," Rocco instructed quite calmly. With that, the four of them—Lisa, Rocco, and Eddie, with Izzy in his arms, coat still covering her head—took off running across the parking lot. Eddie was practically dragging Lisa while holding on to Izzy. All João could do was watch them depart, wondering if he should risk his life to chase after them, or stay with Natalia and call for help. He chose the safer and smarter course.

Meanwhile, the squad jumped into the cranky old truck, and as Rocco ignited the engine, Eddie looked around to see how many witnesses were out there. The security guard was now standing over the scene, but Rocco assured them he would wait before calling it in, seeing how he was an accomplice now and Natalia's wound wasn't life-threatening. But more concerning were the patrons and employees of the restaurants. Folks began to pour out and wander over to the playground to see why they heard loud yelling—in English, no less—and gunshots. Some people started to scream as they took in the bloody mess.

"We need to get the hell out of here! Now, Rocco!" Eddie insisted in the sternest voice he could muster.

As they screeched out of the parking lot, through the exit, and past the now-empty security booths, Eddie removed the coat from Izzy's head and looked her in the eye. "Hey, little girl. You know I love you so much! Remember, Lisa?"

"Yes, Daddy."

"Hi... Izzy," Lisa was shell-shocked, never having been anywhere close to this kind of carnage. But she was starting to come to her senses, knowing she had to be strong for Izzy.

Eddie knew he had to take the pressure off, continuing, "This is our friend, Uncle Rocco. He's American just like you and me. The four of us are going to go on a really big, cool trip now, like a fun camping trip, then a plane ride back to California. Are you ready for an adventure?"

## 22

THE SURREALITY OF it all quickly became a harsh a reality. Two Americans in Brazil with no intention other than the safe but illegal return of a toddler girl were now accessories to both an attempted murder and an actual homicide. To say things turned for the worst was quite an understatement, and the couple felt that realization all too quickly.

Lisa was the first to question the sanity of the entire endeavor. To not let Izzy hear a word, she moved herself within whispering distance of Eddie, and let him have it. "Do you know what just fucking happened, Eddie? I mean, do you really *know*?"

"Lisa, you need to relax," Eddie whispered back. "Rocco will get us out of this. You need to trust me."

"Trust you? Are you kidding me? All I can think about is lethal injection! We are going to death row in Brazil!"

"First of all, there is no death row in Brazil. Well, I don't think there is, anyway. Secondly, like I said, Rocco will—"

"Fuck Rocco!" Lisa raised her voice, and Rocco immediately snapped his head back and gave a stare. Izzy also heard this and looked up, shocked, even if she didn't fully understand the words.

"Lisa, calm down," Rocco insisted. "I know you are scared right now, but you need to be an adult about this. I've seen and been through far worse, believe me. Plus, you're scaring the little girl." Rocco then looked down at Izzy and winked.

"An adult? I don't think you understand what just happened out there. I don't care how many other soldiers you've killed. That was—"

"That was fireworks!" interrupted Eddie, shooting Lisa an evil eye, then moving his gaze down to Izzy. "Fireworks are fun, right, Izzy?"

"Yeah! I like them!" Izzy responded, unaware of the intensity of the situation.

Eddie then raised his eyes back up to Lisa and whispered in Lisa's ear, "You need to hold it together, Lisa, for Izzy's sake! We are now a crew, an escape team, and we need to stick together to get out of here."

"Eddie, it was our fault that Don did that! We planted the idea in his head about you and Natalia."

"Shhh! Quiet down!" Eddie was speaking as low as possible, as he understood what might happen if Rocco heard that particular conversation. "That's guilt talking to you, Lisa. We might have played with his mind a bit, but it wasn't us who went and pulled the trigger!"

Lisa had nothing left to say and nestled herself against the window of the truck to ponder what she had gotten herself into.

As Rocco drove, he wanted to make sure the team knew who was in control and that he was unfazed by the trouble. "Listen up. We can still hold our own fate in our hands and complete the rest of the plan. Number-one goal now is getting us out of the country and back home to the States. No matter what transpired up to this point, we are still somehow making it from point A to point B. Plus, we have little Izzy. It worked. We made the grab; now we need to put the rest behind us, along with this whole godforsaken country."

"Agreed 100 percent," Eddie concurred while simultaneously nudging Lisa in the arm.

"Sure. Get me the hell out of here... *please!*" Lisa had no other choice but to agree.

First things first: they had to rid themselves of the old beater truck and switch to the unassuming van that was holding their bags and other needed items. Ditching cars in Brazil is easier than you think, even—and sometimes especially—old piece-of-garbage trucks. The abundance of poor, homeless folks would gladly take the vehicles off their hands rather than travel by bus, donkey, or whatever other method of transportation available.

They hid the van on the other side of the lake in another parking structure housing an immense grocery store. Truthfully, it wasn't really *hiding*, but there were a couple of reasons for that. First, miraculously, there were no cameras in the parking lot, so making a switch from one car to another in a crowded lot wouldn't raise too many eyebrows. Second, it was safe. You leave a van full of bags, clothes, camping components, and whatnot in a lesser-crowded area, the vehicle and all the belongings in it would be gone within an hour.

The best route to the store was to circumvent the entire lake, to the south side, where a small bridge spanned the narrow body of water. Such an old bridge, maybe even the first to cross the lake, meant no high-tech security cameras there either. Navigating across the bridge undetected was a breeze; they just needed to get to the grocery store lot before the police tracked them down. This had to happen hastily, though. The police in Brasília are known for quickly throwing up roadblocks; therefore, they were definitely working against the clock.

Rocco steered quickly into the parking lot. Their white getaway van with blacked-out windows sat right where they'd left it. They were one step ahead so far but needed to make the switch quickly and ditch that damn truck. And that's just what they did. Eddie grabbed the keys, Izzy, and Lisa's hand.

"See you at the spot," he told Rocco, and he urged the rest of the team into the van. Izzy was wiped at this point, so they set her up in a little comfortable array of bags and clothes in the back to let her sleep off the nightmare she'd just experienced. They just hoped she actually believed the whole ordeal was truly fireworks (and a dream).

Rocco tore out of the parking lot like his wheels were on fire. Nobody gave two thoughts to it, though, knowing they'd rather have him get to the spot loudly than to be caught by the police driving slowly. Izzy was asleep in the back, and with Lisa in the front seat, Eddie confessed his fear too as everything was starting to sink in as the adrenaline wore off. "Listen, I do know what went down there was bad, but we're so close, babe! We need to get a handle on this, get the fuck out of here, and in the future, I'll be paying for the psychiatrist to help with the PTSD."

"You're going to make a joke right now, Eddie? This shit is crazy! We need to get out of this country now! Eddie, I'm scared."

"I know. Sorry. Trying to deal with it too. The last thing I want to do is end up in some Brazilian prison. That won't go over well—American gringo in a South American prison. Believe me, I've heard the stories. Look... here's the positive thing about it. You saw what Rocco did back there? All instinct. He is a professional. I trust him completely now. We need to just stick to the plan."

"Yeah, he is in it knee-deep with us now too. But why did it take him so long to get to us in the first place? We could have grabbed Izzy and been out of there before Don even showed up!"

Eddie thought about that too. But in the end, he didn't have the energy to think or ask Rocco why he was late. He was just going to accept the gratefulness he felt that Rocco was there at all. "I don't know, Lisa, but I'll tell you, it seems Don had been following Natalia around at least all day today if not longer. That dude was nuts. We can't ever let Rocco know about our Don Plan—he could lose it on us. Agreed?"

"Yes. We can't say a word."

As they drove toward the turnoff road now on the north side of the lake, where a series of streams ran off to dense shrubbery and trees, Eddie saw tire marks careening off the paved path into a cut of bushes. He knew this was Rocco and the truck, and right on cue, Rocco came running out from within, yelling at Eddie to open the door for him to jump inside.

One might think ditching a getaway truck that was involved in a major crime, fully intact, not scrubbed down, wasn't the smartest thing in the world. Then again, one might not know Brazil. Leaving that kind of evidence in the United States, somebody would call it in, and there would be CSI, FBI, and whatever other acronyms crawling all over the scene. Brazil is different. Much different. Abandoning the truck in a spot like this, filled with poor, homeless people, then making a little fuss and noise to actually draw more people to it, worked out in their favor. Chances were extremely high that there would be a fight over the abandoned truck, followed by some deal-making, on to the winner acquiring his new piece of property, washing it, cleaning it, maybe even painting it, then selling it off in full or piece by piece to pay for his family's groceries for the next month or two. No need to get the cops involved here.

Now in a clean van, with Izzy in hand, the next move was escaping the city, before the Brasília police threw up what's called a blitz—road closures and checkpoints. Quite honestly, the crew had no idea who saw what at the scene of the crime. For all they knew, the cops were looking for some little favela kids who'd botched a robbery. The more likely scenario was Uncle João was already in the military police headquarters, and the whole damn Brazilian Army could be looking for them.

There weren't many roads out of Brasília, and one might assume they would take the better, safer highway toward the bigger metropolitan cities like Rio or *São Paulo* given that options for international flights were really only available from those two cities. But for the authorities to follow this line of reasoning would be a huge mistake, because that is where they were going to try their luck southbound, first through the state of Paraná, down to the western side of the state of Rio Grande do Sul, into the extreme southern border with Argentina and Uruguay. That's where they planned to cross the border and depart the country entirely, then pivot directions, by air, and head north to the States.

Escaping the city of Brasília had been fairly easy so far. They only saw a smattering of police dotted along the roads, and there were no blitz searches setup anywhere. Quite luckily, the disorganization of the system in Brazil was really working to their advantage. But this was where it got dicey. Highway 153 routed them south, but it was a main artery, and they could have been stopped at any time. But not by the police—they didn't have the budget to roam around patrolling highways in the lost lands of the interior of Brazil—the team was more worried about criminals. A van like theirs could be seen as a potential vehicle filled to the brim with goodies that could provide a month's worth of income to a desperate family. This escape was going to be sketchy.

Nightfall came upon them, and it wasn't any run-of-the-mill darkness. Out there in the middle of Brazil, the darkness was like being locked in a closet. Eddie wasn't the only one feeling trapped inside the wilderness... and much like the closet, he felt very claustrophobic there. Maybe it was the combination of the total blackout darkness, plus being in a van with other people, holding the feeling that the entirety of Brazil was coming for them, crashing down from all around.

When they pulled the van over, nobody really even knew what state they were in, physically or mentally. Tossing out all cell phones before they departed Brasília left them with some navigational barriers, to say the least. Road signs on the artery weren't in abundance, as there would be on, say, Interstate 80 in the United States. Rocco believed they were in Rio Grande do Sul, although the other two could have argued for any other southern state. Looking around the van, Eddie could still see the terror in Lisa's eyes, the nervous attention Rocco was giving to the world outside of the van, and then something amazing. Izzy was having the time of her life. She didn't seem to get it, and luckily enough, maybe she didn't realize her mother was gone forever. And to her, she was camping with her father, with whom she hadn't hung out in a long time.

"Izzy, do you want any more chips?" Eddie asked, trying to constantly spoil her with junk food since he knew she hadn't had anything like that in months.

"No, Daddy. Can I have a soda?"

"Sure, honey. This trip is for F-U-N! Anything you want!"

But right then, out of the left side of the van, they heard the most wicked howl ever heeded at that range.

"Must be some kind of tiger or cougar," Rocco explained, quite proud of his knowledge. Who knew if those kinds of cats existed the wilderness of Brazil where they were parked.

"A tiger, Uncle Rocco? Where?" Izzy looked around.

Eddie shot Rocco a mad-dog look and calmed Izzy down. "Izzy, for sure! This is a big wilderness park like back in California. It's completely safe. We get to camp and see a lot of exotic animals! Cool, huh?"

"I wanna see tigers! Where? Where?"

"We'll keep our eyes open, but not too long, because we have to get a lot of rest for another drive tomorrow."

"Daddy, can Uncle Rocco show me animals? I like Uncle Rocco!"

"Of course, honey. Promise."

Rocco seemed genuinely taken aback. The whole drive down she had been gravitating to him. She obviously sensed that his presence came with excitement, or at the very least a change from her current life, which was a superior result to a less-desired outcome. And Izzy reminded Rocco of his own nephews. He loved them dearly, and she took him back to a time when he was able to pass the days with that family of his own. Maybe having a little one around started to soften Rocco's edges. But maybe the team didn't need Rocco to be soft.

BACK IN BRASÍLIA, while Natalia recovered in the hospital, her family had been hard at work, calling every politician they knew, cashing in every political chip they had. Natalia had instructed them to do whatever was possible, to capture the Americans and safely return her daughter. João was pissed beyond all measure, which was completely understandable, and he was out for blood. He insisted the whole event was a planned homicide attempt. He wasn't privy to the Don Plan, so to him, all the Americans were in on it together.

The police, however, were clueless. Different policing organizations existed within each city, including branches of the military police and the civil police. Despite the obviousness in their titles, deciphering the responsibilities between the different bodies was more difficult than solving world hunger. Being a high-value case, jurisdiction in this matter was handed to the professionals laboring long days within the military police.

The disorganization was startling, but this being Brasília, the news of an attempted murder on a daughter from a prominent family, an American dead at the same scene, and the kidnapping of a Brazilian girl had reached all the way to the top. Natalia's father made so many waves with the politicians that the president of Brazil had been briefed, and her first order of business was to get the US embassy into the fold, not because she wanted to involve the Americans but because she knew she held some leverage now—not quite an outcome the US embassy desired with the trade deal pending.

The US ambassador decided to send good ol' Frank James to go clean up the mess. Of course, Frank was not too pleased at having to leave important trade negotiations to deal with an irate, highly connected family of an injured Brazilian citizen, especially since all signs pointed to the culprit being an American who, to add the cherry on top, was in the embassy jail a short time earlier.

Natalia had been interviewed, but the real move was to meet with João, who left the scene unscathed while witnessing the entire ordeal. The thought was that he might be a bit more clear-minded. Frank already recognized that the outcome of that inquisition could be biased, but he had to go through the motions regardless.

"Thank you for coming. I know you are still busy with Natalia in the hospital, but I ask you to let us help you. Let us help each other." Frank started with his questioning of João, but João was not alone; he'd brought with him representatives from the military police, and just to make it even more of a pain in Frank's ass, João asked Javier, the *great* lawyer, to come along for support.

Before João could even get a word out, Javier said, "Mr. James, let me start by telling you this. I know Eddie Watters extremely well. I represented him for a short time before I knew that he was out to cause trouble for the Pacheco family. Mr. Watters is completely unhinged. He told me several times that I should do 'whatever it takes' to retrieve his daughter. I guess we have now seen what that means."

"Thank you, Javier. I do understand that, and I also spoke to Mr. Watters several times, and he showed signs of stress around the issue. But at the same time, I do realize that the girl was taken away from him unlawfully—"

"That has never been determined in a court of law," Javier argued.

"Nevertheless, just know that we will completely support the search for Mr. Watters, and as an American citizen, I hope you will take the correct course of action when he is caught—meaning that the US embassy should be completely involved with this case."

"That is bullshit! This gringo is going to prison!" the official military police detective decided to pipe up.

"And I believe the girl involved, now within Mr. Watters's custody, is also an American citizen, which means this whole thing has to be handled quite delicately," Frank continued.

João decided to involve himself in the discussion, and in his best broken English, he said something meaning, "I don't care what country he is from. I want him caught, and I don't care if you bring Eddie back dead or alive! My niece is Brazilian, and this piece of shit stole her, then tried to kill my sister out of revenge!"

"So, João, it was Eddie Watters who shot your sister?"

"No. It was an entire ambush. He must have agreed with Natalia's boyfriend, Don Thompson, to do it as part of their plan!"

"Wait. So Natalia's boyfriend pulled the trigger, but then Mr. Watters killed him after?"

João could only reply, "No, another gringo shot Don. He looked like a soldier—big guy with muscles. He looked like an assassin."

The light bulb in Frank's head went off, but he didn't want to play his cards yet. "So, Mr. Pacheco, you are saying Don Thompson shot Natalia, then a soldier-assassin killed Don? But why would he do that?"

The Brazilian detective assumed he knew the plot and replied, "It is obvious: Mr. Watters and Mr. Thompson planned a murder. Don Thompson was an extremely jealous man, from what João has told us. There are three people with two motives. Once Don was convinced to kill Natalia, Mr. Watters must have hired someone to ... how does the saying go in English? 'Tie up any loose ends.' We are going to find these two killers, and they will pay a heavy price!"

*Those fucking marines*, Frank thought as he walked back to his office after escorting his guests out of the building. Frank had been around the diplomatic game long enough to have connections of his own. American soldiers leave their respective branches of the armed forces possessing the tricks of the trade, and knowing how to apply them correctly allows for contract work in this exact type of situation: assassin for hire. However, a private citizen like Eddie certainly did not have the connections or the communications pipeline to even find these types of people. The only way he could have hooked this up would be through fellow diplomatic or military resources in country. In this case, it meant the marines.

But who could it be? Frank stormed back to the security room to ask for recent tapes of when Eddie and company visited the embassy. As the recordings progressed, he noticed a few certain interactions.

"I know what's happening now," Frank muttered to himself.

It was Bobby in the waiting room, whispering back and forth with Eddie, ever so undercover but in too close a proximity to each other for a trained eye to see they were communicating.

"That little shit Bobby," he mumbled. "Doesn't he know these kinds of operations run through me?"

Frank made his way over to Bobby's post to initiate the confrontation. "Bobby, how is the life of a marine in Brazil today?"

"Very pleasant, sir. How is your day, Mr. James?"

"Fine, fine. All good. Well, not so good. Actually, I'm quite stressed because... well, I was wondering. I need you to come back to my office. I need to discuss some security issues with the ambassador, and they recommended speaking to you first since you are the ranking marine here, and quite honestly, I like you."

"Sure thing, sir!"

The two marched back to the main building, down the white hallway, and into Frank's office. Frank decided the right course of action was to not be the nice guy. In other words, be direct as possible.

"So, Bobby, before we talk about the ambassador, I wanted to ask you about another little situation, if you don't mind."

"Anything you'd like, sir." Bobby was quite unaware that he was walking right into a trap. Of course, he'd heard about the chaos at Pontão, but there was no way to connect that back to him. Rocco was a professional, after all.

"You know, Bobby, I have been in this game quite a long time. I know a lot of things and see a lot of things. One thing I noticed the other night that frankly struck me as odd was that when we were out back for that little embassy party—you know, playing pool and having a few beers... anyway, when we were there, I noticed you had a very nice, brand-new watch on. Quite expensive for someone at your pay grade."

"Yes, sir, a very nice watch. My girlfriend here bought it for me. She comes from a family with a bit of money."

"Ah yes, your girlfriend. But I wonder, Bobby, I was told you and your girlfriend broke up several months ago. She must have won you back by buying you nice gifts, huh?"

"Well, yes. Maybe, sir. We reconciled, and she bought me this."

"So, Bobby, that same girlfriend of yours, I just happened to see her the other night with another marine. What's his name? Sam?" Of course, Frank was lying, but Bobby didn't know that.

"No, they are just friends... I think, sir."

"That's funny, because they seemed to be very *close* friends over there behind the wall."

Bobby started to stutter a bit. "Well, uh, sir, I don't know. If that's true, I'm pretty pissed off right now!" He was stonewalling much better than anticipated, and Frank's patience was now all but lost.

"Cut the crap, Bobby! Where did you get the money for that watch?"

"Sir, I told you—"

"Bullshit, Bobby! You think I don't have access to security tapes? You think I don't have the same resources down here as you do? Let me tell you something! I know everything that goes down around here, and I know everyone! Now tell me, where the fuck is Rocco?"

That little speech accomplished the objective, and Bobby broke, agreeing to help Frank find Rocco and team in exchange for forgiveness, letting Bobby off the hook. After all, Frank was more upset that the operation didn't receive his blessing so he could redeem a partial referral fee. In the end, however, it was better for everyone in the embassy if the Americans found the suspects first, rather than the Brazilians. Nobody wanted to see a soldier like Rocco in some Brazilian prison for the rest of his life.

ON THE OTHER side of town, João, Javier, and the whole Brazilian police force turned into full search-and-destroy mode. João gave descriptions of everyone and decided not to let fate lie in the hands of the Brazilian or American government. In the past hours, he had been able to whip up support from a lot of his hoodlum friends, all armed to the teeth, to go find and kill his ex-brother-in-law. But little did he know Eddie and the crew were hauling ass to the southern border, and every kilometer left behind was one more away from the bullshit going on in Brasília… and one more closer to being free and clear.

# 23

FINALLY ARRIVING IN Rio Grande do Sul, Eddie and the crew had spent the past few days dodging various towns along the way, only to stop to buy gas and fuel, all paid for in cash. Those back roads in Brazil were horrendous; the team wondered how people could live a life outside of the major cities. Most of the towns along the route had no plumbing or barely any running water. But they were doing their best, despite the environment.

The border of Uruguay was their craftiest bet; a small town named Chuí straddles the two countries, and for the average tourist, immigration is a breeze. Speeding down the road a few kilometers out, Rocco and Eddie began discussing the crossing. "Rocco, how the hell are we going to not only convince the Brazilians to let us exit but the Uruguayans to let us in?"

"No problems there at all. Only way they cause a stir is if they are actually looking for us. That being the case, it's all money, my friend. This whole continent thrives on corruption. It's going to be easier than you think—"

*Bam!* The car immediately came to a screeching halt as they hit something in the middle of the road.

"Damn! What was that?" Eddie yelled.

"I have no idea!" shouted Rocco. "But shit, man, whatever we hit just fucked up our van!"

"What the—!" Lisa cried out, jolted awake from a nap that had her escaping the situation. "Rocco! Eddie! Did we get shot? What happened?"

"Hold tight!" Rocco commanded as he jumped out of the car, gun in hand, ready to shoot whatever the hell just hit them in case it was still alive.

Eddie followed right behind him only to have Lisa grab him by the shoulder and say, "Don't go out there, Eddie. Stay here!"

"It's okay. I don't see anything out the window. Stay with Izzy. I'll be right back."

Lisa understood that part of her role was now 50 percent to be Eddie's rock and 50 percent to be Izzy's. The girl was going to need a mother now, and she could thank the heavens they had sent Lisa.

Eddie crawled out the car and saw their left front tire blown away, covered with blood along the fender, down to the driver's-side door. He looked down at biggest cat he'd ever seen in his life.

"It's a damn jaguar," said Rocco, "and it's still moving!"

The creature was on three legs, bleeding profusely, and as it turned its head toward them in a daze, it began to growl with a profound nastiness. It leaped a little at them like it was going to pounce, even though it was only half-alive.

Right at that moment, Izzy looked out of the window and shouted, "Daddy! Animal park!"

Lisa snatched Izzy back, and Eddie jumped back in the van as Rocco yelled, "Stay there with the girl!" After all, Izzy had been around more death that week than any kid should be exposed to in a lifetime. Rocco placed six rounds into the animal with short, quick bursts. Holstering his gun, he moved around the van and hollered at the crew to lock Izzy in and to help move the carcass.

"Eddie, we can't let Izzy see this!" exclaimed Lisa, covering Izzy's ears. So instead, they put the van in neutral and pushed it backward. On three wheels, they parked the van far enough away from the dead creature so Izzy couldn't take a curious glance.

"I'm telling you, Eddie, this is the kind of shit we have to deal with. There are all kinds of animals like this running around. That thing could have killed us even after being steamrollered by the van!" Rocco explained like an expert.

Rocco was right; they had to plan for all the variables. But now they were stuck practically in the middle of nowhere with a disabled van sitting on three working tires.

To make matters worse, Izzy did notice the stress of the situation, and her immediate worry targeted not only her dad but, interestedly enough, Rocco. "Uncle Rocco! Daddy! Okay?"

Eddie could see that Rocco was moved, and he wondered if Rocco had ever had someone care for him like this.

"Yes, Ms. Izzy," Rocco said, kneeling. "Everything is wonderful."

Izzy ran over to Eddie and jumped up and down, swatting at him. Then she looked at Rocco and sprinted to him, flailing her arms then giving him a giant high five. "Good, Uncle Rocco! You're my friend now!"

Rocco reflected on what a really cool little kid Izzy was. Everyone noticed how positive it was to see him break down his rough exterior. Sensing he might have needed that right at that very point in his life was quite uplifting. A little ray of sunshine billowing through the omnipresent, dark cloud that was hanging above the van.

Waiting into the late afternoon for some vehicle to flag down, they noticed a buzzing sound coming from somewhere in the back of the van. Eddie searched through the belongings, and a furious anger started to overtake him with what he saw. Typical Eddie, not thinking but reacting, he grabbed the device and threw his hand right into Rocco's face.

"You brought a cell phone, Rocco? What the fuck, man!"

"First, get your hand out of my face before I tear it from your arm. Second, it's a satellite phone, and it's completely secure and untraceable. Locating us from that phone is impossible, and only a few of my partners know it exists or even have the number. It's for critical emergencies only. I won't even use it to help us with the van predicament we're in, because we can figure our way out of this without involving anyone else and their attention."

Eddie immediately backed off and shot Lisa a bewildered glance.

She looked back and stated the obvious, "Well, if it's ringing now, it can't be good news." She was right, and they all waited tensely to see what was in store next for the ill-fated team.

Rocco hit the Receive button and answered with, "Go."

"Rocco, it's me, Brian. I have news."

Brian was one of Rocco's closest partners in the clandestine business. For him to be calling meant something truly was afoot. "Tell me."

"They know you were involved with the scene there in Brasília. I received a call from one of our friends in the embassy. They want to talk. The entire Brazilian police force is looking for you guys."

"Brian, I don't trust them, and you know that. But you need to relay something to them right away. I did *not* shoot any Brazilians. And that other American—he wasn't a part of our plan. Nobody was supposed to die. It was a simple grab of the kid and get the hell out. You need to tell them it was the other American who hurt the mother."

"They already know that, Rocco, but I have someone here who wants to speak with you. I'm sorry, Rocco, but he threatened to completely shut us down globally. He is promising to work with you here."

"Rocco! This is Frank James."

"Fuck, Brian!" shouted Rocco. "Frank, I know you are always in the loop on these, but this was a *private* assignment. Simple snatch, then pay a few border guards and get the family back to the States. We did *not* plan on anyone getting killed or injured!"

Frank knew how to choose his words wisely. "Rocco, listen to me. You should have notified me. I give you a lot of business, and it works when we are all on the same page."

"I'm sorry, Frank. I was going to send word once we were out of Brazil, but I never know who's listening on the other line."

"Rocco, this could completely fuck up our military sale with the Brazilians. You did this without consulting me. Now look what happened. That is not how you treat business partners!"

"Frank, we're in deep shit down here. I am telling you, and you have to believe me—that crazy ex-boyfriend was the instigator with the guns flying. Yes, I put a bullet in him, only because he was about to light everyone up."

Frank thought it through long and hard. Rocco just corroborated João's story. Yes, there was a confrontation, but who was he to fault a father for what he'd done? As far as he could tell, the true criminal, the one who attempted to murder Brazilian, deserved what he got in the end. By the hands of an American hero, no less. Also, he liked having his network of ex–Navy SEALs available for his dirty work. He didn't want to screw up the global team he relied on in very heavy situations. He realized that if he hung Rocco out to dry, the rest of the team would be unavailable to him going forward. On the other hand, the Brazilians would never let it go. They were out for blood.

"Rocco, listen to me," explained Frank. "Do not go to any border crossing and try to bribe the guards. You, Mr. Watters, and that girl are all plastered on every crossing. We need to get you out another way, and we need to make it look like you never got out. Where are you now?"

"Frank, thank you. We need all the help we can get. I'm not going to tell you our position over this line, but our van is shit, and we're stuck. We'll make our way out of it, but tell all your buddies despite the security, we are headed for Uruguay."

"Rocco! Why did you say that over the phone!" Eddie yelled as Rocco powered off the phone.

"Because they know anyway, and if someone was listening they will be on their way south. We're now headed north."

Now that the whole plan was flushed down the toilet, they needed to adopt a new idea. Everyone realized what a piece of crap

Frank James was, but they also understood that he was their only hope. And if Frank let Rocco flutter in the wind, his black-market Navy SEAL contractors might not find that too pleasing. So yes, it was in Frank's best interest to get the team home alive, but they needed to make absolutely certain. They decided to respect Frank's plan while agreeing to follow it smartly.

But first things first: they had to get all their possessions out of the van and find a way north—way north and way fast. Traveling those roads was both risky and time-consuming. They needed an airplane.

They moved as many of their belongings as possible down the road, realizing their only course of action was to wait for a ride. The sun was high in the sky, almost a complete, perpendicular line from the pavement they were sitting on. Rocco was thinking, Lisa was sweating, Eddie was burning, and Izzy... well, Izzy decided to dance around in a circle.

"She really is a cute bundle of joy!" Rocco exclaimed, stating the obvious to Eddie, who just nodded and put his head down on his bent knees.

Lisa leaned over and rubbed Eddie's back. She had made peace with the whirlwind tornado she found herself in, almost strangely now enjoying the excitement of it all. "You know, Eddie, all those people back home are getting up and going to work. Look at us... we're on the run in a third-world country, having no clue if we will even last the next five minutes, let alone get out of here alive."

"Yeah, fun stuff, eh?" Eddie replied.

The tables had turned, and Eddie was now the stressed and depressed one. Lisa would play the role of motivator for the time being.

"Catch, Uncle Rocco!" Meanwhile, Izzy had been finding little pebbles and chucking them at her new best friend, and Rocco was more than happy to oblige, enjoying the little game with his new adopted niece.

From the distance, they were almost just a normal family on vacation experiencing some car trouble. Zooming in on the bunch, this household was far from normal, a family in the midst of chaos. Finally benefiting from a stroke of luck, a standard little Volkswagen Golf approached from a few kilometers ahead, slowing down and stopping as they waved it down. Eddie instructed the driver in Portuguese that he would give him five hundred American dollars to drive them to the nearest farm. They were setting their newly devised plan into action, hoping this time it would go off without a hitch.

THE CATTLE INDUSTRY in southern Brazil is thriving. Most of the beef in South America comes from this fertile region. The gauchos who work the farms usually are employed by large ranch owners. Paid a significant salary for their skill set, their demand increases according to the beef market—and, of course, it's always thriving. These farms gave the struggling Americans the perfect backdrop for their next adventure.

Eddie and company purposely abandoned the van, including their fingerprints and evidence, so the authorities would know where they were headed. Before the Volkswagen came to their rescue, they also left a trail of items, such as clothes, food, and the like, leading off into the wilderness beyond the road. They utilized some of the jaguar's carcass and stamped blood across the highway along the same path as their trail. Anyone with any investigative experience might think they'd hit the animal, leading it to attack them, only for the humans to escape into the open land fearing for their lives. They would have seen that they killed the jaguar but also recognize there were many other wild predators beyond the road. With a lack of water, the heat, and the natural wildlife, it was a fifty-fifty chance they'd make it out of there alive. The police could spend a day searching the countryside for dead bodies, giving the crew an extra twenty-four hours or so in front of the chase.

The four gringos piled into the tiny clown car was almost humorous. The driver of the Volkswagen transported them to the outskirts of one of the biggest ranches in the south, happily letting them out. By now their possessions had all but disappeared, save for the clothes on their backs and Rocco's gun with plenty of ammunition.

As the driver waited for his payment, Eddie handed him $500, plus another $500, and instructed him not to tell a soul about it. And just to be sure, Rocco pulled out his gun, pointed it at the driver's head, and in Portuguese said, "To make sure you truly don't say a word about who you picked up, I am going to take your wallet. I will now know who you are, which means I will know where you and your family live. If anybody finds out about us, I am going to kill all of you!" He tapped his gun on the driver's temple. The old man was scared shitless, so they were pretty confident the secret was safe with him.

This of course frightened Izzy a bit too, but it had to be done, and Eddie explained to Izzy that it was only a water gun and Rocco was just teasing the guy. But the bigger issue was that he now needed to convince her how the rest of the game would be played. Thinking outside the box, he resorted to describing the adventure as a game to alleviate any of her stress.

But if it was a game to Izzy, it was quite the opposite to the adults. They were going to have to sneak across the giant farm filled with marvelous cows grazing away, and make their way down the road to the hangar where the farmer had a pesticide-spraying airplane for the estate's soybean and corn crop.

Brazil is one of the top pesticide-spraying nations in the world, buying up all the banned products for use where other nations have laws against those same chemicals. And Eddie's team hit the jackpot. A ranch of this size usually retains a locally built, Embraer EMB 202 Ipanema model agricultural aircraft to spray their crops from a low altitude. But this particular hangar housed a modified Zenair CH 801, meaning there were four seats instead of two, and better yet, it was a short-field runway. They didn't need any farmers chasing after them down some lengthy runway! Because of Rocco's navy days, flying an airplane of that size would not present any issues. Back to aerodynamic and piloting basics, downgrading from an F/A-18 to a propeller-driven agricultural aircraft would be a breeze.

Between the plane and the posse was about three hundred yards of open land. Rocco, Lisa, and Eddie were all in great shape—or at least they had been before the trip to Brazil—and they were still fit enough to handle a run like that. The bad news was that Eddie was going to have to carry Izzy on the sprint.

"On three, we go," Rocco instructed. They peeked around in every direction to see what they were going to have to deal with. A few gauchos and farmhands were out and about, but they were nothing to worry about seeing how they were perched on a little upland, meaning the run would be downhill to the plane. They prayed that the plane was fueled up. Eddie explained to Izzy that the next sequence in the game was going to be a thrilling one.

"Three, two, one...go!" Rocco shouted, and they exploded off the little perch and went full-steam ahead to the plane. Several farmers turned their heads, thinking they were witnessing some bat-shit crazy locals, not four gringos on the lam. But the farmhands also refused to do anything about it; they weren't compensated enough to get involved with whatever the hell was happening.

Rocco was the first to the plane, followed by Lisa, as Eddie brought up the rear with Izzy wrapped around him. Rocco yanked the airplane door open with full force, and Lisa jumped in the back, while Eddie threw Izzy into her arms and then crawled across the left side to the right. The pilot in command was sitting in the front left seat, who for this flight was going to be Captain Rocco. Igniting the engine, Rocco immediately positioned the flaps down full for takeoff and pushed the throttle forward. No weight and balance checks or flight plan there—they were going to wing it.

Initiating their accelerated taxi toward the little takeoff strip, they moved to the departure position at the end of the strip. At the same moment came several men running toward the plane from the left. It must have been the ranch owner and some of his closest men.

"Oh, shit, Rocco! This is getting real! We need to get the hell out of here now!" Eddie shouted over the sound of the propeller.

Izzy's nervousness was cutting through the excitement, and Lisa jumped in and provided a calming squeeze, wrapping her whole body around the uneasy girl.

"Hang on tight, everyone," Rocco commanded as he held the brakes down and pushed the throttle forward in preparation for a proper short-field takeoff. As the men approached within one hundred yards, the propeller screamed at full force, and Rocco released the brakes while pulling the control wheel back, engaging the elevators.

They were on a grassy runway strip, so lifting the front wheel off the ground during takeoff was essential in gaining enough ground speed to rotate the plane. As the plane accelerated down the strip, the men were in full pursuit behind them. One of them held a rifle, and he broke off his gallop to aim at the plane. The team was moving down the strip at a fast clip as they felt the nose of the plane lifting. They heard gunshots behind them as the rest of the plane rose off the ground. Rocco then pushed the wheel forward a bit to give them the proper airspeed before pulling back again to increase altitude.

"Everyone, heads down!" Rocco yelled, in case one of the bullets came screaming into the cockpit. Gaining more and more altitude, the men fell farther behind in the distance while Rocco turned the plane northeast, using the ailerons and rudder simultaneously in perfect harmony.

Eddie had to give Rocco proper accolades, commenting, "Rocco, very smooth!"

"Thanks, man. I have one thousand hours in a Cessna, and this is pretty damn close. To be honest, I completely guessed the takeoff speed needed, but hell, it worked!"

"Nice job, Rocco!" Lisa shouted as Izzy clapped her hands and screamed, "Yay!" her nervousness subsiding.

"Don't get too excited yet," responded Rocco. "We only have enough fuel to get us about four hours up the country—it's not going to help us too much. Eddie, hand me my sat phone. Now we're going to need some help."

FLYING AT ABOUT ten thousand feet, the team looked down and observed the farmlands of southern Brazil, which were not unlike the heartland in the United States, with squared-off pieces of land where one could identify the irrigation circles. It was not quite as symmetrical and organized as the views over, say, Kansas or Nebraska, but pretty damn close. Eddie couldn't help but wonder who was waiting for them below.

"Natalia's family must have stirred up the hornet's nest by now, and I know Frank has tipped the authorities off that we headed south," Eddie commented as they flew along.

"Well, from my chat with Brian, it looks like Frank is being the diplomat that he is, playing one side while having a separate agenda. There seems to be a modern-day lynch mob on their way to have their hanging party, but we're not going to be there. We'll probably fly right over them, unbeknownst to the raging group of police, army, and Natalia's family and friends below," Rocco replied, correctly as usual.

Rocco was smart enough to completely rip the plane's transponder out and chuck it out the window right after takeoff. If that farmer reported the missing plane—and surely he did—the authorities weren't going to track them by a squawking transponder. If that were the case, the authorities would be led to some unsuspecting dupe many kilometers away.

Eddie sat deep in thought, constantly reminding himself, *We continue to take two steps back with every step forward. Was I really involved in that murder scene? How did this become what it now is? Are we going to make it out alive? But I feel like we have destiny on our side. We will make it home. I know we will. The power of positivity.*

But right then, the sputtering. It sounded like the engine was struggling to keep the propeller moving.

"So, I have some good news and bad news for you all," Rocco declared over the noise of the engine dying out. "Good news is,

I think we are close to Curitiba. Bad news, we're out of gas and we're gonna have to make a loss-of-engine landing."

Curitiba is a modern city that over the years has made great strides. South of Brasília but in proximity to São Paulo, it's considered one of the greenest cities on the planet. The citizens of Curitiba are proud of the advancements they have made on the green technology front, with efficient public transportation, ethanol-based vehicles, and legislation that will continue to advance them. Demographically speaking, the city is inhabited by German descendants, so there is an abundance of blond hair, blue-eyed, gringo-looking Brazilians. This would help the team blend in a bit, but first they had to make it there alive.

Rocco adjusted the plane to its optimal glide slope, or at least what he thought it might be in terms of throttle and pitch. These prop planes were actually pretty easy to handle without an engine. Extremely light, the aircraft basically becomes an engine-less glider with any loss of power. There were plenty of open fields below, so they hoped there wouldn't be any problem finding somewhere open to land safely.

Zero fuel was being advanced to the engine, commencing their controlled descent. Rocco adjusted the airspeed slightly and circled around a few fields as they slowly lost altitude. Moving the flaps into a short-field-landing position, he chose an approximately half-square-mile spot where they would land the struggling bird.

"No need to worry, everybody," Rocco reminded them as Eddie looked back to see Izzy tearing up.

"Don't worry, little girl, this is all a part of the game!" he reminded her, as did Lisa.

Lisa's face had turned completely white too, and Eddie couldn't help but wonder if she was thinking what a huge mistake he was. After all, she could have been sitting on some Southern California beach, drinking a beer and grabbing a tan. Instead, she'd witnessed a murder, was on the run from the police in a third-world country, and now was about to do her best to survive a crash landing in an airplane.

"Never a dull moment, you have to admit!" Eddie said as he grabbed Lisa's hands and held on to them tightly.

"You owe me big time," she said, "like for the rest of your life!"

Approaching a hundred feet from touching down, they braced themselves by placing their heads between their arms and legs. Slower and slower they descended, with the ground creeping up ever so slightly. The wheels below started to smack against the tall grass, and then boom! Bouncing off the ground, Rocco pulled the wheel back, trying to keep the nose from touching down and causing a front flip. Boom! Again, they bounced and then hopped up and down in the field. Smacking his head against the windshield with a loud thump, blood rushed from Eddie's cut. As they rolled through the field, bush and grass became overwhelming, slamming against them, limiting the visibility to three feet. Smash, smack—the windshield started to crack. Lisa completely covered Izzy.

"You guys okay?" Eddie cried out as their speed began to drop and the force of the landing was lessened.

"We're good!" Lisa replied, with grateful tears flowing.

Izzy looked like she had seen a ghost, but a smile crossed her face as the plane settled in. She then raised her hands over her head, clapping and yelling, "Again! Again!"

"I told her it was like Disneyland!" Lisa clarified.

"Holy crap, yes!" Rocco jumped out of the plane with full excitement. "That was awesome, huh, little girl? Whoo-hoo!"

It was the first they'd witnessed Rocco with some encouraging emotion. Maybe the stress had been getting to him too, but he was just too macho to show it. But he sure was releasing it now. Jumping up and down a few times, he thrust his fists into the air. The rest of the team laughed it up and cheered because, what the hell, the guy just successfully crash-landed a plane he'd never flown before in his entire life. Nice work, Rocco.

As they piled out of the plane, jubilant from the situation, happiness quickly subsided.

"It's getting ridiculous how we keep winding up in these scenarios and even more absurd that we can always squirm our way out," Eddie observed.

"Yes. And now we walk," Rocco responded.

Throwing Izzy on his shoulders, with Lisa at his side, actually holding on to his arm very lovingly, and with Rocco to his left, Eddie began walking. It was going to be a long one. Thankfully, they were just beyond the outskirts of the city, though they still faced quite a distance. Not wanting to take the risk of tracking down another car and hitchhiking, they decided their feet would be their transportation. The key was stealth; they would descend upon Curitiba from the fields, as opposed to the main road.

The grass became denser with every kilometer, almost like a rain forest in some parts. It going to be tough to do without any interactions with locals. They were all extremely thirsty, and while there was plenty of fresh flowing water, the last thing they needed was a case of dysentery while trying to escape the country. They'd have to wait till the city and hit some store for supplies.

"Rocco, what's the plan? How the hell are we going to get all the way to northern Brazil?" Eddie inquired.

"That plan is down the drain, my man. Way north we have friends. It was going to be easier to get out from there. So now, we'll just have to bring our friends here. I'm sick of this adventure, and I'm not going anywhere else. We will leave the country from Curitiba."

A stern statement indeed. It was time to see how solid he was with the follow-through.

# 24

**W**HAT SEEMED LIKE hours upon hours of slow moving had now become progress. As they crept along through the brush of the never-ending fields, the tall grass swayed and smacked any exposed skin on their withering bodies. The need for water was such an understatement that nobody dared to be the first to complain. In fact, they knew they should thank their lucky stars for even making it that far. But with every minute passed, the weight of their present state of being increased. Kidnapping, murder, crash landings... was this a novel, or was it truly real life? The answer: it was both. It was Eddie's Life Book—a combination of normalcy and fiction, all wrapped together with the ending yet to be authored.

Approaching the first outposts of the city, suffering with thirst and with a hungry kid, they saw what looked to finally be a sign of civilization and headed straight for the nearest convenience store. Lisa stayed behind the store and insisted on keeping Izzy, allowing her rest. Eddie and Rocco popped into the store and threw down some water bottles and chips on the counter with a thud. Money was running low. Eddie had spent almost every Brazilian penny he'd converted, and after the expense of the last few weeks, plus paying Rocco, an outrageous thought passed through his mind: Why not add robbery to my rap sheet? What's it going to hurt? But he knew better, of course. Even with all that he'd been through, he still maintained a moral compass. Yes, he would have to answer for his sins at some point, but for today, he would make that future conversation easier and just pay the man with the last change he could find in his pocket.

The four gathered behind the convenience store to chow down like animals. The strain of the trip was finally starting to take its toll on Izzy. She wasn't as happy and jovial as normal, but nevertheless, they had to press on. Frank and Brian had set up a private jet for them to leave the country, and it wasn't cheap. Somehow, some way, if they did indeed make it out of the country, Eddie would have to find a way to pay Frank back. But money would have to be the second-place finisher once again, because they had a goal, and they were nearing the completion of that goal. Hopefully.

"Listen," instructed Rocco, "we are going to make our way to a private airport, where our plane will be waiting. We need to get onto the tarmac without going through the usual airport entrance, so we're going to essentially have to break in. The plane will sit in a hangar on the southwest side of the airport, where we will then rendezvous with our pilot, who will smuggle us out of the country. Easy."

"This sounds too uneventful for what we're used to, Rocco. What about breaking into an airport, though? That doesn't sound like something to sleep on," Lisa said.

Lisa was right. It did sound too easy. How could that be? One step at a time. They just needed to get to the airport first in one piece, which was easier said than done. It wasn't like they could just pull out their phones and use Google Maps. Rocco had received information about the general area of the town it was in... but that was it.

Deciding they'd had enough of walking, something had to give. Eddie couldn't carry Izzy any longer, and her little legs were just too tired to walk any distance. They were going to have to use public transportation. It was risky, but they were so close, so they thought, Screw it.

Returning inside the convenience store, Eddie bought hats and sunglasses to hide their faces a bit. But the store worker decided he wanted to strike up a conversation. He noticed right away that Eddie was not Brazilian. Eddie found a Curious George cashier full of questions. He lied to the cashier, telling him they were South African... anything to confuse him enough in case the cops did find a scent. But this cashier now represented a potential variable to the plan.

"Rocco, should we pay him off?" Eddie leaned over and whispered.

"Leave him a nice tip and tell him not to mention us. Just get the directions to the nearest train or subway station, and that's it," Rocco instructed as he slipped out the door to leave Eddie on his own.

Floating through their minds was plain and pure impatience. Eddie truly hoped that feeling wasn't going to get them into deep trouble. He recognized, as did Rocco, that they were starting to make mistakes. They should have continued the mission, by foot, super stealthily, making their way to the airport. Instead, they were going to hop on public transportation and hope the Brazilian surveillance cameras weren't sophisticated enough to set off any alarms. Big gamble for sure.

They made their way by bus to the nearest train stop and boarded the carriage. With exhaustion setting in, they looked to get from point A to point B as quickly as possible and with the least number of steps taken. However, the consequences of rapid transportation meant that they had actually arrived at the airfield too quickly. Brian and Frank James had set up the rendezvous for twelve hours later, so they had twelve hours to kill—in other words, to find a place to crash.

The airfield was just over a hill to the west of their current location, where they would pass the night as a homeless family. There were no Marriotts to check into and order room service. Taking shifts, sleeping in the bushes of the open park, and eating little fried delectables from the local bakery would be their undertaking—that and ensuring survival with the other homeless crowd in proximity. Eddie was scared to death for Lisa and Izzy. It was no place for grown men, let alone a stepmother and her little toddler.

Rocco and Eddie decided on two six-hour watches, arming themselves with the gun just in case anything or anyone peculiar was about. The first shift was Eddie's, and he'd never been so nervous in his life. Lisa wrapped her body around Izzy, as Eddie stationed himself right next to them, gun cocked and ready to fire. Cold as could be, as Curitiba is at night, Rocco placed his jacket over the two of them and then curled up about five feet away.

"Good night, Lisa. I love you." Eddie hovered over Lisa's head, whispering in her ear. "Homeward bound. We are almost there."

Lisa kept her eyes closed, but the side of her mouth rose to present a half smile. "I love you too, Eddie." She dozed off.

Eddie was left to ponder his own thoughts and reflect on his life. Where do I go from here? My daughter's mother was shot, and her acting stepfather is dead ... because of me. Was it because of me? Should I have done nothing at all and let her kidnap my daughter and move to another country? She brought this upon herself, did she not? I hope Izzy will understand what happened when she is old enough. Will she hate me? And what about Lisa? How in the hell could she have stuck with me through all this shit? She really does love me, doesn't she? I will never leave her side, ever. I finally found my soul mate this time. His eyes started to flutter as the thoughts were moving further and further away from his full attention, but he knew he had to fight hard to stay awake.

SIX HOURS PASSED, and Eddie's shift was calm and quiet. Although it was Rocco's turn, Eddie decided to let him continue to sleep. He had tricked his body to be at full alert, so even as tired as he was, the two most important girls in his life were lying there so vulnerable. He wanted to be the one to protect them. Plus, life was better when Rocco was rested and on his game.

Off in the distance, Eddie heard some rustling. He leaped up and flashed his weapon in the hopes that whoever was snooping around would see it and convey to his buddies that they were carrying and not to be hassled. The noise crept closer, and the shape of a body appeared, probably five foot eight, sneaking around. Fuck this, Eddie thought, firing the gun straight in the air towards the sky, crushing the midnight silence. The intruder sprinted off just as Lisa and Rocco both jumped to attention.

"I got this. Don't worry," Eddie uttered quietly. He didn't want anyone nearby to hear English being spoken.

Rocco was visibly startled, grabbing the gun out of his hands to take a defensive position.

"Lisa, go back to sleep," Eddie instructed, knowing it was a fruitless recommendation.

"What was that?" she asked, quite alarmed.

"Don't worry. Whatever it was is not coming back."

Rocco decided it was better if he held watch the remainder of the night, but Eddie insisted on staying there right by his side, through daybreak. And that couldn't come quickly enough. It's always around 4:00 a.m. or 5:00 a.m. when the bitter chill hits, regardless of location in the world. It seems odd that the middle of the night stays relatively warm, but as soon as the sun starts to come up, the air turns frigid. Shivering and shaking like a sick ward in the hospital, the whole gang felt the pain of the cold. The mission went from standing guard, morphing into the search for coffee and hot chocolate. Izzy was still out, but the three adults needed some warm beverages. Finding an early-opening bakery, Eddie grabbed a few french rolls, cheese, and some coffee.

Sipping their beverages, they waited for Izzy to wake out of her much-needed slumber. Finally, with about an hour to go before the rendezvous, Eddie gently shook Izzy awake.

"Time to make the doughnuts!" he joked as she opened her little eyes.

She smiled up and asked, "Daddy, are we still playing the game?"

"Yes, sweetie. This is the final round!"

"Good. I don't like this game anymore!"

"Neither do I ... neither do I."

"Uncle Rocco, did we win?" Izzy shifted her attention to him. Rocco was laser-focused on the mission but made time for the little girl who was really starting to look up to him.

"Not quite yet, little one, but we will."

The four bandits moved up slowly upon the outer fencing of the small airfield. The hangar, housing their escape plane, was directly through the fence and just to the left. It wasn't much of a fence—not really serving its purpose of keeping anyone out. There was no barbed wire or any of that jazz, so a simple up and over did the trick. There was absolutely zero movement around the airfield, and everything just had that eerie feeling. Something was off.

The good news was, as they pressed themselves up against the outside wall of the hangar, peeking around the edge, they saw that the hangar door was slightly open, just wide enough to be able to slip through. It seemed as if they really were expected, and the hope was that whomever moved around inside of the hangar was playing for the same team.

Encumbered by the trash all over the side of the taxiways, they forced their way to the front of the hangar. Rocco slid the hangar door open just a bit more to see what appeared to be some range of government-procured Learjet. Frank James and various staff with a few marines stood there in front of the jet, and Frank immediately waved his hand, saying, "You made it! Wow, I honestly didn't think you would!"

"Neither did we."

Who was that? Eddie glanced over to see where that voice was coming from, and out of the shadows walked a Brazilian official, probably from the military police or maybe the president's office.

Who knew? What was he doing here? More bodies appeared from the shadows of the hangar walls—uniformed and armed police. And João.

"What the fuck?" The words formed on Eddie's lips.

Rocco immediately blazed his weapon, pointing straight at the official's head, prompting the others to unholster their firearms and aim for Rocco.

"*Calma*, Mr. Rocco. No need for that!" stated the official like he really meant it.

"Bullshit! Frank, what the fuck is going on here?" Rocco looked ready to bring hell on anyone standing in the hangar. And why not? They had obviously been duped.

Frank stepped in to offer his two cents. "Like I said, I honestly didn't think you would make it. It's your fault in the end, Rocco. Why the fuck would you use public transportation?"

"That was yesterday, Frank. These guys don't have the technology to pick up on that, or us, that quickly, unless they had help, you motherfucker!"

"Wait a minute, Rocco." Frank tensed up. "I'm here, aren't I, with the plane as promised?"

Eddie decided to chime in. "You're a two-faced liar, Mr. James! I saw that the minute I met you!"

Izzy started to tear up, obviously sensing that men with guns ablaze was a scary situation. She was terrified, and so was the rest of the team.

Rocco could feel this. He looked down at her and placed his hand on her head, saying, "We're okay, Izzy. I promise you, you're going home with your dad today."

Lisa simultaneously kicked her mothering nature in, picking Izzy up and holding on to her for dear life.

"Not so fast!" shouted the official. "The girl is coming with us."

"Come here, Izzy." Now it was João's turn. "Time to go back to Grandpa's house."

"Stay back, João," Eddie warned, staring straight at him. "I'll be dead before she goes with you. I AM HER FATHER!"

And with that, João took a step forward, while Rocco responded by pointing his gun at João's head.

"Easy, everybody. Easy." Frank broke the tension, but not for long. "Rocco, it's over."

"You lied to us, but why? You went through all the trouble to get a plane here, and you still lied?" asked Rocco, becoming angrier.

"I didn't lie, Rocco. I am providing the plane. Our friends here asked for our help. I told them there would be no formal intelligence assistance from us, but as a good show of faith, we could provide some data, and they could use it anyway they wanted. They wanted our image-capturing technology, which I gave them. I fulfilled my end of the bargain with them. I didn't think you would be stupid enough to get caught on camera, on a train, two miles away."

"Enough with this!" The Brazilian official was getting antsy. "I don't care about this little girl. You shot a Brazilian citizen. You're coming with me!" He looked at both Rocco and Eddie, unsure of whom he should really focus on.

"We're not going anywhere!" Rocco blurted out over his raised gun.

Several of the uniformed personnel started pointing their weapons back and forth between Rocco and Eddie. Lisa turned her back to shield Izzy from any stray bullets.

"My daughter is here! Are you all crazy?" Eddie couldn't contain himself.

They were so close to scoring their freedom but somehow still nowhere near the goal line.

"If any of you make one fucking move, I will blow Mr. João's head right to the sky. Then you *will* have a murdered Brazilian under your watch." Rocco meant business.

"And why don't we just shoot you, then, Mr. Rocco?" the Brazilian asked.

Frank James finally stepped in. "Because if you kill an American in front of me, you will have to kill me too. I will make it my mission to destroy you and your career." Eddie looked over at Frank and gave him a nod, as did Rocco. It seemed Frank was a master of diplomacy, and there was no way anyone was killing a diplomat.

Frank didn't rat them out either, per se, but he had to give the Brazilians something, which was some technology. He was right; they were stupid enough to get lazy. And after all, he did show with the plane.

Rocco looked over at Lisa and Izzy, then at Eddie, then at the rest of the scene. He was deep in pondering. Something was going on in his head, but what?

Finally, Rocco glared at the Brazilian and decided it was time to make a deal. "If I may, I am here to tell you that I am the shooter. Mr. Watters and his family had nothing to do with any of that, and João over there should know that. Eddie wouldn't... do that to Izzy's mom. In fact, he also knows that I did nothing to harm Natalia, but it's okay. I am willing to be your scapegoat. I will go down for this. I will take your public hanging. I will take all of the blame, and you can take me in without incident, but you have to let those three get on that plane and return home."

"Bullshit!" yelled João.

"Shut up!" the Brazilian official directed right at João. Then he walked slowly to Lisa, put himself within view of Izzy, and asked, "Little girl, is this your dad?" He pointed his finger at Eddie.

"Yes," she responded the best way a toddler could, sniffling from her tears and fear.

Then he looked at Rocco and asked, "Why would you do that, if you don't mind me asking? Do you know what they do to murdering gringos in prison down here?"

"It doesn't matter why."

"I can't let you do that, Rocco," Eddie jumped in. "I can't have that on my conscience."

Rocco strode over to Eddie, peered over at Lisa and then down at Izzy, and in a slow, almost sad voice, he said, "Eddie, I remember my nephews, but I never see them. I am a loner. But this little girl has touched my heart. I can't let her go through any more bullshit. She needs to go home now with her family. I will be fine. I know people. I am a Navy SEAL. I am a warrior. Take her home, and take good care of her." Then he looked right down at Izzy and said, "The game is over, Izzy. You won. I will never forget you."

Izzy glanced up through her tear-filled eyes, saying, "Don't go, Uncle Rocco!"

"It's time for my new game, little girl."

"Will you visit?"

"I promise, Izzy."

She gave him a giant bear hug.

Rocco almost had to unlatch Izzy, and then he shifted his head over to the Brazilians. "So, do we have a deal?"

THE PLANE RIDE home was surreal. Was it possible to feel sadness, guilt, and jubilation at the same time? For Eddie, it was. There were opposite ends of the spectrum of emotions all rolled into one butterfly-filled gut. Constantly surveilling Izzy and Lisa, then staring out the window, Eddie once again found himself overcome with thought. *Northern border of Brazil... the thick rain forest below us. We are actually heading home. My ex-wife, Izzy's mother, should be out of the picture now. How should I feel about that? She is Izzy's mother, after all, but she has brought me so much pain. I am sad for her and her family, but in the end, I have Izzy back. Is that wrong? Is it an equal trade? My suffering gone, Izzy back with her father... but am I not doing the same thing she did to me? No, it is not a fair exchange. Natalia didn't deserve to get hurt, but she did. She picked that crazy boyfriend, Don, not me. She put this whole damn thing into motion, not me. I must come to grips with that. But how?*

Furthermore, the Rocco factor was really tearing up his soul. He just gave his life for Eddie and his family. This was not lost on Eddie's wandering thoughts either. *Is he going to rot away in some prison? A gringo in a Latin American justice system—that's definitely bad. My family and I will be in his debt forever. And I'll tell you one thing: I will continue the fight. This time, it will be to get Rocco out and back home. No man left behind. The game is unfinished, on temporary hold, to get my daughter home, and Rocco will be next.*

"What are you thinking about?" asked Lisa, witnessing Eddie deep in his own mind, with the weight of the world obviously on his shoulders.

"I'm thinking about Rocco. I mean, I'm happy. This is our family now, and with the boys and now Izzy, we are complete. But we can't leave him there, can we?"

"Yes, we are complete. Forever. Rocco made his choice... and he chose Izzy."

"But, Lisa, I will have to come back, you realize. Rocco gave up his life for us."

"That's not a good idea, Eddie. You should never go back to that country... ever! Plus, Rocco has so many connections, I'm sure he will find a way out."

"I know, I know. But I can't help but feel ashamed for letting him do that for us. I am a man, and another man just gave up his freedom and his life for us. I need to rectify this. I need to get him out."

"Eddie, can we just enjoy what we have now? Look at your daughter over there—that beautiful little girl is back home with her dad, where she belongs. Be happy for that!"

Lisa was right on that. Eddie had spent hundreds of thousands of dollars and probably years off his life, but now they were going home.

"But what about... you know who?" he asked, meaning Natalia. "Can we live with what happened to her and Don?"

"Now is not the time or place, Eddie. For now, we focus on Izzy. We have plenty of time ahead of us to sort out a way to cope with that stress. Try to get some sleep."

Eddie knew that was impossible, both the coping and the sleep, but he would try, because that was all he had left within him.

BACK IN BRAZIL, there was a media circus around capturing the criminal American. First, Rocco was processed through that bedlam, then the prison system. For Natalia's family, they couldn't help but feel slighted. Rocco was taking the fall, but it didn't damper the pain of losing Izzy.

João continued to sit up late at night, plotting his revenge. Rocco was not only going to jail for his role but he was going to have to pay the ultimate price... his life. He must. Furthermore, he knew he *would* get his niece back, and every American involved would get what they had coming, one way or another. It was just a matter of time and patience.

As the trio landed back in California, the sweet smell of the Los Angeles smog cover never tasted so good. Eddie had made a decision to live and experience everything to come, good and bad, positive and negative. His immediate next move was to focus on the family while he figured out the Rocco situation and how he could help.

On to the next story in his Life Book. Not yet complete in its entirety, he knew there was much left to be written. One thing was for sure: there would be plenty of sensational stories to share in the book, when he turned old and gray and held the desire for his grandkids to understand their family's history. His American-born grandkids, that is.

# About the Author

Red, White & Betrayal is A.J. Wood's first novel though he has written a children's book and had several articles published in various business journals. A.J. strives to achieve his passion: balancing experience and creativity to enable great storytelling. He has traveled and lived overseas and enjoys exploring the boundaries of myriad situations possible in the ex-pat universe. A.J. lives in California, is married, and has two children and two step-children. When not writing, A.J. coaches almost every youth sport with a focus on basketball. The best gift he can give to his children, A.J. believes, is an interest in reading, and he is working hard to make sure that his kids share his passion and appreciate every day in a world of boundless curiosity. He hopes you enjoy *Red, White & Betrayal* and look forward to his future novels.